AS IT NEVER WAS

A JAKE HOUSER MYSTERY (BOOK #3)

BO THUNBOE

WESTON PRESS, LLC

Published in 2019 by Weston Press, LLC

Cover Design by Jeroen ten Berge

ISBN: 978-1-949632-05-7 (trade paperback)
ISBN: 978-1-949632-04-0 (ebook)

Weston Press, LLC
Naperville, IL
www.thunboe.com

For Diane

ALSO BY BO THUNBOE

PROLOGUE

July 5, 2010
Mount Logan, Illinois

Benchley slowed the van to match the boy's pace. He trudged
along the sidewalk a block ahead of them pulling a blue wagon
piled high with tightly rolled newspapers. His sweat-soaked T-
shirt clung to his body and his faded jeans were snug on his hips
and buttocks. He was a soft one, but plenty of men liked that.

Benchley pulled his eyes off the boy and scanned the neighborhood, squinting against the brightness. It was deserted.
Everyone was inside lazing away the burning-hot day. Many were
no doubt nursing hangovers. But even if someone looked out a
window they would see nothing unusual, just a dirty white van
like a hundred others that delivered appliances and fixed
plumbing and installed carpet. Invisible for all practical purposes.

The van hit a pothole and the loud creak of its suspension sent
an extra spike of tension straight up Benchley's spine. He'd war-
gamed this operation a thousand times, and snatching the boy up
was the high-risk moment. After that it was just the long drive

home—duct tape as needed—and he'd have the boy alone in the basement.

"That's definitely him, Mr. B." Thomas rubbed his hands on his thighs.

"Yes it is." Benchley normally dealt in runaways and street kids. Boys no one would miss because they were already gone. One of his older boys would lure them in, and Benchley would bend them into who he wanted them to be. A formula that worked. But if he fulfilled this request, his future would grow with the rise of the man who made it.

"You're sure he'll get in the van?" Benchley asked.

Thomas nodded, then licked his lips, his face glowing with anticipation. "He liked me. A lot."

"I believe it," Benchley said, smiling at Thomas's confidence. He was a great recruiter. He'd followed this boy into an arcade, then read the boy and gave him what he needed. That had turned out to be the basics: talking and laughing and smiling and touching.

Getting the boy—Mark—to come along voluntarily would greatly reduce their risk on this end. But it wouldn't make a difference on the other end. Once Benchley had him in the basement, he would bend the boy's mind until he believed with all his heart and soul that he wanted to do all the things Benchley would ask him to do.

The boy stopped in the deep shade of an oak tree, dropped the wagon's handle, and wiped the sweat from his face.

Benchley checked the rearview and then the side mirrors. Still clear. He edged the van onto the shoulder and stopped. He threw his arm over the back of his seat and turned around. "Tracy?"

"Hang on, Mr. B." Tracy's voice had finally changed to match his matured body, and the deeper tone still sometimes caught Benchley by surprise. Tracy looked out the back windows, craning his head from side to side to get the widest possible view. "All clear in the back. Like the whole town is sleeping one off."

"Seth?"

Seth sat opposite the sliding door, holding a roll of duct tape. "Let's do it."

Benchley looked out his side window and saw nothing moving, just a long row of tired houses sleeping away the heat. "Get ready." He took his foot off the brake, and the van eased forward.

"Wait!" Thomas leaned forward and put both hands on the dash.

Benchley braked, and the van stopped with a squeaking lurch. Ahead, the boy kicked at the wagon, then looked around like he didn't want to be caught doing it. His gaze traveled over the van without pausing.

Invisible.

The boy picked up the handle and backed the wagon toward a big bush. He lifted its lower branches and pushed the wagon underneath. When he dropped the branches, the wagon disappeared. After taking another quick look around, he continued down the sidewalk, past a garage, and turned in behind it.

"He went down the alley!" Tracy said. "This is perfect!"

Benchley tweaked the gas pedal, and the big van surged forward. He swung wide, cut the wheel, and nosed into the alley. The boy was a few garages ahead of them, kicking at some shredded paper scattered on the gravel, his hands in his pockets.

Benchley stopped. "What's he doing?"

"Looking for duds," Thomas said.

"What's that?" asked Seth.

"Firecrackers that didn't go off."

The boy bent and sifted through the paper. He picked something up, examined it, then stuffed it in his pocket before walking on.

This is it.

A flood of adrenaline surged through Benchley. His heart thumped so hard against his breastbone he could feel it. He took his foot off the brake, and the van rolled forward. "Seth? You ready with the duct tape?"

"Ready."

Gravel crunched and popped under the van's tires. The boy flinched away from the sound, stepping into the weeds growing down the edge of the alley. Benchley pulled up next to him. When the boy stopped suddenly, Benchley hit the brakes. The van jerked to a noisy stop.

The boy raised his face to the window, squinting against the sun. His face glistened with sweat, and he wiped it out of his eyes.

Damn. He is beautiful.

Thomas powered his window down, and the boy's face lit up with ecstatic recognition. Thomas was right—the boy was ripe.

The boy stepped over to the van. "Hey, Thomas!"

"What's up, Mark?" Thomas held out a fist, and they bumped. "Taking a break from the paper route?"

"Yeah. I'm heading over to get a cold pop at Larsen's. Do you live along here?" Mark stood on his tiptoes and looked past Thomas. "That your dad?"

Benchley gave the boy a small wave and a smile. He had the AC cranking, and the cold air flowing out the window raised goose pimples on the boy's hairless forearms. Benchley caught himself licking his lips and pulled his tongue back into his mouth.

"Yeah," Thomas said. "We were just headed to get a soda, too. Want to hop in and come with us?"

Mark smiled wide. "Okay."

Tracy opened the sliding door, and Mark climbed inside. The door slid shut behind him, smooth and silent.

Mark blinked, likely seeing little in the relative darkness of the cargo van. Benchley smiled and nodded, then left it to the boys.

They knew what to do. He'd trained them well.

1

DECEMBER 2017

"I just need the money, is what it is."

Detective Jake Houser pulled his eyes off the people clustered in the long shadows thrown by the rundown buildings lining the street and turned back to the banger sitting in the passenger seat. Smoke's hands moved constantly, his long fingers sweeping over the dashboard, tapping the buttons on the radio, playing a silent tune on the tiny keys of the gold zipper of his puffy coat. The sharp odors of citrus and cedar from his body spray were almost strong enough to mask the reefer stench coming off him. Jake powered the windows down a couple inches, and a sliver of cool night air snaked through the Mustang and flushed out most of the reek.

"I can't pay you unless you're official." Jake waved the note card again. "All you have to do is fill this out." There was more to becoming a confidential informant than filling out the card, but the Supreme Court said lying was a cop's right. The completed card would generate a CI number and initiate a background investigation. Not to confirm Smoke was clean—he was a banger and would have a criminal record—but to confirm his identity and affiliation. Then they would test the information Smoke sold them. If it was good, they would buy more. Eventually they hoped

5

it would help them find and eliminate the source of the heroin that had killed three teens at Weston South High School.

But first the card.

Smoke's eyes shot to the wad of bills sticking out of the pocket of Jake's corduroy jacket. Jake always showed the money when recruiting a CI. Smoke shook his head, the motion folding the skin on his neck and distorting his gang tattoo. "I don't like the word 'official.' Like you gots a file on me."

"No file." Another lie. There would be a file full of ass-covering paperwork, including the background check, payments made, and information collected. And of course, how many arrests resulted from Smoke's information. "Just this little card with your name on it and the CI number assigned to you. The card is buried away where no one can see it. I just use your number to pay you. It's an accounting thing to make sure I don't steal the money." That line always helped close the deal; bangers didn't trust cops and loved to hear their own bosses didn't either.

Jake shrugged and held the card in front of Smoke. "Easy peasy."

"Easy peasy!" Smoke shook his head again, his eyes coming back to the money. "You the whitest guy I ever met." His gaze darted from the money to the card. It was only a matter of time now.

Jake waited, his attention shifting back to the neighborhood. Pockets of people loitered under streetlights. A tight pack of noisy teens spilled out of the convenience store on the opposite corner, laughing and hooting. The activity and the brown faces and the tired storefronts of Kirwin's east side reminded him of his first beat in Chicago, and he realized, suddenly, that he missed it. Not the city, but patrol. Working a beat and learning the people, places, and activities of the community. Becoming a part of it and connecting with the residents and shopkeepers and streetwalkers and homeless. Connections were critical to doing the job and to finding the right people to recruit as informants.

It was one of those old connections that had led Jake to Smoke.

A CI Jake recruited way back then was now a high-ranking minister in a south-side set of the Easties. He wanted his gang out of the heroin business, so he arranged this meeting with his cousin. A Kirwin banger as a CI would be a big win for the department—*if* he produced actionable intel.

Smoke's hands froze, and his gaze fixed on something through the windshield.

"What is it?" Jake pulled the transmission into gear and turned the wheel away from the curb. Ready to move.

"Them's my boys just strolled up." Smoke pointed across the park to a trio of baggy-panted black men posturing on the corner while a pair of curvy Latinas walked through the light spilling from a storefront.

"I'll drive around behind the bank."

"No. They're busy with the ladies, so we're good." Smoke's hands went back to the zipper on his puffy coat, pulling it up and down in fast little tugs that ripped out a tune. Familiar, but just beyond the edge of Jake's recognition. Then he got it. *Jingle Bells.*

"Dre says you're cool, so you're cool. He told me some of the shit you did. The people you took down for him. I can't figure why you'd leave Chi-rak for that dead-ass town of yours, but I never have understood white people, so whatever."

Jake hadn't taken anyone down for Dre, but Smoke was heading where Jake wanted him to go, so he let it be. He put the car back in park. "I have other things to do, Smoke. You in or out?" He pushed the money deeper into his pocket so it didn't show and waved the note card again.

Smoke's eyes bounced to the card and back to the pocket. Then he snatched the card from Jake's hand.

"There's a pen there in the door pocket," Jake said. "Once you fill this out I can pay you for those names."

Smoke scooped up the pen and went to work, the card on his knee, his long fingers clamped around the pen like he'd never used one before. Jake left him to it and let his eyes wander the area.

It was early December, but winter hadn't yet made its way to northern Illinois. During the short sunny days the temperature pushed up to an almost-balmy fifty degrees. The weatherman said it would all end soon and they could expect record snowfall by the end of the month. Then these street corners would be buried under mountains of snow and ice, and everyone would be inside.

"Here you go." Smoke waved the card in Jake's face.

Smart-ass.

Jake took the card and scanned it. Smoke's block printing was crooked and cramped, but it was legible and the form was complete. "Your real name's Dillon?"

"Don't gimme no shit, *Jake*." Smoke smiled. "My moms was into Westerns." He held up a hand and rubbed his fingers together. "Gimme the cheddar."

Jake pulled the wad of twenties from his pocket and Smoke snatched it away. He flipped through the bills, folding and smoothing them and then doing it again. A green blur.

"So," Jake said. "Tell me."

"Los Toros Locos."

Smoke grabbed the door handle. Jake shot out his right arm, pushed Smoke against the seat, and plucked the cash from his hand in one burst of fluid motion.

"Da hell, *Jake*!"

"I didn't pay for the name of your rival gang." Jake gestured to the door. "Get out."

"Wait now!" Smoke's eyes tracked the cash in Jake's hand, his tongue darting across his lips. "That's true shit."

"I need names and places. In Weston."

Smoke pulled his eyes off the money and swung them around the park, then to his homies on the opposite corner. "Can't have that coming back at me."

"We know what we're doing." Jake waited.

"They's the ones pushing that shit into Weston. Ain't want us to even get started, five-oh. Plenty of money in stank. Low risk. Hell, it's prac-a-tack-ally legal. You come down hard on those boys, we rethink getting into it."

"Specific names and places."

"Specifics gets a guy killed," Smoke said. But he wanted the money and coughed up the names of two Toros and the Weston bar they sold from. Sellers, not suppliers, but it was a place to start.

Jake handed over the cash. "Call me when you're ready to earn more."

Smoke ducked out of the car and pushed the door shut gently behind him.

Jake dropped the Mustang into gear and pulled away, the tuned exhaust burbling back at him off the curb. He lowered the windows all the way to flush out Smoke's stench as he circled the park and drove back toward Weston. Glancing at the dashboard clock, he wondered whether his boss, Deputy Chief Braff, would still be at the station at nearly six-thirty p.m.

He had just pulled his phone out to call Braff when it vibrated with an incoming call. He checked the screen. It wasn't Braff, but he took the call anyway.

Jake paid his debts.

The Siebert family lived near the back of the Cress Creek subdivision, one of the first golf course communities in the country. It was a picturesque neighborhood of winding streets and cul-de-sacs laced around the course and normally bustled with golfers and runners and children playing. Tonight, though, despite the mild weather, the place was almost still, the only movement an occasional commuter driving home and the false motion of twinkling Christmas lights.

Jake parked the Mustang on the curb opposite the Siebert house. He pulled his gun in its holster from the inside of his waistband and locked it in the glove compartment, feeling happy to get rid of it. It was a tool of his trade, and he would carry it until the job was done with him, but then he would be done with guns.

As he climbed out of the low bucket seat, the quiet struck him. The last time he'd been here—to interview Paul Siebert about a robbery—the Sieberts' five teenage boys were locked in a loud game of street basketball.

That seemed like a long time ago.

As he approached the house, the blinds in the dining room moved, clattering softly as they hit the glass. He stepped onto the stoop and waited for the person at the window to answer the door.

The storm door reflected Jake in his standard I'm-not-a-plain-clothes-detective outfit—faded jeans, roper boots, and a green quarter-zip under a gray corduroy jacket—then the image was replaced by Linda Siebert stepping up to the glass, Paul behind her with a hand on her shoulder.

Both tried for a smile, and failed.

Linda pushed the storm door open. "I'm glad you could come." Her face was flushed and her voice breathy. She grabbed his arm and pulled him inside.

"Sure." Jake met her gaze, but her eyes flitted away. He turned to Paul. The man's mouth was a grim line. "Hey, Paul."

Paul reached around his wife and shook Jake's hand. "Thanks for coming, Jake. We—"

"I'll tell him." Linda grabbed Jake's hand and pulled him down the hallway toward the back of the house. Her hand was damp, and a few tendrils of hair were curled wet and dark against her neck.

The house was silent except for their footsteps on the oak floors. No cooking smells came from the kitchen although it was dinnertime. "Where are the boys? And Annie?"

"Annie took her brothers out for pizza," Paul said from behind them.

Linda kept moving, her grip tight and her pace quick. She led him into the family room, then released his hand. It was a comfortable space, with a thick Persian-style rug centered on the hardwood and all the furniture angled toward a giant flat screen in the far corner. The TV was off and the room was dim, lit only by a floor lamp in the corner and light spilling in from the kitchen.

Jake sat in a leather club chair and the Sieberts took the couch. It was their show, so he waited for them to get to it, wondering if their issue would be about their foster boys, or perhaps about the foster system itself.

"It's about Mark," Linda said, her wide brown eyes locked on Jake's. She grabbed Paul's hand and gripped it between both of hers.

"Mark?" Jake repeated, surprised.

"You know about Mark? That he was... taken?" Paul asked.

"Just the basics. What was in the papers."

After his first meeting with the Sieberts, Jake had researched them online. Seven years earlier, when the Sieberts lived hundreds of miles away in downstate Mount Logan, their son Mark had disappeared without a trace. Their entire community rose up to search for him, but without success. Months later a transient drunk confessed to killing the boy and burying him in the Shawnee National Forest. Despite a massive search, they never found his body.

"Those news people will burn in hell!" Linda's face twisted, then she pressed her lips together and closed her eyes tight.

Paul squeezed her hand. "A man came to—"

"I said I'd tell it." Linda pushed Paul's hand away and clutched her long fingers into a hard knot of knuckles. Her eyes closed and her lips moved silently. A prayer, maybe. Then her eyes popped open and locked onto Jake's, and her mouth pulled into a wide smile. "Mark is alive!"

Alive? A man had confessed to killing the boy. Jake looked to Paul for some explanation, but his eyes were on his wife.

"What makes you think that, Linda?" Jake asked, leaning forward.

"I don't *think* it," she said. "I know it."

"Please explain."

"A man came here to the house. His name was Robert Miller. *He* told me." She grabbed Paul's hand again and pulled it onto her lap. "He said Mark was... a good man." She broke into sobs, but recovered. "I... he's a *man*. Eighteen years old. I still think of him as the boy he was when he was taken from us."

"If Mark is alive why didn't he come with this guy?" Jake asked.

Linda's eyes welled with tears and she coughed out another sob, then looked at Paul.

"Miller told Linda that the first time they came to the house

Mark saw the boys out front and he... he thought we'd replaced him. Miller said Mark wouldn't come back after that."

A genius explanation, Jake thought. Not only credible, but perfectly tuned to generate serious guilt. Only a master con man could have come up with that.

"I told him to tell Mark that wasn't true," Linda said. "Our foster sons don't replace him. *Nothing* could replace him, and we'd never even try!"

"Did he have any proof that Mark is alive?" Jake asked. "A picture? Anything?"

Linda shook her head, then blurted, "But he knew things! *That's* how he proved it. That we open the gifts in our stockings on Christmas Eve and that we eat Swedish sausage with applesauce and about our cabin. How else would he know all those family details except if Mark told him?"

Because he was working a con with someone who knew the family. An insider. Or even the killer. Even the man's name, "Robert Miller," sounded fake.

"What do you think, Paul?"

"He wasn't here," Linda said.

Paul nodded. "I wasn't here, like Linda said. But he might be like those other nuts and sickos who contacted us back when Mark disappeared. You wouldn't believe them all."

"He wasn't like them," Linda insisted.

"Did Miller explain where Mark has been for seven years?"

"I asked him that. I did," Linda said. "But he said it wasn't safe for me to know because the people involved were powerful and dangerous." Tears now streamed down her cheeks. "I pushed him as hard as I dared—he was all jittery and I was afraid he'd leave—but he wouldn't tell me."

First Miller flooded them with guilt, then he pushed fear. Classic con.

"What did Miller want from you?" Jake asked. But all cons— short ones and long ones—chased the same thing: money.

"Our help," Paul said.

"How much did he ask for?"

"He didn't ask for money," Linda said.

Not yet, thought Jake. But he would, and the more time he invested in conning them, the more he'd try to pull out of them. "What help did he ask for?"

"He wanted to use our cabin on Rend Lake, but we sold it when we moved up here."

A place to stay? *Until when*, Jake wondered. Until it became safe for "Mark" to come home?

"How did Miller leave things? Are you supposed to call him? Did he give you a phone number?"

"No," said Linda. "Annie came home with the boys while we were talking, and it freaked him out. He literally jumped up and ran out of here when they came in."

"Did you see what he was driving?"

"I asked the boys," Paul said. "They said it was a four-door car. Dark green."

"Linda," Jake began, his voice gentle. "This guy is probably a con artist. I'll find him and drag him into the station and—"

"Not the police," Linda said, her eyes fierce. "Just you."

"I *am* the police. If I work—"

"Just you!"

"If he's a con man," Jake persisted, "dragging him into the station will scare him off."

"That'll scare him off even if he's *not* a con man," Paul said.

"Paul, Linda..." Jake spoke as kindly as he could. "A man confessed to killing Mark. If I dig into this, it will only bring your pain back, and Mark will still be dead."

"He is *not* dead," Linda said, her eyes sparking with fervor. "He's alive. He visited me here."

3

Benchley spent a moment with each photo before tossing it into the fireplace. There were a lot of memories here of the beautiful boys he'd bent and used and profited from before selling them off. Everyone liked his boys because they obeyed and they pleased and they earned.

He fed another photo to the fire. The heat from the coals blackened and curled the edges, then the photo burst into flames, the little inferno heating Benchley's face. He blinked away the dryness.

Goddamn Reznik and the mess he made in DC.

Thomas came back from that last trip sullen and uncooperative. Deprogrammed after almost *ten years* of loyal service. And then the goddamn tweets started. And since they continued even after Benchley locked Thomas in the basement, he was sure they hadn't come from inside this operation. Which meant they'd come from Reznik's disaster.

He picked up the note Andy left after breaking Thomas out of the basement.

Liar!

Benchley didn't dispute the label, but without context he didn't know *which* lie had pissed Andy off. Hell, he still didn't understand how Andy could even recognize a lie. He was perhaps Benchley's best work, the only boy he trusted enough to keep—other than Seth—when he sold the rest off to Denver.

He crushed the note and tossed it on the fire. The flames licked up around the ball until an edge caught, and then the whole wad burst into a satisfying little blaze.

Screw you, Andy.

Benchley got back to the photos, taking a moment to remember his time in the basement with each boy before adding the picture to the fire. He hated to destroy these photos, but they were the only things left linking him to what the tweeter was alleging. His memories would have to be enough.

Well, the only things left that were still in his possession. There were also the files Andy and Thomas had stolen from him. He needed to get those back. Especially the secret file he had made on Reznik with a few choice photos of Reznik frolicking with underage boys. If push came to shove, that would keep the man's mouth shut.

He fed in another photo. A blond with freckles across his abdomen and long slender fingers. Daniel. Thomas had coaxed him into the van out of an alley in Cedar Rapids. He'd burned out in less than a year—some boys weren't as tough as others—but it had been a good year.

Benchley's phone shuddered in his pocket. Reznik. With a sigh, he answered.

The congressman jumped right into it. "This damn twitterer keeps adding that *Washington Post* reporter to his goddamn tweets. Tagging him, or whatever the hell it's called."

Benchley set down the photos. "A *Post* reporter won't pick up the story until he can confirm it completely."

They'd had this conversation at least ten times. So far the tweets contained nothing a real reporter could latch on to—no names, no dates. Just sensational claims of Washington power brokers having drug-fueled orgies with underage boys.

"You're *sure* Thomas isn't the tweeter?"

"I'm sure. This is on you."

Benchley had pumped Thomas full of a drug cocktail he'd developed when he was in the Army, and it was still the closest thing to a truth serum the US had. Thomas fought it, but Benchley pulled a few useful pieces of information out of him before Andy broke him out. Including that other boys had already been at the party house when Thomas got there. Boys Benchley didn't own, from a source he didn't know.

"I knew another provider who wanted to get in here, to DC, so..."

Benchley said nothing, because he'd said it all before. Reznik should have stuck to what he was good at—politics and politicking—and left operations to Benchley.

"We need to *do* something," Reznik said.

Benchley agreed; action was always better than inaction. "I've kept an eye on Tracy James."

"James?"

As if he didn't know. Reznik was good at putting his past behind him—except when he was calling in a favor—but Benchley knew the man hadn't forgotten James. That was just a starting position while he waited to hear why Benchley brought it up.

"After seven years in prison, he accepted his first visitor," Benchley said. "A storefront Bible-thumper. Thomas must have sent the guy."

The other useful thing Benchley had pulled out of Thomas was that this disaster somehow revolved around Tracy James. Which was more proof that it was all about Reznik. Benchley had immediately cashed in a few favors to get eyes on Tracy James twenty-four-seven, and the long shot had paid off.

A dull grating came over the line. The congressman grinding those brilliant white teeth, as wide and flat as a horse's. The grinding stopped when Reznik asked, "Can you snatch up this visitor and do your mind voodoo on him and find Thomas?"

Reznik had never really understood what Benchley did or how he did it. The full bending took time and only worked on the immature brains of young teens and pre-teens. And although the truth serum worked on anyone, it wasn't one hundred percent, and the subject always remembered what happened while under its effects. Benchley couldn't use it on a person he had to return to the population.

"The preacher is untouchable," he said.

"This is no time to get soft."

"I'm not touching him," Benchley said. He couldn't disappear a preacher—even one from a low-rent storefront in Rockford—without attracting attention. So far the tweeter was solely focused on DC, and Benchley wanted his attention to stay there.

"Maybe I should send an intelligence operative."

"Can you do that?" Benchley asked. Reznik had leveraged his relationship with the new president to land the chairmanship of the House Intelligence Committee. The position had given him new authorities, but it had also pumped him full of a new and irrationally high level of confidence.

"The intelligence community needs a friend like me right now."

"How would it work? Don't those guys have handlers?"

"I can get it done."

Benchley chewed the idea and decided he liked it. "Okay. I'll find Thomas, then you send your operative to bring him in."

"Has he used the files?"

"No."

"Let me know if he does," Reznik said, then the line went dead.

Benchley picked up the photos and flipped through them. He'd broken in and bent some beautiful boys. And he would again. When this whole thing was behind him, he would find some new boys and build his operation back up. He'd stay here in the Heartland where he knew the players and already owned dozens of them. *If* he got the files back. Without them, he'd have to work slowly, re-accumulating the leverage he loved to wield.

Benchley tossed the rest of the photos onto the coals. Flames sprouted underneath them, then light flared and a wave of heat washed over him.

Thomas would pay for that.

4

____

Jake shot Paul a glance, but he looked as surprised by Linda's claim as Jake was.

"Mark visited you?" Paul asked her. "When? Why didn't you tell me? What—"

"Just stop!" Linda shouted.

Paul did.

Jake pushed himself back from the edge of his chair, giving Linda space, waiting for her to explain.

"I'm sorry." Linda took an audible breath, then her words came out in a rush. "I didn't tell you because I wasn't sure, but now I *am* sure. Now that I *know* he's alive, I'm sure. And back then, it was two years ago, we weren't... together like we are now. Things were bad. I wasn't right."

She wasn't sure *then*, but she was *now*? Jake looked at Paul, but the man said nothing, just gave a slow gentle nod, his eyes sad.

"Let's take a step back, Linda," Jake said. "Tell us about when you saw this man who might have been Mark." He kept his voice low and calm, but it didn't soothe her.

"Not 'might have been.' It *was* Mark." Linda sprang up from the couch, pushed past Jake, and paced in front of the patio doors.

20

"I know this sounds crazy. But when it happened I just... I wasn't sure."

"You weren't sure the man was Mark?" Jake asked.

"No!" She covered her face with her hands.

"Honey!" Paul started to rise from the couch, but Linda jabbed her open hands at him to tell him to stay where he was. He sat back down.

"I *was* sure it was Mark, but I... I wasn't sure whether he was actually *here*." Linda pointed at Paul. "Tell him how it was back then. How I was. I just can't."

Paul nodded slowly, then turned to Jake. "We moved up here after what happened with Mark. That helped for a while. But then that thing after the robbery..." Paul shook his head. "We kind of... lost Linda. Not sleeping. Not eating. She had, like, waking nightmares. Mark coming to her. Sometimes he was dead. Sometimes alive." He pushed back into the couch. "It's just been in the last year or so—with medication, and then we took in the boys—that everything straightened out."

"So I wasn't even sure the visit really happened," Linda said. "But if Mark is alive now, he was alive then. It *was* real. It *is* real. Mark is alive."

Her reasoning was circular. The truth of each of the two claims —that Mark visited her then and that he was alive now— depended on the other being true. "It might have been one of the waking nightmares you were having," Jake suggested.

She shook her head. "It wasn't."

"Tell us about the visit," Jake said.

She told the story.

Two years before, the doorbell rang in the middle of the day. Annie was at school and Paul was at work, and their five foster children were still a year from moving in. Linda answered the door and a young man stood there. Right away she knew it was Mark, even though it didn't look exactly like him.

"He was just about all grown up." Linda put her hands on her cheeks. "He had a little beard. He was a short, chubby bunny when he was young, but he'd grown out of that and had the wide shoulders all the Siebert men have."

She pulled him inside, and he explained he was there to tell them he was okay and she didn't need to worry about him. He apologized for what had happened.

"That's the way he put it. For *what happened*." Linda's eyes squeezed shut.

"Did he say what *had* happened to him?"

She shook her head. "He said he couldn't tell me. But he wouldn't say why not."

"Was he alone?"

"There was a car outside. When he left I could see someone else was driving."

"Was it Robert Miller?"

"I don't know."

"Why didn't you tell me about this?" Paul asked. His voice sad, not angry.

"I just wasn't sure back then." She started pacing again.

"You *were* sure," Jake said. "You were sure it *wasn't* real, or you would have told Paul."

"I..." She nodded. "Yes. But now I know it *did* happen. He was here."

"Did Miller mention the visit? Or did you ask him about it?"

"I didn't have to ask him!"

"You said the boy looked different than Mark. How did he convince you he was Mark?"

"He didn't have to *convince* me. He was my *son*. I knew it." She pounded her chest with a fist. "I felt it."

"Did Mark have any distinctive birthmarks?"

"A blotch on his left hip," Paul said, patting his own hip.

"Did this boy offer to show you his birthmark?"

"Did he offer to show it to me?" Linda said. "I honestly didn't think to ask to see it." Her hand went to her face.

Four indicators of deception clustered together within seconds of his question: repeating the question, responding with a non-answer statement, touching her face, and the reference to her own honesty. And the lie was right there in her claim of honesty. She *had* thought of asking to see the boy's birthmark.

But she didn't ask.

She'd been so hopeful for so long that she wanted to believe her son was alive and standing in front of her. She didn't want to test it and risk proving otherwise.

"It was him, Paul. I could see it in his eyes and his chin, just like yours. But he didn't smile. Mark's smile could light up the world."

Jake found himself nodding. Her obvious pain in revealing her mental struggles convinced him she at least *thought* she was telling the truth.

He stood. "I'll talk to Miller."

Linda came and grabbed his hands. "Just you. No police." She squeezed. "Please."

"Just me," Jake agreed. "And if he's a con man I'll convince him to leave town."

"And when you decide he's not a con man, what then?"

"Then?" If it wasn't a con, then Mark was alive, the guy in prison was a liar, and the cops in Mount Logan were going to crap themselves. "If Robert Miller is telling the truth, I will bring Mark home."

Paul stood and shook Jake's hand. "Thank you, Jake."

"Do you have anything more on Miller than his name?" Jake asked. "Any mention of where he might have gone when he left here?"

"He said he's staying at a boarding house," Linda offered.

"Boarding houses are illegal in Weston."

"Well, that's what he said." She shrugged, then her eyes widened with a memory. "By the phone company. Does that help?"

"It does." Jake knew the place. A rundown foursquare on the north edge of downtown. A speculator had bought it and was renting out rooms to generate cash while he waited for someone to overpay him for the lot. Probably earned enough rent to pay off an ordinance violation if the city bothered to cite him.

"Can I have a copy of your most recent picture of Mark?"

Linda pulled a framed photo off the fireplace mantel. A school photo of a round-faced boy with long eyelashes. Jake took a picture of it with his phone.

"What does Robert Miller look like?"

"Tall and thin, with brown eyes and thick dark hair. Cut short but floppy on top the way the boys do it now. He's maybe twenty, twenty-two. In there."

"Okay. I'll get on this tomorrow afternoon." Jake glanced at his watch. "I have court in the morning, and I need to take the rest of tonight to prepare. But call me if you hear from Miller."

"Thank you." Linda clasped her hands together and brought them to her chin, her eyes pinching closed. "I knew—*we* knew— you'd help us."

5

———

As soon as Jake was out the door he started to regret the terms of his involvement. He should have insisted on making his participation official. When a cop did something on the side for a friend, it always came back to bite him in the ass. But he'd made a promise. He'd work on Miller and keep his badge in his pocket.

As he drove across Ogden Avenue, his stomach reminded him he had nothing to eat at home, so he stopped for a sandwich at Reggie's Subs. While he ate, he tried to focus on the grand jury testimony he would give in the morning, but Linda's story kept intruding. Mark Siebert's body had never been found, so technically he *could* still be alive. But it was unlikely. A murder confession without a body would have made the Mount Logan PD take a very hard look at whatever the killer offered to corroborate his story.

As Jake left the sandwich shop, he intended to head home and start preparing for court, but as he pulled away he decided to take a quick drive past the boarding house. It would only take a minute and maybe he'd get lucky, spot the con man getting out of his car, and running the plate would reveal something determinative.

He slowed as he approached the house. It sat on a deep corner lot with the front facing Main Street and a detached garage fifty feet behind it facing Franklin. The two overhead garage doors were gone, each replaced by vertical wood siding with a small window. Four cars crowded the driveway, three sedans and a coupe. But none of them were green.

He pulled to the curb just short of the driveway and took out his phone to call in all the license plate numbers, but his promise to the Sieberts stopped him. Running four plates would attract official attention.

He put the phone away.

Might as well knock on his door while I'm here.

Jake walked along the street, the back yard opening to his view as he skirted the cars on the driveway. The grass was thin, an ancient maple shading it too deeply to let the sun hit it. A worn picnic table anchored the middle of the space, and beside it a scattering of lawn chairs surrounded a fire pit. Three men sat at the table, two with their backs to him, one facing him. Oblivious, laughing. Passing a bottle, and from the smell, a joint. All had long hair, one in clumpy blond dreadlocks.

Jake was past the sidewalk and nearly upon them when the man facing him stiffened, then warned his friends in a loud stage whisper, "Five-oh."

The other two turned his way, one stubbing the joint out against the table leg, a ribbon of smoke curling up around his arm before a puff of wind dispersed it.

Jake's phone vibrated in his pocket. He stopped on the thin grass a few feet from the men, and pulled it out. Anna McKay, the assistant state's attorney prosecuting the case he was testifying in the next day. He stepped back out to the street and answered.

"Houser."

"You ready? You work through those questions I gave you?"

"I will be."

"Will be? You should have it all buttoned up by now."

He smiled as he walked around the backs of the parked cars. "I do, don't worry."

"We need this indictment. My boss has the heat on."

"Mine too," Jake said. An understatement. The influx of heroin into Weston had caught the department unprepared and they were scrambling. "I'm heading home to work on it right now."

"You want me to come over and run you through your testimony?"

He did want her to come over, but not to run through his testimony. She was curvy and athletic and at a post-football-game bonfire a few weeks before they'd spent hours talking and ended up in a teenager-style clench. The problem was, she was too good for a one-nighter, and Jake wasn't sure he had more than that in him. He'd tried that, just a few months before, and that relationship had ended before it really got moving. Maybe he would spend the rest of his life as the lonely widower. His tribute to his late wife, Mary. One she would have never asked of him. She would have—

"Jake?"

"No," he said. "We've been over it. I'll be ready."

"You're on at ten."

"I remember."

"We need to nail this guy, Jake." Her voice thickened with emotion. "We need your best."

"You'll have it."

Jake got back in the Mustang and headed for home. As he passed the house a man came out of the back door. Tall and slender with thick black hair. Young. Robert Miller. Jake slowed, pulled his phone out, and took a picture.

Miller skirted the picnic table, stepped onto the square of wood decking in front of the door to the garage apartment, and went inside.

Jake nearly parked again, but he needed to focus on his testimony for tomorrow. All eyes were on this case, and if the indictment failed, fingers would point and heads would roll.

Robert Miller would have to wait.

* * *

Jake's house was a small ranch less than a mile south of downtown. It had a two-and-a-half car garage connected to the house by a big breezeway the previous owner had boxed in with cheap paneling and storm windows and floored with AstroTurf, as if the entire room was nothing but a doormat to drag your feet across on the way into the house. Jake had ripped out the fake turf, but he still didn't have a plan for the space. It made the most sense to open it up with screens and a wood-burning fireplace for fall gatherings, but he didn't like entertaining. And his struggle with this decision was just an echo of his struggles with the whole project.

He bought the house intending to rehab it into a place of his own. His first step had been to gut most of the interior, creating a new great room with a volume ceiling that accounted for half the house's total footprint. The skin of the space was now finished—drywall up and sanded and primed—but he'd gotten stuck at that stage of renovation and done almost nothing over the last month.

Maybe keeping this house as his own instead of flipping it was a mistake. It had everything he thought he'd wanted—a fantastic location, a good footprint, and a yard small enough not to require endless yard work—but it just didn't feel like home.

Inside, Jake hung his jacket over the back of a folding chair at the card table in the near corner. Another card table sat over the pipes where the sink would go—that one held his coffee maker and toaster—and a low table by the front window held his stereo. The only other piece of furniture in the room was the gold refrigerator that came with the place. He tuned the radio to a country station and grabbed a bottle of beer from the fridge.

Sitting at the card table, he flipped open his laptop. As he signed into the department system, the house groaned, a protracted sound that had started after he'd ripped out the chimney. It was less frequent now that the supporting beams were in place, but it still startled him. He shrugged off the eerie noise and got to work.

He sent an email with Smoke's hot tip to the opioid task force leader. He would send it on to the right people and follow up to keep the complicated organism that was the multi-jurisdiction investigation moving at its typical snail's pace. Eventually an undercover vice officer would make some controlled buys from the two dealers to confirm Smoke's credibility. If that panned out, they'd make bigger buys and start flipping their way up the distribution chain.

Jake took a photo of the CI card with his phone so he'd have Smoke's number, just in case. Then he pushed the laptop away and pulled his case binder over from the far side of the table and got to work reviewing the Storch case one more time.

McKay had said she needed his best.

And that's what he would give her.

6

—————

Jake read through his narrative summary and his notes from every interview, re-living the slow accumulation of information. Twin eighth-grade girls, Jada and Jasmine Jefferson, had brought heroin to school. The school called it in—only marijuana was handled internally—and Jake was assigned the case.

The twins' mom, Imani, refused to let the girls talk to him at first, so he went at it from the outside. He talked with teachers and classmates and neighbors and relatives and friends. Piecing together what he learned led him to Jeffrey Storch, a seldom-employed mechanic who lived next door to the girls. With his focus on Storch, Jake then re-interviewed the neighbors. He learned Storch had used drugs, including heroin, to entice several of them into having sex with him. Jake shared the information with Imani, which convinced her to let him talk to the girls. Under gentle questioning, both told Jake the same story: Storch introduced them to the drug and then used it to coerce sex from them.

Their mom was devastated and finally consented to letting the girls testify, but only in front of the grand jury. It would be a closed proceeding, and would take place in secret so that Storch wouldn't even know it was happening. But Storch wasn't the real target—just a stop along the way. Once they had a grand jury indictment—for both the drug charges and the sex charges—Assistant State's Attorney Anna McKay would convince Storch to flip, and then Jake could chase arrests up the distribution chain. As long as Storch cooperated fully, he'd never do time, and the sex charges would be deferred. The county would trade away justice for the Jefferson girls in exchange for a shot at stemming the flow of heroin into Paget County. A drugs-for-sex transaction that was inevitable because the girls lived in a politically insignificant and poor slice of town while the children overdosing belonged to families of the politically connected and financially powerful.

Jake's stomach twisted and he took a pull from the bottle, but the cold beer did little to soothe him. He let his anger simmer for a long minute, then pushed it aside. To survive working in the justice system he had to focus on his part and let the other players do theirs. His part was to investigate and present evidence. The decision on what happened next, and the responsibility for it, belonged to someone else.

When he was done preparing his testimony, he opened another beer and sat back down at the table and searched for information on Mark Siebert's abduction. The articles he found were familiar because he'd done this same research back when he first met the Sieberts. Notably, there was almost no information about the confessed killer, David Smith. The man had refused to talk to the press and they'd been unable to dig up any background on him. In an anniversary article, Smith's public defender revealed that Smith had refused to talk about his past even to him, even to help develop mitigating factors for sentencing. He simply pled guilty and accepted the prosecutor's offer of thirty years in prison.

Jake kept googling, linking Mark Siebert's name with different words—abduction, murder, conviction—but found nothing new until he added the word *missing*. Halfway down the list of results was a link to a website on missing children. There he found a brief summary of Mark's case, with an age progression showing how he might look today as an eighteen-year-old—his jaw wider and his face thinner with eyes deeper set. It was interesting, but it didn't provide any new information.

Jake got up from the table and stood at the front window, looking at the distant bulk of the Weston Central football stadium. He had learned that he thought more clearly when he was looking across a distance.

If Mark Siebert is still alive, where has he been and why did a man confess to killing him? Who is Robert Miller, and how is he connected to Mark Siebert? Did Mark Siebert actually visit his mom two years ago?

Jake went back through his conversation with the Sieberts, and he caught something: Linda didn't bring up the visit from Mark until Jake said he was sure Miller was a con man. Did she concoct the story on the spot to convince him to help?

He chewed on it and found two reasons to believe her. First, if the story was a lie she wouldn't have admitted to once doubting the visit had occurred; she would have just said it happened, period. Second, she would have said she *had* seen the visitor's birthmark.

So, a man *did* visit Linda Siebert, and she did believe it was Mark.

Jake let that conclusion settle. He found it solid.

After hoping and praying for so long, Linda didn't wanted to ask the man a question that would expose him as a liar. And she didn't tell Paul the story, to avoid him talking her out of believing her son was alive. She wanted to hang on to that belief, so she kept it to herself.

Until now.

Until Robert Miller showed up to confirm what she felt when she met the man two years ago.

Could the man really have been Mark? For a moment, the possibility sent a pulse of excitement through Jake, but reality flooded back in. David Smith had confessed to killing Mark. Why would he do that if it wasn't true?

7

———

Jake rose early the next morning and dove right back into the Storch materials over a cup of coffee. When he'd worked through it all he ran his four-mile route along the Paget River—it was a beautiful day, cool and dry—then showered, ate a bowl of oatmeal, and headed for the courthouse. Rush hour was over, so the drive to Glenbard was fast and easy. He badged himself through security and took the escalators up to the criminal courts on the fourth floor.

He saw a lot of people he knew from the law enforcement community—cops and sheriff deputies and attorneys—and gave each a nod or a brief greeting. The defendants not in custody also crowded the halls with their families and friends. A crowd of reporters, cameras left outside by court rule, clustered around the largest courtroom where a crooked politician was on trial. Jake arrived at the grand jury room ten minutes early and waited on the bench in the hallway while mentally spooling through his testimony.

Within a few minutes the door swung open and Assistant State's Attorney Anna McKay came outside. She wore the same color scheme as nearly every female attorney on the floor—black over black with black shoes—but on her it looked stylish. Tailored.

She smiled when she saw him, her face shining with confidence. She wore a hint of makeup brushed over her freckled cheeks and her blond hair was pulled into a tight ponytail.

"So far, so good." She looked around and her face lost its glow. "Have you seen Imani and the girls?"

"No. What time are they supposed to be here?"

Anna looked at her watch, then glanced up and down the hall once more. "Now."

Jake joined her in scanning the hallway. "How did your opening go?" he asked, just to make conversation. It could only have gone well. The grand jury is completely the state's attorney's show; the prosecuting attorney calls for it to meet and decides what to present and is the only lawyer there. The criminal defendant isn't invited and can't attend.

Her smile came back. "I had every single juror nodding along by the time I finished. They were appalled at what Storch has done and can't wait to indict him."

"Before they've even heard the evidence," Jake noted.

"I laid it all out in my opening."

"Miss McKay?" a voice said behind them.

"Imani! I was starting to worry." Anna's face regained its glow. "And call me Anna. We're past last names at this point."

Imani Jefferson was a statuesque woman who wore her coal-black hair in a long braid. Jake had met with her and her daughters many times during his investigation into Jeffrey Storch, but now she wouldn't even look at him. That wasn't good.

"Miss McKay, it's because I like you—and the girls like you—that I came. But they're not coming, and I'm not testifying."

"What?" Anna crossed her arms, then uncrossed them and looked around. "Let's talk in here."

She led Imani into the alcove next to the grand jury room. It was a small space with a padded bench running around the three perimeter walls. Jake followed the women in.

Anna shot Jake a pained look, then leaned forward. "Tell me what's wrong, Imani."

"Nothing's wrong. We just decided—I decided... what I mean is, I don't want them to have to talk about it ever again. And that's that. We've moved out of that place and we never have to see that bastard again."

"What about the other girls in the neighborhood?"

"I feel bad about that, but I'm not *their* mother. They've got their own mothers, and some of them have dads, too. Me, it's just me, and I'm not going to have my girls carry the weight for the whole damn place."

Anna shook her head and looked to Jake.

"Did Mr. Storch threaten you or the girls, Miss Jefferson?" Jake asked.

The grand jury proceeding was secret, but secrets got out. And the girls themselves might have spilled it to a friend, who spilled it to another, and on around the block until Storch heard the news.

Imani shook her head. "Like I said, we already moved so Storch has no hold over us. But neither do you. We just aren't going to do it. That's all, Detective. You and me, we talked about doing right and that I'd know what's right in my gut, and this thing I'm doing here is what feels right. For my girls. And that's what I got to care about. Doing right for the rest of them and getting him punished, that's on you. That's not on my baby girls."

"We can't do it without you—"

"Whether you can or can't is up to you," Imani said.

"We can subpoena you," Anna said. "And the girls."

Imani took a step back, cocked a hip, and shook her head. "That's what you gonna do? Send a deputy sheriff out to wrestle us into a squad car and drag us here? A white deputy, no doubt. Your boss got the stomach for that?"

Anna's boss definitely did *not* have the stomach for that. Nor did Anna, Jake was sure. It was an empty threat born of her frustration at not being able to punish Storch for what he'd done.

"I—"

Imani lifted a hand and cut Anna off. "I'm sorry about this,

Miss McKay. I am. But this is how it is, and your talking isn't going to change my mind. I've prayed on it and talked to my pastor."

That was that.

Imani Jefferson strode away. The milling throngs of attorneys and their clients parted before her.

"I need to call my boss."

Jake stepped back out into the hall to give her some privacy.

Had Storch—or someone up the heroin distribution chain— threatened her? If she'd been pressured, it meant Storch knew they were on to him, which introduced further complications. But he'd sensed no fear from Imani, just determination. Which meant Storch and those above him were still in the dark. Their plan to leverage Storch could still work.

If they could get an indictment without the Jeffersons' testimony.

"He says to go for it," Anna said as she emerged from the alcove, stuffing her phone back in her pocket.

"It's a long shot," said Jake.

She sighed. "Don't I know it."

* * *

The grand jury room lacked both the formality and the dignity of a courtroom. No judge was present, so there was no elevated desk from which he or she would look down. And because there was no defense attorney or client, there was no formally arranged area behind a "bar" with matching tables for the prosecution and defense. Instead there were just two elevated tiers of chairs with small desks for the sixteen grand jurors, and a long table fronting them where the prosecuting attorney sat with whatever witness was giving testimony. More classroom than courtroom.

Jake sat behind the table with Anna. He knew from observing her over several trials that sitting didn't suit her. She liked to stand and stride, and looked good doing both.

The jurors had been talking among themselves when Jake and

Anna walked in, but now they quieted down. It was one of Anna's tactics—letting her silence suck them in, not speaking until all eyes were on her. It was very effective at engaging people who often didn't want to engage.

Anna stood. Popping up with a suddenness that caused a woman in the front row to jerk back with a start.

"Before we begin with Detective Houser's testimony—you'll remember he is the detective who investigated the entire case and spoke to all the witnesses, including Imani Jefferson and her twin daughters, Jasmine and Jada—I need to share some unfortunate news."

She paused, scanning the expectant faces.

"Mrs. Jefferson had just informed me that she and her daughters will not be participating in this process. But because Detective Houser conducted the entire—"

"Not participating? What does that mean?" The voice came from the second row. A woman in her thirties with blunt-cut hair and small square glasses that made her face look too round.

"They won't be here to give testimony."

"But that's not really their choice, right?" This from a chubby white guy with a gray goatee hiding his double chin. He had raised his hand and left it up. "You said in the beginning that we have the power to ask questions of whoever we want, right? We can use a subpoena to make them come in." He dropped his hand.

"We don't force thirteen-year-old girls to testify about being sexually assaulted," Anna said.

"Well what about the drugs part of it then? We can get them to tell us about him using the drugs on them to get... what he wanted."

"The two things go together," Anna said.

"So how are we gonna decide?" Goatee asked.

"Detective Houser will lay out our entire case, including everything the girls would have testified to."

"That's good enough?" asked a skinny man with his hair in a bun. "Aren't there rules about getting it from the horse's mouth?"

"Not here."

"What do you mean by that?" Goatee asked.

"In this room, we can proceed with Detective Houser's testimony as to what the Jefferson girls told him. When you return an indictment, we can arrest Mr. Storch."

Bun again: "Are these two girls... what with the J names... going to testify at trial? Hell, that'd be worse than talking to us, I expect."

"The vast majority of cases resolve before trial," Anna said. "By plea agreement."

"So you expect us to help you trick this Storch fella into thinking he might have to go to trial where Jada and Jasmine—what the hell kind of names are those anyway—would tell about him?" Bun was pressing now.

"No trickery here," Anna said patiently. "You listen to Detective Houser and our forensic witnesses on the drugs, and you make your decision."

"You're wasting our time," Goatee said.

Square Specs nodded, and several others joined her.

Anna ignored the nods, and they got started.

While she was taking Jake through what the twins had told him, Goatee interrupted. "Only the girls can say what happened between them and Mr. Storch."

"They did say. They told me and I confirmed parts of their stories with nearly two dozen people."

"But those bits were just details, right? None of them others saw the sex or the drugs I'm guessing, or they'd be in here telling it."

"That's true," Jake admitted.

Anna got things back on track so Jake could get in the rest of his testimony, but by then they both knew it was a waste of time.

This grand jury would not indict Jeffrey Storch.

* * *

After Jake's testimony, he and Anna met in the hall.

"I'll finish up with the forensics on the drugs," Anna said, "but we both know how that's going to turn out." Her eyes drilled into his, sharing her pain. "That bastard has gotten away with statutory rape."

"So far," Jake said.

"He'll do it again, you know." She folded her arms and spun to stalk away, but three steps later she turned on her heel and strode back to him. "Have you ever been out there—of course you have. That neighborhood is full of broken families. Ripe pickings for Storch."

"We'll find another way to get him."

She barked out a scoff and shook her head.

"Call me when the jury's made its decision," he said.

She pulled on a weak, sad smile, and he left her there, pacing, waiting for the forensic tech to arrive.

A cold wind kicked up as Jake exited the building and dark clouds banked across the sky. The weather matched his mood. But he couldn't blame Imani for wanting to protect her daughters. If he had a family, he'd probably do the same. Hunching his shoulders against the chill, he hustled back to the Mustang and drove south to Weston.

His stomach rumbled, and he pawed through his glove box and found a protein bar. It chewed like granular paste and didn't taste any better, but it would keep him moving. He washed it down with the bottle of water he kept in the console.

When he pulled to the curb across the street from the boarding house, he sat for a minute, eyeing the building, the engine ticking away its heat. The place was still. The yard empty. Both windows on the driveway side of the converted garage were dark. A black car was parked in front of the left window. The Siebert boys had told their dad that Miller's car was dark green, but eyewitnesses were often wrong, so Robert Miller might be inside.

Jake got out of the Mustang, crossed the street, and stepped onto the little wood deck in front of the door. The door was old, its white paint cracked and peeling to reveal gray wood, and it held a window split into three horizontal panes. A curtain printed with faded yellow flowers blocked his view inside.

He knocked.

Nothing.

A hard triple rap.

Still nothing.

He pulled his small flashlight out of his blazer's pocket and shined it through the window. The beam cut through the thin curtain fabric well enough for him to see shapes inside. A couch, a chair, a kitchen counter. Nothing moved.

"What are you doing?"

Jake spun, bringing the flashlight's beam up to shine on the face of a twenty-something white guy wearing dreadlocks and a tie-dyed T-shirt under a worn jean jacket. One of the guys from the picnic table the night before. He had a backpack over one shoulder, and both hands gripped the strap.

"You a peeping Tom or... get that light out of my eyes."

Jake shut off the light and put it back in his pocket. "I'm looking for the guy who's staying here."

"I'm calling the cops." Dreadlocks pulled out his phone.

Jake pulled back his blazer to show the badge on his belt.

"Oh." Dreadlocks stuffed his phone back in his pocket. "They packed up and left."

They.

"When did they leave?"

Dreadlocks shrugged, then glanced at the main house. "You should talk to Carl."

"He run the place?"

"Why do you want those guys? They some kind of master criminals hiding out in suburbia?" He laughed.

Jake stepped into the man's personal space, already crowded with body odor. "You were telling me about Carl."

"He's inside. He's always inside." Dreadlocks stepped back and pointed to the house. "Dude's obsessed with TV."

"I'll go talk to him." Jake stepped forward again. "Did Robert tell you why they were leaving?"

The man shifted on his feet, his eyes skittering away from Jake's.

"Spill it."

"We told him that five-oh came by last night. That was you, right? They left this morning." Dreadlocks shrugged. "Guess they didn't want to talk to you."

Damn. I spooked them.

"They coming back?" Jake asked.

Another shrug.

"How many were there?"

"Three, maybe? I don't know. They stayed in the room."

"Thanks for your help."

"I just... Okay." Dreadlocks turned away and walked east on Franklin, heading for the college.

As Jake watched him cross Main Street, he kicked himself. Being seen last night had been a big mistake. He'd ruined an opportunity to confront Miller and get the Sieberts their answer. Maybe forever, if Miller didn't come back.

He turned back to the door, then looked up and down the street. Dreadlocks was out of sight, and the neighborhood was still. He tried the knob.

It was locked, but the doorknob was loose and the door rattled in the jam when he shook it, moving back and forth more than a quarter inch. The knob looked original to the garage, a key to lock it on this side and a simple twister on the other. An inclined latch bolt to let the door close easily. No dead bolt. Why bother? It was only a garage.

He could bypass the lock with a credit card. But going in without a warrant meant anything he found would be useless in court, and any information he developed from what he found— which the law called fruit of the poisonous tree—would be useless too. But he wasn't working a case here. He wasn't collecting evidence. He was doing a favor for a friend—getting to the truth.

Of course, that meant going in would be a crime: trespassing, or maybe breaking and entering. Burglary, if he took something.

He looked around again, but he was still alone. It was his own damn fault he'd missed Miller the night before. He needed to make up for that and salvage the situation the best he could by finding something inside that would help him get to the truth.

He pushed the door to increase the gap at the jamb, and slid a credit card in by the knob. Within a few seconds, he'd sprung the lock. Looking around one last time, he pushed the door open, swallowed a lump in his throat, and slipped inside, closing the door behind him.

It was dark, all the drapes closed. He ran his hand along the wall until he found the switch and flipped it up. A cheap ceiling fixture came on, casting only a dim wash of light over the room. It would have to do because he didn't want to open the drapes.

Little had been done to convert the garage into a livable space. It was still just one large room about twenty feet square, with a bathroom walled into the corner. The far side held a small kitchenette with a round table and four chairs, with a set of bunk beds on the wall to his left. Closer to the door, a sofa and wingback chair faced a TV. A door-less closet was boxed between the two windows—and clothes hung on the hangers.

Someone planned to return.

In the closet three items were pushed to one side of the rod: a pair of Levis, size 30-34, and two flannel shirts, size large. A set of shelves ran up the left side of the closet, and one of these held three pairs of boxers and two pairs of socks. Jake fingered all the pockets and found nothing.

He turned to the tiny bathroom next, and flipped the light. A ceiling fixture with a built-in fan started with a whir that was as soft as the light. A shaving kit sat on the back of the toilet. It held a collection of toiletries any man might use.

Jake returned to the main room. He looked under every piece

of furniture, in every drawer and cabinet, under every cushion, and between the mattresses and box springs. He opened the fold-out couch and ran his hand over the thin scratchy blanket. But he found only a few days' worth of the *Daily Herald* stacked on the floor, and in the fridge, two beers left from a six-pack of Corona and half a pizza in a Domino's box.

He sat in the wingback. If two or three men had been staying here, they were gone now. But the one who'd left his clothes behind must be coming back.

As if his thought had conjured the man, the doorknob turned.

8

Jake sprang up from the chair and faced the door. The sunlight flooding into the room was so bright he couldn't make out who stood in the doorway.

"Oh, I thought you'd all gone." A sharp, nasal voice. "Wait, you're not one of the boys. Who—what are you doing here?"

"How are you?" Jake asked, buying time to think. This wasn't Miller, so it must be Carl, the man Dreadlocks said ran the place. Jake was in deep shit unless he could talk his way clear.

"Fine," Carl answered.

As Jake's eyes adjusted to the light, he got a better look at Carl. He wore shiny black sweatpants puddled on leather slippers and a food-stained fleece jacket. His hair was a long, matted mass of wiry gray that melded into an untrimmed beard. His glasses had thick lenses and large plastic frames. He held a piece of paper in one hand and a crowded key ring in the other.

"You with the boys?" Carl asked.

Jake considered accepting that explanation for his presence, but he had questions for Carl that a friend of the boys would not need to ask. "No," he said. "I'm with the city, Carl." He pulled out his notebook, flipped it open, and pretended to read from the page. "I'm responding to a complaint that you have eight unrelated people living here together. That makes this a boarding house, and that's too many boarders."

Carl swallowed, then took a step back. "Maybe I should call the owner?"

"You are Carl, right? You're the man I want to talk to."

"Okay. I guess."

"How many boys were in this room?"

"Just Robert and his friends."

"How many?"

"The room's the same price no matter what."

"How many?"

"Three, maybe? But they left this morning so maybe my numbers are okay now?"

Jake pointed at the closet. "Clothes were left behind."

"Robert said he's coming back in a couple days. He paid in advance."

Jake pulled out his phone, brought up the picture he'd taken of Mark's school photo, and held it out toward Carl. "Did one of them look like this guy? Or like his older brother?"

The man took his time looking, moving his glasses in and out with one hand. "I don't... well, maybe. These guys were all a lot skinnier than this kid."

"Where did the boys come from?"

"Well..." Carl scratched his chin through the wiry beard. "I don't think they ever did say. No reason to, I guess."

"How'd they find you?"

"Craigslist, like everybody else." Carl squinted through his glasses, the lenses distorting his eyes. "I'm supposed to call the owner if somebody asks me a bunch of questions. Should I call him?"

"I don't want you to get in any trouble, Carl."

"Sure. Okay. That's good with me. There's actually eight guys plus me. That's counting the guys out here, if'n there's three of them. So maybe six now if Robert is here alone. Awfully nice fella." Carl scratched at his beard again, the paper he held snagging on the wiry hairs.

"What's that, Carl?"

"Oh," he said. "I come out here to give Robert this message." He rattled the paper. "Guess I'll leave it on the table."

Jake held out his hand. Carl hesitated, then handed it over.

Jake read it out loud. "*Hawkeye called: If it's true, what about my momma?*" He looked up at Carl. "If what's true?"

"I wondered on that so I asked him, but he said Robert would know."

"This the only name he gave you? Hawkeye?"

"Yep."

"When did he call?"

"Like, maybe an hour ago."

"Why'd he call you and not Robert directly on his cell phone?"

"He didn't call me."

Jake held up the paper.

"I got a cell phone too, you know. Everybody got one nowadays. But the house here still has its own phone. For house business."

"Show me."

"The phone?"

"Yes."

"Well..." Carl fidgeted, his hands scratching his sides. "I guess I can if you need to see it. It's in the house."

"I'll follow you."

Jake shut off the light, closed the door, and followed Carl across the yard. The man shuffled instead of walked, the legs of his nylon sweatpants *wisp-wisping* together. He was careful on the squeaky stairs up the rear porch.

The back door, crossed at eye level with a diagonal string of diamond-shaped windows, opened into a small foyer. To the left a set of worn wooden steps rose to the second floor; to the right the foyer opened into the kitchen. Carl led him that way. It was tired and dated—laminate countertops, yellow appliances, the design worn off the linoleum in paths around the kitchen table—and it smelled like overcooked noodles and tomato sauce. But it was clean, and a teetering array of cookware was stacked upside down in the left-hand side of a double sink. A wide archway in the far wall opened into the front room where a TV blared a talk show, women's voices talking over one another.

Carl pointed at the phone on the wall, a long cord spiraling down from it toward the floor. "Told you. The house has its own phone." He stepped over to the archway, and his eyes went blank as they found the television.

"Any other calls since the one from Hawkeye?"

"What's that?"

Jake repeated himself.

"No. No one hardly never uses that phone because everyone has a cell phone." Distracted by the TV, he stepped through the archway, leaving Jake alone.

Jake picked up the phone. It was gold plastic with the dirt of decades worn into the finish. No screen, so there was no caller ID. But most landlines had something almost as good.

He dialed *69, a standard landline calling feature that automatically dialed the last number to have called into the phone. A professional-sounding woman's voice with a smooth southern lilt answered after a single ring.

"Big Rend River Correctional."

Jake was momentarily speechless. That was the prison where David Smith was locked up for killing Mark Siebert.

"This is Big Rend River Correctional," the woman repeated.

"Where are you located?" Jake asked. He knew, but wanted to be sure.

"We're in Lincoln County, a few miles south of Mount Logan, Illinois."

Jake identified himself and explained that he needed to know who had made the call he was returning.

"I have no idea if that is even possible, Detective."

"Aren't all inmate calls logged and recorded?"

"I think so," she said. "But the number you called isn't part of the inmate phone system. It's for the prison library."

"Are you the librarian?"

"No, sir. I'm with the answering service. The librarian forwards the phone here when she's not in. She works part-time."

"Are the calls on the library number recorded?"

"Outgoing calls? I doubt it, but we only handle the inbound calls here so I can't say for certain."

"Thank you." Jake hung up.

David Smith was in Big Rend River Correctional, and someone calling himself "Hawkeye" called this house from Big Rend, asking for Robert Miller.

The conclusion was obvious: Smith was Hawkeye. The man who'd confessed to murdering Mark Siebert was working with the man who'd claimed Mark Siebert was still alive. It wasn't a certainty, but anything else required Jake to accept a giant coincidence, and he didn't do that, not when investigating crime.

Which meant this whole thing was a con. Miller had gotten his inside information from Smith, who'd gotten it straight from Mark Siebert before he killed him.

Jake found Carl standing in front of the television, his eyes locked on the screen where a crowd of women talked over each other in excitement about what some movie star wore on the red carpet.

"Carl? Thanks for the help."

Carl waved a hand, and Jake left him there, caught in the beam.

* * *

On the way home, questions ran through Jake's mind. If Miller and Smith were working together, why would Smith call the landline and not Miller's cell? Like Carl said, everyone had a cell phone. Maybe Smith didn't have Miller's number? But he somehow had the *house* number?

Robert Miller wasn't around to answer those questions—and that was Jake's fault. But David Smith could also answer them, and he wasn't going anywhere. When working a case Jake knew that if he kept moving—just kept working his leads—answers would come. Treating this favor to the Sieberts like a case was the only way he knew how to do it. He swung by the house, packed an overnight bag, and headed for the highway.

* * *

Jake got on the East-West Tollway at Weston Road and settled in for the long run to Mount Logan—four hours and twenty minutes away according to the map on his smartphone. A few miles east he caught 355 South, and he was bombing along when his phone rang.

"Houser."

"Deputy Chief Braff is looking for you," said Erin. She was the department's civilian investigator, and because Jake avoided the station and its politics as much as possible, she was also his eyes and ears there. "Wants to know about the grand jury."

"I'm glad you called," Jake said. "I need you to put me down for some PTO time. The rest of today and all of tomorrow."

"Will do, but give me something for the boss."

He told her about Imani Jefferson refusing to let her girls testify and that the indictment would likely fail. "But there is good news. I landed a new CI—tell Braff it's the guy we talked about—and he gave me two names I already passed on to the task force."

"A bad news, good news report."

"Better than a bad news, bad news report. Hey, I left the CI card on my kitchen table. Can you stop by and get that plugged in and a CI number assigned, and give the number to the task force?"

"Sure. What's the PTO time for?"

"Remember Paul Siebert? The guy who was robbed outside the liquor store?"

"Sure."

"His son was abducted and murdered seven years ago down in Mount Logan. I'm taking a quick look at it for the Sieberts."

"What can I do?"

Jake considered. He was already driving four hours to talk to Smith. He might as well talk to the people who investigated and prosecuted Smith while he was at it. The more threads he pulled on, the better chance he had that something would unravel. It was more than the Sieberts had asked for, and more than he had promised them—but even thinking that way undervalued what Paul Siebert had done for Jake. And he knew he could count on Erin without worrying about blowback. They'd been friends since kindergarten.

"This isn't police business and it needs to stay that way, but I could use a little help." He asked her to find him a hotel room in Mount Logan, collect contact information on the local law enforcement people involved in the Siebert case, and set up his visit with David Smith at Big Rend.

"I'll call you back."

After the call, Jake's energy spiked with his decision to widen his investigation. It was the right way to handle it because it gave him a better chance of seeing the whole picture. His thoughts spun through what he knew about Miller and Smith.

The call to the boarding house had to be from Smith, but how would the two men know each other? Miller would have been only a teenager when Smith went to prison. Jake considered calling Erin back and asking her to research Miller, but he'd asked enough of her already. And he had another resource for this. He made the call.

"Paget County Cleaners!" Levi answered in his ever-cheerful voice.

Jake had met Levi a few months before while looking into the strong-arm robbery of Paul Siebert in the cleaners' parking lot. When he learned what a wizard Levi was with the Internet, Jake recruited him as an unofficial and unpaid Internet investigator. Levi loved it so much he had since enrolled in Paget Community

College's Private Investigator Program, which gave him access to subscription-only databases that made his results faster and better.

"Hey, Levi."

"Detective Houser! I hope you're calling with something for me to do."

"I am." Jake told Levi about Robert Miller's visit to the Sieberts and the little else he knew about the man. "I'd like you to dive into this guy and see what you can find."

"Do you think he could be telling the truth?"

"Very unlikely. A man confessed and is in prison for it."

"Then that's a really ugly thing to do to the poor parents. I'll jump right on it."

"Thanks, Levi."

9

Benchley re-read the email, optimism making his heart race. His hunch had paid off: Tracy James had made five phone calls in a row from the prison library. Three of the numbers—the second, third, and fifth—shared the same exchange: 355. None of the calls lasted more than twenty seconds, except the last one, which lasted nearly four minutes. The boy must have been calling around looking for someone and found them at that last number.

That someone had to be Thomas.

With Benchley's files.

He googled the exchange and learned it belonged to Weston, Illinois. He typed the last number into his laptop, and Google spit out a long string of results all offering the same information. The number was for a landline at 101 North Main Street.

"I've got you now."

He had a vague memory that Weston was one of the suburbs that spread out around Chicago. He spun his chair and pulled the Illinois almanac out of the credenza. He was old school when it came to maps and always liked to put his finger on where he was going. He slapped the big floppy book down on his desk, flipped through to the index, and turned to the pages listed for Weston. He ran his thumb up the middle of the book to flatten the fold then traced the coordinates in from the margins. Bingo! Weston was about thirty miles straight west of Chicago, where the suburbs began to thin out. Just beyond its edge sat Kirwin, a big city straddling the Wolf River.

He snatched up his phone and made a call. It was time for the congressman to wield the power he claimed to have and get back both Thomas and the files.

Reznik answered. "Benchley?"

"Yes. I've found—"

"Hang on." Silence, then Reznik's deep voice droning away from the phone. A pair, or maybe three distant voices responded before a door closed. The congressman returned to the phone. "That twittering bastard spewed out a new thread about us," he whined, his voice losing its usual deep thrum. "He listed three specific dates when parties were held at the 'Love Shack,' as he calls it. All three were right. He's got someone on the inside."

Benchley said nothing. He had seen the tweet. His boys had only been at the last of the parties listed. That was where they ran into the other boys Reznik had brought in from who-knew-where, provided by who-knew-who. Reznik's "expansion" of the operation had destroyed it and now might bring them both down.

"Why did you call?" Reznik finally asked.

"Tracy called a number in Weston, Illinois."

"What's in Weston?"

"He was calling Thomas."

"An assumption."

"He made the call the very next time he had access to the phone after the preacher's visit."

A pause. "It could be, then. What's your plan?" Excitement pumped the volume of Reznik's voice.

"For you to send an operative. Why have the power if you're not going to use it?" That was a direct quote from the congressman's recent appearance on a Sunday morning political show where the host quizzed him about a rumored return to the black ops programs of the past.

A longer pause, accompanied by the familiar gurgle of Reznik pouring himself a glass of Maker's Mark. It sounded like a tall one. A slurp, then the faint rasping of the congressman's teeth grinding. Another slurp.

"I'll bring in an asset," Reznik said. "But I'm starting him off back home."

"Thomas could disappear again," Benchley warned. But he knew it was pointless to argue. Reznik thought changing his mind was weakness and simply didn't do it.

"Can Thomas tell a coherent story after all the work you've done on him?"

"I don't know," Benchley admitted. Whatever had happened in DC had a profound impact on the boy.

"The little shithead is as guilty as the rest of us."

That was true. Bending the boys until they participated in the same corruption done to them was part of Benchley's operational design. But it wouldn't help them if Thomas decided to talk anyway.

"Let me know when you're sure it's Thomas," the congressman said. "If it is him, I'll send the asset up there as soon as he's done with what I need him to do back home."

10

Jake was approaching Kankakee when his phone rang, interrupting a song about lost love that was flooding his head with memories of his wife. Those memories were a blessing and a curse, because every trip down that memory lane ended with Mary sprawled on the gallery floor, throat gaping open, her life spilling onto the tile floor.

It was Levi.

Jake cleared his throat of the tremor Mary's memory often put there. "Did you find anything interesting?"

"Did you know there are twenty-one thousand, six hundred and fifteen people in the United States with the name Robert Miller?"

Jake sighed. Levi liked to soften bad news with a trivia lead-in.

"I'm sorry, Detective." The energy in Levi's voice made the apology sound insincere. "I've tried linking together every name and place you gave me, but I found nothing helpful. The name is just too common."

"Thanks for the effort, Levi. Sorry we didn't have a license plate number for you." The plate number would have given them the address where the car was registered, and maybe even another name if Miller didn't own the car. "I'll text you when I have more."

"The name David Smith is even *more* common. Thirty-four thousand, two hundred and thirty-nine people have that name. In fact, I did some research, and found that these two names—Robert Miller and David Smith—are among the top ten most common names in the country. I don't know enough math to calculate the odds, but it would seem unlikely the two names would pop up together in one case. They might be fake."

"Thanks, Levi. Great work. "

After the call, Jake pinged Levi's idea around. If David Smith *was* a fake name, the man using it had adopted it seven years ago and not even the longest con was planned seven years in advance. Which meant Smith didn't adopt the name for a con, but to hide his identity. A man confessing to murder and accepting a plea deal for thirty years in prison doesn't need to hide his identity because his life is basically over.

So he didn't do it for himself. He took the fake name to protect someone else. Probably to protect his family from the shame of being related to a murdering pedophile. Jake shook his head. He was overthinking it. Lots of people had common names—that's why they were common. Levi was just working too hard to pull meaning from the two very common names because he knew Jake's rule against coincidence when investigating a murder.

The important fact was that David Smith had called Robert Miller, and that connection meant the two had something going on.

David Smith could tell Jake exactly what.

* * *

Benchley pushed the button on his desk, and the buzzer sounded faintly in Seth's distant room.

As he waited, he wondered if he'd made a mistake in not telling Reznik about the secret file full of the congressman's own perversions—perhaps he should have leveraged that to spur more urgent action. But one thing he'd learned in the Army was that during the action you couldn't dwell on what you'd done or failed to do, you had to move forward with what you had. Could-have-beens had to wait for the after-action debriefing.

He knew where Thomas was, and he had his own resource. He would act now. He couldn't take a chance on Thomas leaving Weston.

"Yeah, boss?" Seth bounded into the room with his usual wide smile and enthusiasm. He wore shorts and a tank top, sweat gleaming on his hard-muscled body. The sight usually thrummed a cord in Benchley. But not now.

"We have him, my boy. I found Thomas."

"That's good! Right, boss?" Seth was no simpleton. His IQ tested at a solid eighty-seven, which was well above imbecile and plenty good enough to follow instructions and do a simple job.

"Very good." Benchley smiled back, which was all the positive reinforcement the boy had ever needed. "We have help coming, but I need you to keep an eye on Thomas until it gets there."

"Sure thing, boss." Seth sat down in the leather wingback across the desk from Benchley. "Anything you need."

Benchley smiled again. He couldn't help it. Seth's strong natural desire to please others, coupled with Benchley's thought reform, had made him the perfect asset. He'd been in high demand until he'd grown too big. Now Benchley had Seth all to himself.

Benchley took the boy through what he wanted him to do, going over it several times to make sure he had it right. Seth would confirm Thomas was there, then keep an eye on him until Reznik's operative came north to help them get both Thomas and the files back.

Then Benchley would put Thomas in the basement and work on him until he knew exactly what the hell had happened in DC.

* * *

The Mustang ate up the miles as the sun dropped, burnt orange spreading under thinning cloud cover as it approached the horizon. Just past Champaign, Jake got another call.

"Houser."

"How about stopping by for a little paperwork?"

Jake grinned at having a legitimate excuse not to. "Sorry, Coog. I'm out of town."

Bill Coogan had been Jake's best friend since the summer before second grade. Even before the Coogans' moving truck was fully unloaded, the two boys had hatched their first adventure. They'd been nearly inseparable since, even going to college and law school together. Coogan was both a CPA and a lawyer and handled the real estate trust Jake inherited when his mom died. It generated a lot of paperwork.

"Where are you headed?" Coog asked.

"Mount Logan. Listen to this." Jake laid it all out, glad to be talking with the one person who knew the entire story about his earlier encounter with the Sieberts.

"Sounds like you believe her about her son visiting her."

"I believe that *she* believes it. But Paul said she was having some mental problems at the time. Delusions, or hallucinations."

"Well, whether that visit happened or not, I agree that Smith and Miller must know each other. Any ideas how? You said Miller is young, and Smith has been in prison for seven years?"

"I have the same question," Jake admitted.

Before hanging up, their conversation turned to the Bears and their new quarterback. It was a short discussion, because they both agreed this new QB had a long way to go to be worth what the Bears had given for him. But the Bears didn't need an elite QB; they won with defense.

Jake kept the pedal down, the sun at the horizon, the bright burning ball pinching away and the light fading to gray. Dark came early, and fast, this time of year.

The phone rang again. "Houser."

"PTO time is all set," Erin said. "DC Braff was happy for you to finally use some days."

Braff had been pushing Jake to take time off since an officer-involved shooting the month before. The powers that be had declared the shooting justified, but the department still wanted Jake to take time off to "recover." Jake didn't need to "recover" from the shooting; he'd done exactly the right thing. It was the rest of that case that haunted him. But keeping busy with work was the best remedy for that.

"I paved the way for you at the prison. You can show anytime from nine to five tomorrow. And for tonight I made you a reservation at the Regal Inn on south Tenth Street. Get off 57 on Broadway. Go east to Tenth, then south a couple blocks to the motel."

"No chain hotels?"

"Out by the highway, but I know how you like to get off the beaten path."

"Thanks." Jake slipped into the left lane and powered past a long line of trucks chasing each other south.

"I sent you an email with the contact information on the prosecutor and the rest. The public defender died two years ago. Drunk driving. I took a look at the original news reports about the boy and reached out to an acquaintance."

"Erin, I'm not working a case here. I can't have—"

"Don't worry. This is a friend of a friend. She works at the recorder's office down there. She told me the state's attorney was worried about political fallout if the case went bad, so he made his first assistant handle it. That guy, Nelson, was eyeing a state rep or senate seat—she couldn't remember which. He milked the case for media attention but didn't 'know his ass from his elbow' according to her. Lucked out when a patrol cop busted a drunk who then confessed. Case closed."

"Didn't the papers credit the investigation with solving the case?"

"This Nelson guy grabbed as much glory as he could, naturally, but my new friend said everybody down there knew the truth. All the names and contact information are in the email. The lead detective retired, and she said he probably won't want to talk to you." Erin laughed. "Can I go home now, boss?"

"Thanks, Erin."

"Call me if you have any questions about the material I sent you."

Jake checked his speed again; it had edged up over ninety. He set the cruise control at sixty-eight and settled back. He had an hour to go, and then he could start chasing answers.

11

Blasting through the tunnel of light bored by the Mustang's headlights, Jake circled around Effingham, went past Salem, and finally reached the outskirts of Mount Logan. He flicked off the cruise control and left the highway, following Erin's directions to the hotel. It was late, and traffic was sparse. Christmas trees sparkled in front windows and lights glimmered along roof lines, but the city's only decorations were around the courthouse square—an inflated Santa Claus and lights strung from the building down to the ground.

The motel was a two-story building in an area hosting a mix of retail and industrial businesses. It was set perpendicular to the street with the lobby on the near end and a freshly paved parking lot with bright white lines. Jake pulled up to the lobby and went inside. Country music was piped over hidden speakers, and a pair of fake leather chairs sat under a window, a coffee pot on a table between them. A smiling woman with gray hair welcomed him from behind an oak counter that cut the small room in half.

Jake told her his name and that he had a reservation, and her smile faltered before she got it back. Erin must have had a rare failure in making an instant friend of everyone she talked to. Or maybe this woman just didn't like a guy who thought he was too important to make his own reservation.

The woman—her nametag said Sheila—took his credit card, swiped it, and gave him a key. Jake was stepping away from the counter when she stopped him.

"Hold on now." She grabbed a sheet of paper from under the counter and slapped it down in front of him. "Your secretary asked me to print you out a map of where you're going while you're here working on your story."

Story. Something Erin said had led Sheila to believe Jake was a writer of some kind. He decided to leave it alone; it was a good cover—writers were as nosy as cops, so the misunderstanding might avoid some interest in what he was doing in town.

"You're right here." Sheila poked at a red circle at the bottom edge of the map. "Up here is where the courthouse is at." Jake had driven past it on his way in. She jabbed at another red mark straight north of the motel. "And this here is the police station."

"And Big Rend Correctional?"

"Straight south on this same road about twelve miles." She scrawled a red arrow pointing to the edge of the page. "Down near the college."

"Any place to grab a quick burger nearby?"

"The Burger King's about half a mile south right down this road." She raised an arm and pointed over his shoulder, smiling now. "Walking distance if you want to stretch your legs. Everything else is back out near the highway."

Jake thanked the woman, took the map, and went back out the door. She had put him in a first-floor unit near the other end of the building, with a door opening to the parking lot. The room was clean and warm, with two double beds. He freshened up, unpacked his laptop, clicked into the free Wi-Fi, and downloaded his email. Erin's email contained the substance of their call plus the names and contact information for the people he wanted to talk to. He jotted them into his notebook before leaving to track down a burger. He left the light on in his room

—a habit he'd developed as a man who lived alone. It was his way of knocking some of the coldness out of a place on his return.

* * *

Drill's satellite phone vibrated against his canteen, throwing up a sharp metallic beat that ruined the stillness. The sun had already fallen behind the jagged rock spine to the west and the temperature was dropping fast. A great night for sleeping outside in the clean desert air. He was probably the only person camping overnight in this part of the Superstition Wilderness.

"Drill." It wasn't his real name, but he used it on the satellite phone.

"It's Spec."

Of course it was Spec; no one else had this number. "What is it?"

"We need you to take an op."

Drill had just gotten back from an operation in a steamy subtropical hellhole, but asking for time to recuperate would only remind Spec of his age. The man was already hinting at Drill's retirement. "When?"

"Right now."

Now? Twilight was fading too fast. Hiking off-trail in the dark was a bad idea. And he was already unpacked, his sleeping bag unrolled on the wide flat space at the mouth of the abandoned mining tunnel he'd found years before. As far as he could tell he was the only person on the planet who knew it was here, a mile off-trail, hidden in a fold in a canyon wall, its tailings pile camouflaged by desert scrub.

"Where?"

"Illinois. Downstate."

Drill's grip on the phone tightened. He'd never been assigned an op in the homeland. There was a whole different set of agencies for that.

Spec, as usual, couldn't handle the silence. "We go where our skills are needed."

One of Spec's favorite lines, but it didn't explain anything.

"When can you be there?" Spec asked.

"Give me a minute to check a few things." Drill didn't need to check anything. He knew how long it would take him to get from here to anywhere on the planet. But Spec didn't need to know that. "How far downstate?"

A coyote screamed into the darkness. The sound echoed off the canyon walls before fading away.

"Mount Logan. Basically the middle of the state."

Which meant flying into St. Louis. "Then tomorrow afternoon is the best I can do from where I am."

"Where are—No, strike that."

Strike that. The ones who came up through law school loved saying that.

"It's stricken," Drill said.

"I'll post the information to the board."

The call ended, and Drill lay back down on his sleeping bag, his head propped on his backpack. He had one night to enjoy the sounds and smells of the desert at night, then it was back to work.

He was tempted to wonder why his agency was handling a homeland operation, but he pushed such thoughts aside. Asking why was Spec's job.

Drill's job was to execute his orders.

12

Jake decided to follow Sheila's suggestion and walk to dinner. Winter was getting a late start, so he wore only his windbreaker over his button-down. He was cold at first, but once he got moving he warmed up, and the cool air was refreshing after the long drive.

After a couple blocks the road dropped down to a two-lane blacktop lined with concrete-block commercial buildings and empty lots. Many of the buildings looked abandoned. A sidewalk hugged the curb most of the way, then petered out into crushed stone before reappearing a half block farther on. It was deeply dark; the streetlights were placed far apart and many of them had burned out. There were more abandoned buildings in this stretch, including a couple of shuttered churches, plus one giant warehouse of a bar with a weed-choked parking lot.

By the time the Burger King sign finally came into sight. Jake figured he had walked close to a mile. But he no longer felt foggy from the drive so it had done him some good.

The restaurant was inside a BP gas station that also housed a Circle K convenience store. The place was apparently a local hot spot, and Jake got a feel for the town as he wolfed down a Whopper Junior and a side salad. People wore boots and flannel and denim, and he didn't see a single pair of jeans sagging below a boy's ass or pair of yoga pants hiked up a girl's crack. He finished eating and then started walking north, back to his car. He'd hit the police station tonight.

* * *

Jake walked faster on the way back to the motel. The temperature had dropped another couple degrees, and he zipped up his windbreaker to hold his body heat in.

Miller and Smith were running a con, that was absolutely clear. Smith abducted Mark and kept him alive long enough to learn the private details about the Siebert family. Then Smith gave those details to Miller to use on Linda Seibert. That all made sense, but it didn't explain how the men knew each other or why they'd waited seven years to launch the con. And what would Smith get out of it—a few bucks in his commissary account?

Jake stumbled over the cracked pavement around a storm drain as he crossed a street but regained his footing with a quick hop onto the sidewalk.

And there were other mysteries. Smith had called the boarding house's landline, which implied that he didn't have Miller's cell phone number. That was strange. And then there was the message itself: *Hawkeye called: If it's true, what about my momma?* What did that mean? And why the nickname?

Jake walked past an abandoned gas station, then stepped closer to the road to negotiate his way around a cluster of trucks in front of a waste-hauling company. The trucks stank of rotting garbage and he held his breath against the stench. He had just edged around a garbage truck parked close to the street when someone grabbed his right wrist and yanked him toward the building.

Jake set his feet against the pull, but gravel rolled under his shoes. So he stepped toward his attacker instead, lifting his captured arm high and grabbing the man's hands with his free hand. He turned his back into the man and brought his hands down fast over his shoulders while jackknifing at the waist. The man grunted as his gut pressed against Jake's back, gravel scattered as his feet left the ground, then he sailed over Jake in a low sprawling arc that ended on the packed gravel. The impact drove the breath from his lungs in a loud gasp that Jake barely registered before he spotted a blur coming from between the trucks.

Jake moved into the new threat, his brain deciphering the shifting shadows.

He brought his hands together and forced them between the grasping arms. His palms finding a rough chin; Jake grabbed the jaw with his right hand and snaked his left around the back of the head. Their bodies came together, and Jake pulled his left hand down and jammed the chin up with his right, cranking the head around.

Standing up tall to relieve the pressure on his neck, the new attacker grabbed at Jake's wrists. But when a cracking sounded in the man's neck, he let go and turned his body with Jake's twist. Jake moved behind him and bounced the man's knees and hips forward with a hip bump, and the man collapsed backwards. Jake spun him onto his stomach while guiding him to the ground, then put his foot on the man's neck and held him there.

It was over so quickly Jake wasn't even breathing hard. But the adrenaline would catch up to him.

"Hold still," Jake growled when the man started to scrabble at the ground, his feet pushing. Jake twisted his foot to get the man's chin under his toe, then pressed his face into the gravel. The squirming stopped.

He eyed the first man, barely visible in the deep shadows, sprawled loosely on the gravel. He looked like he was out. Both men wore faded jeans, work boots, and flannel shirts. The local uniform.

A scuttle sounded across the gravel from deeper in the shadows, and a harsh whisper carried through the still air. "What's taking them so long?"

The man under Jake's foot bunched his muscles and pulled his arms underneath his body.

Jake leaned more weight onto the man's chin and pushed two knuckles against his temple. "Make a sound or move a muscle, and I'll put a nine-millimeter round through your brain."

The man went still.

Two car doors closed with soft thuds, and the first man started to move—groaning and rolling back and forth like a turtle trying to right itself. Footsteps approached. Another groan, louder now.

It was time for Jake to go.

He darted into the street and took off northward at a sprint, his rubber-soled shoes nearly silent on the blacktop. He was under the next street light when loud voices—three, maybe four— erupted behind him. He kept moving.

The first two blocks were wide open, the buildings set back from the street. On the third block Jake veered up onto the sidewalk in front of a two-story red brick building, then ducked down the alley beside it, and stopped, leaning against the wall. Sweat was now beading on his face, and he breathed deeply to replenish his oxygen. Probably the fastest quarter-mile he'd ever run.

Within a few breaths his heartbeat slowed and his breathing eased. He stuck his head around the edge of the wall and looked back the way he'd come. No one in sight.

A shout, then a car door slammed. He leaned against the building and took a couple more breaths before heading north again.

An engine started behind him, a throaty rumble of a souped- up engine and an aftermarket exhaust system, then tires squealed as the engine revved. Jake ducked west at the next street and cut up an alley running behind the buildings fronting Tenth. It was unlit and deeply shadowed, and he dodged from building to dumpster to bush until the alley ended at an east-west street. There was no alley on the other side.

The engine was still somewhere south of him, the exhaust cracking loud as the driver gunned it.

Jake jogged east to Ninth Street, then north until he saw the sign for the motel poking into the sky to his left. He ducked west at the next street and continued straight to his car in the motel lot. He caught movement in the office as he got in. The person backlit in the window matched Sheila's height and shape.

He opened the glove compartment and took a long moment to think it through before picking up his Glock. He didn't know what those men intended, but they had him outnumbered, and he couldn't count on getting lucky a second time.

He pulled the Glock from the plastic holster that clipped to his belt, then dropped the magazine to check the load. Ten nine-millimeter rounds. He slapped the magazine back in and pulled back the slide to seat a bullet in the barrel. Ready for action. Leaving the holster in the glove compartment, he put the gun in the right-hand pocket of his windbreaker. Available, but concealed.

The now-familiar engine rumbled, coming north on Tenth Street, and another joined it. Jake put his hand in his pocket and wrapped it around the gun, then stepped out of his car and stood, waiting and watching.

A minute later two old Chevy pickups cruised by, a pair of flannel-clad men in each. The passengers gave him a long look as they drove past. The lead truck, bright orange with giant rear tires, was the noisy one.

Jake shot a look at the office, but the light had gone out and Sheila's shadow was gone.

He slid back into the Mustang's leather bucket seat and slammed the door. The solid *chunk* when he closed himself inside the steel cocoon flooded him with relief. He fired up the car and thought about chasing the trucks, but quickly decided against it.

Now that he had the gun, he might be tempted to use it.

He backed out of his parking spot and took off with a sharp bark of his tires. On the way north he rolled down his windows to let the flush of cool air dry his post-action sweat. He passed the tiered limestone courthouse centered on its own block. The police station was only a block and a half beyond it on the opposite side of the street. Jake parked in the lot next to the station and took a minute to consider what had just happened.

He'd seen no one else walking along that stretch of road, so no robber would choose that spot to lie in wait for a passerby. Besides, the men who attacked him were too old for random violence, too clean, and too...something. But if the attack wasn't random, then it was a setup, which seemed equally unlikely. Sheila was the only person in town who knew he was here, and she didn't know why. And even if she did, why would looking into Mark Siebert's abduction generate that much animosity?

And it all happened so fast he didn't get a good enough look at the men to identify them. All he could describe was the most generic guy in this community: big, white, husky, wearing flannel and needing a shave. He'd seen a dozen men like that while eating his burger. It was an embarrassing lack of detail for a seasoned investigator.

He looked through the windshield at the police station. Reporting the attack would label him a victim and change the whole dynamic of his visit. He didn't want that.

He'd keep it to himself.

And it wouldn't happen again, because now he was ready.

13

———

Jake put his right hand in the pocket with his gun and walked across the lot toward the police station, a block of red brick that looked like a repurposed warehouse. A sign on the steel door facing the lot directed him around to a single-story metal-and-brick addition facing Tenth Street.

The glass front door opened onto a bleak space that stank of pine air freshener. Bare walls and worn tile flooring hosted a half dozen empty chairs pushed up against the walls. The far wall held a door and a pass-through service window.

A woman clutching a bundle of files to her chest walked past the window and spotted him. She tilted her head down to look at him over the glasses perched on the end of her nose. "What can I do for you?" Her voice held the hint of an accusation; he wasn't from around here and she knew it. She didn't put the files down.

"Hope you can help me. I'd like to speak to Detective Roman Greer and Officer Steve Brakur." If the retired Greer was a tough nut, maybe channeling the request through the department would help open the detective up.

The woman's lips pursed. "Stirring *that* up again." She dropped her files onto the desk under the window with a *thwump*. "Name?"

"Jake Houser."

She pushed a button on the desk phone. "Chief, there's a Jake Houser here asking for Detective Greer and Officer Brakur."

The reply was too distorted for Jake to decipher.

"He'll be with you in a minute. Take a seat." The woman turned and disappeared.

Jake took one look at the hard chairs and stayed on his feet. After the hours in the car, the street brawl, and the sprint up Tenth Street, his back and thighs were stiffening. He paced around the small room, flexed his shoulders, and did a few leg lifts. The adrenaline had burned off and a post-action exhaustion was working through him.

The door next to the window was swung open by a uniformed man of about fifty, with gray hair cut short on the sides and a little longer on top. His uniform shirt was severely wrinkled, and his equipment belt hung heavy with a Glock 17, spare magazines and handcuffs, and a radio with cord snaking up to a mic clipped to an epaulet on his shirt. The full complement of a patrolman's equipment.

"I'm Chief Bell," he said. "You might as well come on back."

"Thank you, Chief." Jake said. "I'm—"

"Save it."

The chief moved like an athlete, light on his feet, as he led the way down a corridor framed by cubicles with seven-foot walls. He stopped outside a door and held his hand out to usher Jake into what was apparently his office. The room was well used, the carpeting worn, the wood furniture scuffed and scratched. Three walls were busy with framed photos, the last with a wide bookshelf filled to bursting with binders, stacks of printouts, and a set of Illinois statutes. A faint odor of old sweat overlaid it all.

Jake took the lone seat in front of the desk and the chief plopped down in a leather chair behind the desk.

"Brakur and Greer, huh?" Bell said. "So you're here about Mark Siebert."

"Yes, I—"

"You're a cop," Bell said, but it wasn't a question.

"Yes. But I'm not here in my official capacity." Jake fished his badge out of his pocket and set it on the desk.

The chief snatched it up. "Weston? You're pretty damn far outside your jurisdiction." The chief's voice was harsh, but then softened. "Weston is where Paul and Linda went ... well, after." Bell pulled a pen from a coffee cup with a Bears logo and wrote Jake's name and badge number onto his desk blotter. Then he tossed the badge and it slid across the desk and off onto Jake's lap. "Why are you here?"

The softness in the chief's voice when he said the Sieberts' names encouraged Jake to open up a bit. "Paul's a friend. He asked me to take a last look at it. Unofficially."

Bell pushed up from his chair and stepped over to the bookshelf. He pulled down a small gold-tone trophy with a quarterback perched on top and put it on the desk in front of Jake. "Only time I ever beat Paul at anything was the long pass contest a bank held when we were in eighth grade. In the finals it was just him and me. Two guys left in a contest that covered the entire southern half of the state, and we lived within a block of each other. I beat him by less than a foot. I'll tell you what I can."

"Thank you, Chief. And will you put me together with Greer and Brakur?"

"Brakur takes his dinner break at nine by the courthouse. I'll radio him and have him tell you his story."

Jake glanced at his watch; he needed to get moving. "And Greer?"

Bell lifted his hands as if in surrender. "That old bastard retired a few years back. You're on your own with him."

"Okay, I'll follow up. But first, what can you tell me about the case? Did you work it yourself?"

"It was my first major case as chief. I—" Bell shook his head and sat back down. "Didn't sleep for months."

"But you solved it."

Bell's eyes met Jake's, then dropped away. "I'd rather have the boy back than his killer in prison." He grimaced. "Smith was an odd sort. Like all of them that like young boys, I suppose. Gave us the confession and that was about it. I watched through the glass while Greer worked him." He shook his head. "About made me sick just looking at him."

"I'd like to see the murder book."

The chief's brow furrowed, then he looked away. "Records clerk is gone for the day. I wouldn't know how to find it in that maze. Believe me, I've tried before." He shifted in his chair and rubbed his jaw.

Three deception indicators clustered together.

"But if you'll give me your cell number, I'll call you tomorrow."

Jake gave it to him, and the man wrote it under Jake's badge number on the blotter.

Jake stood. "Thank you, Chief. I'd better get moving if I'm going to meet up with Officer Brakur."

They shook, and Jake noted that the chief's hand was now moist and warm from his deceptions.

The man wasn't used to lying.

* * *

Back on the sidewalk, Jake checked his watch. He only had six minutes before Brakur took dinner, but it was a short walk and it would be good to get some blood pumping through his legs; his thighs and hamstrings had tightened further. He put his hand in the pocket with the Glock even though he doubted he'd encounter the flannel-clad men here. The street was well lit with a steady stream of traffic.

The cool night air was still and smelled faintly of wet leaves. As he walked, Jake decided to take a minute to call the retired detective. Greer might say something Brakur could refute or verify.

If Jake could get the retired detective talking.

He found the number in his notebook, then dialed. It rang and rang without going to voicemail, and Jake was just about to end the attempt when someone picked up the phone with a hard fumble that racked his eardrum.

"Hello."

"I'm looking for Roman Greer," Jake said.

"Good for you."

"Are you Roman Greer?"

"Quit playing games and tell me who you are and what you want."

Jake got to the point before he lost the man. "I'm Detective Jake Houser." He hoped to establish rapport—one detective to another. "I'm with the Weston Police Department. I just talked to your chief and he suggested I call you directly."

"Bull." Greer coughed, then hiccupped into the phone. "There's no way Bell told you to call me."

"I'd like to hear about your Siebert investigation. From what I've heard so far, you cracked a tough nut." Most cops liked to talk about their big wins.

The silence that followed was encouraging. He had Greer thinking.

"He was a good kid."

"Everybody liked Mark," Jake said. He needed to keep Greer talking.

He sat down on a low brick wall in front of the First Community Bank parking lot. The occasional car cruised past, its tires a whisper on the street.

"Ah... nice work, Detective. First you butter me up and then you try to draw me in. I know the drill. Firstly, the investigation is all in the book—that's why we put the damn things together. And B, I didn't make the arrest. So talk to Brakur and leave me the hell alone."

A bang, and the line was dead. Multiple people had warned him that Greer wouldn't talk, but Jake was still disappointed.

He put his phone back in his pocket and stood up, brushing the grit he'd picked up from the wall off the seat of his pants. A block ahead, a patrol car pulled to the opposite curb.

He hoped Brakur was more cooperative than Greer.

14

———

As Jake crossed Tenth at Main, the patrol car's headlights flashed on and off. He approached the car, and the passenger window lowered and the driver leaned across the seat.

"You Houser?"

Jake bent down to the window. "Yes. I appreciate you taking the time to meet with me."

"Hop in."

Jake opened the door and slid onto the slick vinyl bench seat. The car smelled of coffee and disinfectant—just like every patrol unit he'd ever driven. A small insulated bag sat on the console between them.

As Brakur radioed in his location and that he would go quiet for dinner, Jake observed him. He had the wide shoulders and thick arms of a weightlifter, and he didn't look bothered about talking with an out-of-town detective.

"So." Brakur turned to Jake. "Chief says to tell you about Smith."

"I'd appreciate it." Jake waited a beat for Brakur to start his story, but he didn't. "Chief Bell said you made the arrest."

Brakur was silent for a moment, probably waiting for an explanation. When Jake didn't provide one, he gave a short nod and started talking.

"I always eat my dinner here on the square." He raised his hands and patted the air in front of him. "It's the busiest intersection in the busiest beat in my town. I was here that night when Smith came stumbling along from Ninth Street." He twisted and pointed east and south. "I saw him in the side mirror first, then watched him stumble back and forth across the sidewalk until he bounced off my rear fender and fell down. I got out and checked him. He was conscious, but reeked of booze."

Jake nodded for him to continue.

"I helped him up, put him in the back of my car, and questioned him."

"You suspected him right away?"

"Not about that. About the drinking. We were having a problem with underage drinking and adults being over-served. I asked for his ID and which bar he'd been to. But he didn't have ID and said he'd been to too many bars to remember. He refused both the field test and the breathalyzer, but I had enough to charge him anyway: falling down in front of me, reeking of booze, and he admitted to being drunk."

"And for the Siebert abduction?" Jake asked. "How did that come about?"

"No great police work on my part. He said 'I'm such a cliché,' I asked him what he meant, and he says, you know, all criminals return to the scene of the crime. So I asked him if he'd been arrested for public intoxication here before." Brakur turned in his seat to look directly at Jake. "He says, not arrested and not drunk, but that he'd been to our town before. When, I ask him. It was hot, he says. You still had your buntings up. It was worth it."

Brakur jabbed a thumb over his shoulder. "We always hang red-white-and-blue buntings on the courthouse for the Fourth. Then he kind of fell asleep and I got out and opened his door and shook him a bit until he was on the edge of waking, and I asked him why it was 'worth it.' And he whispered... 'the most beautiful young boy' and smiled and burped. I remember that distinctly because it smelled like french fries. And then he was out."

Jake nodded, absorbed with the story.

"That previous July Fourth—Mark Siebert disappeared on the fifth—was hot. Just a couple degrees off the record. I called my cousin—he's with Public Works—and he said the buntings came down on the sixth."

"Nicely done, Officer Brakur." It was a slick bit of work that relied on the officer's knowledge of his beat. Something a detective might not have been able to put together as quickly, if at all. "And from that you were able to get a full confession out of him?"

Brakur shook his head. "I read him his rights and took him to the station. The desk sergeant called the chief and he pulled in Detective Greer and the ASA. I gave them my report and I was out of it." He brushed his hands together like he was wiping off crumbs.

"So Greer got the actual confession using your work as the fulcrum to leverage the whole story out of Smith."

"That's the way it worked."

"Would your notes contain any more details?"

"Greer took those, but my memory is tight. That's all of it."

"Which bar served him?"

Brakur gave Jake a hard stare. "Just between us?"

"Okay."

"I was told to drop it. Greer would handle that follow-up."

"But it was your beat." Jake had covered a beat for nearly a decade; he knew Brakur would have wanted to personally handle the follow-up.

"Exactly." Brakur shook his head. "I decided I could use my investigation into the underage drinking and over-serving issues to look into it, and I took a copy of Smith's booking photo along with me. But a week had passed. By then everybody I talked to had seen Smith's picture a hundred times on the tube and in the papers. If Smith had a drink with every person who claimed it, alcohol poisoning would have killed him long before he bumped into my cruiser."

"Did Greer have any better luck at the bars?"

Brakur bit his lip. "He was focused on finding Mark's body. I can't blame him for that."

"You're saying Greer hadn't talked to anyone in the bars?"

"Not a one."

Jake gave Brakur a business card. "Please call me on the cell number there at the bottom if you think of anything else."

"If you're not going to tell me why you're asking," Brakur said, pointing at Jake, "at least show me that gun you have in your right-hand pocket."

Jake laughed. "Your chief didn't notice it at all." He pulled it out, racked the slide to eject the shell, then removed the magazine and handed it to Brakur.

Brakur nodded in apparent approval at the precaution. He took the gun, flipped it over, then gripped it. The subcompact G26 looked like a toy in his big hand. "A good backup. Easy to hide, light. I like it. What's your primary?"

"You're holding it." Jake shrugged. "It shoots well enough to qualify."

Brakur smiled and handed it back. "Well, I hope your trip to my town was worth it."

Jake reloaded the Glock and put it back in his pocket. "It's not over."

Brakur raised his eyebrows. He clearly wanted to ask what more Jake was after, but he kept his questions to himself.

"One last thing," Jake said. "Why still a beat cop?"

Brakur's expression grew serious. "Detective, this is my town, and these are my people. Doing this," he spread his hands in front of him, "is who I am. It's *why* I am."

Jake nodded. Brakur was the real deal. He wasn't in it for the pension or as a stepping-stone to a political position. It was his calling. Keeping the people of his community safe was his mission.

A man after Jake's own heart.

15

Benchley spent the afternoon at his desk, thinking through the what-ifs and maybes of the action to come. There were a lot of variables: Thomas and Andy; Reznik and the operator he was bringing in; Reznik's problem down in Mount Logan; and that damn tweeter. But planning and contingencies were his strength and he kept spinning through the possibilities.

As he worked through them, he realized he had his own problem downstate. He should have silenced Tracy James long ago. He'd correct that, but not until Seth confirmed Thomas actually was in Weston. If Thomas wasn't there, Benchley might need Tracy to find him again.

He wandered upstairs as he puzzled through next steps, then paced the long hallway, looking into the empty rooms and smelling the bleach they'd used to wash them down and the fresh paint on every wall. They had scrambled to get it all done. Eighteen-hour days cleaning, patching peepholes, and painting. Seth working like a demon to pile the furniture in the fire pit out back and erase everything. Nothing here now looked like the pictures in the files Thomas had stolen.

He stopped in the library. He'd put together a lot of deals here with men who all shared this same interest. A network of powerful men Benchley had created, nurtured, leveraged. Now all at risk because of Reznik.

He turned off the lights and went back downstairs. It was dinnertime. He was never hungry during an operation, so he had to force himself to eat on a schedule.

His phone rang in his pocket when he was halfway down the long swooping staircase. He paused to answer.

"Benchley."

"I ain't seen him, boss." Seth's voice had the slow tempo it got when he smoked pot. "But it's definitely him staying here. Him and Andy, maybe one more."

"One more?"

"The guys aren't sure, but they think maybe Thomas has two guys with him."

That had to be wrong, unless that preacher was with them. "What is this place?" Benchley continued down the stairs and headed back to his private office.

"It's a rooming house, like in those old movies you like. Where the drifter comes to town and stays in a spare bedroom at the widow's house. Like that. Only here it's not a lady widow but a weird dude who talks funny. He turned the garage into a little apartment and that's where they were staying. Only Thomas took Andy and the other guy—if there is another guy—someplace else this morning. But he's coming back."

"How can you be sure?"

"The weird dude told the guys living in the house. I made friends with some of them."

"I bet you did." Seth made friends faster than a three-year-old on the playground.

Seth laughed. "It's easy with this Acapulco Gold. These guys are all tokers."

"No one's in the apartment right now?"

"No. It's empty."

Benchley nibbled at the ends of his mustache. The damn files might be sitting in there waiting for him. "Can you get in there and look for the files I told you about?"

"Don't need to, boss."

"Why not?" Benchley pushed through the heavy oak door and into his office. Just stepping inside his private space improved his mood. He strode to the fireplace and watched the glowing coals, their red surging and fading.

"Two of these guys have been in Miller's place already—that's the name Thomas is using, Robert Miller—looking for something to steal, and they say there's nothing in there."

Thomas was using a fake name. No wonder Benchley had been unable to find him. "You didn't tell them about the files, did you?"

"No way, boss. I got these guys talking about him and we made like a game out of who knew more about what stuff he had in his room. Winner got hits of the Gold. It was smooth." Seth chuckled, his voice deep and phlegmy—he'd taken plenty of tokes himself. "Same with the car he took from you. The Impala. Nothing in it worth stealing."

So Thomas was either keeping the files on him, or he'd hid them somewhere. "You find a place to stay?"

"I'm gonna crash in my car. Told these guys I'm staying with my grandma. It's all cool."

"Good work, Seth. Let's talk tomorrow."

After the call, Benchley sat behind his desk, his thoughts turning back to his downstate problem. He'd done a fantastic job twisting Tracy's mind until his reality, his very memories, included killing the Siebert boy. He literally believed he had done it. But it had now been seven years, and the constructs Benchley had built in Tracy's head were susceptible to erosion over time and with maturity. He shouldn't have left that loose end dangling for so long.

His stomach twisted, and he popped a handful of antacids from the plastic jar he kept in the drawer. He chewed the chalky tablets into paste, then washed the slurry down with a slug of whiskey from the flask in his lap drawer.

He tilted his head back and forth, stretching his neck, then made the call.

"Talk."

"It's Benchley."

"Well, well. I was starting to think you'd wrapped up that little enterprise you got going, white man." The voice on the phone was soft and almost lyrical.

"I need something." The quicker he got to it, the quicker he could get off the phone. This guy always made Benchley nervous.

"I gots everything you might need, Whitey. You'll want some of the blessed herb, right? And some racing powder? Maybe some more of them freaky drugs you like. Them are expensive, man. But you know I can get 'em."

"No. I need a... thing taken care of down at Big Rend."

"A *thing*."

"You know people down there, right? Who can get things done?"

"I do." Sudden hardness. "But it's gonna cost you cash, and a pile of it."

"I understand." Benchley opened his lap drawer and ran a finger down the corner of a thick stack of hundreds he'd brought back from Denver. Easy come, easy go. But he wasn't in this for the money.

"Come see me at Winona's on East Second. You know it?"

A shudder ran through Benchley, and he pressed his legs together to quell it. "I'll find it."

"Right now."

The line went dead.

Benchley pocketed the phone, took another slug of the whiskey, and got moving. Waiting wouldn't make it any better.

16

———————

Jake left Brakur with his dinner, recovered his Mustang from the police station, then drove south toward the motel. On the way he spotted an IGA grocery store and stocked up on energy bars. He parked in front of his room and took the gun inside with him.

Stretched out on the bed, he found a Northwestern basketball game on television. But it was a non-conference blowout and Jake's attention wandered. He picked up a postcard propped against the lamp on the nightstand. It featured a glossy picture of the motel, the paintwork bright and the windows sparkling. On the back was a stamp: *Harold and Sheila Siebert, Proprietors*. Siebert. In a town as small as this, they had to be related to Paul.

He put the postcard down, then pulled his laptop up onto his belly and checked his email. Nothing from the task force. Nothing from ASA McKay about the Storch case. He started an email to her about other ways they might go after Storch if the indictment failed, but he couldn't come up with a good plan and ended up deleting it all. Then he wrote about focusing on her own duty and letting the other cogs in the wheels of justice do theirs, but the tone was too heavy. He deleted that too and pushed the laptop onto the other half of the bed. When he had something concrete

85

to suggest, or something witty and interesting to say about the job or about life, he'd try again.

He started flipping through the channels but he couldn't engage with anything because his thoughts kept drifting back to Brakur. Something about the officer's story was niggling away in Jake's brain. He replayed the whole conversation and saw no deception from the man. Brakur had told the truth as he knew it. But somewhere in that story there was an anomaly.

Jake couldn't identify it yet.

But he would.

* * *

Jake woke slowly the next morning, light bleeding around the edges of the curtain and the window rattling from a truck going by out on Tenth Street. He stretched, then yipped when the knot in his back stabbed him with a reminder of the night before. His back was a little touchy from the ten years he'd spent in a squad car.

He got down on the floor and did some careful stretching, and the knot dissolved as his body warmed with the movement. He took two Aleve to keep it at bay, then made coffee with the in-room machine and ate a couple energy bars.

While he showered, he thought about the day ahead. Before heading out to the prison to talk with Smith, he would visit the ASA who'd handled the Siebert case seven years before. According to Erin's research, the man now had a private law practice and had been elected mayor which was apparently only a part-time job in this little town.

Dressed and ready to go, Jake sat at the room's small desk and checked email. An update from ASA McKay: the grand jury had refused to indict Storch. He'd expected it, of course, but the failure still pissed him off.

He pulled his cell phone out and called her. She answered on the first ring.

"No indictment," she said. "Came down yesterday afternoon, but I was too angry to tell you until this morning."

"We figured," Jake said.

"I reached out to the Department of Children and Family Services, and they'll open a case against Imani for neglect because of the heroin, just so someone is keeping an eye on the girls."

"That's all you can do." Pushing beyond your defined role in the criminal justice system led to frustration and burnout. And made enemies.

"Your chief has started with the finger pointing."

"Braff?"

"No, the top guy. Chief Arvind."

"Has the media gotten ahold of it?" The blame game usually started after the media kicked up a stink.

"Not yet. I guess he's just getting ready."

"We'll find another way into the heroin network."

"I know," Anna said. "It's just these little girls—Christ!"

"I landed a new CI that might help." Jake hoped that didn't sound like he was trying to impress her—but maybe he was.

"Who?"

He told her about Smoke without naming him or his gang.

"Let's hope that helps," she said.

Then the line clicked dead. The abruptness felt like an accusation. The Storch case had been his investigation, so it was deserved. But it still hurt.

* * *

Jake stepped outside into a cold fresh morning under a clear blue sky. Then he noticed that his Mustang was slumped in its parking space—all four tires were flat. He put his hand in the pocket of his windbreaker and wrapped it around the Glock, his heart rate kicking up.

Kneeling by a tire, he checked for damage. The valve was slashed, not the tire. He must have slept like a rock not to hear the rush of air when it was cut. He checked the other tires and found the same damage on all four. The flannel-clad men from last night? Or someone else?

He stood back from the car, then noticed a message scrawled on the back window in greasy green and white. It looked like it was written with a bar of Irish Spring soap.

Leave it alone.

Time slowed as the pieces fell together.

Shit.

He made a call and spoke briefly to the man who answered. Then he walked to the lobby and pushed open the glass door.

"Good morning, Mr. Houser." Shelia's voice held anger that made her greeting a lie. "What can I do for you today?"

Jake held out his phone. "Take this call."

"What?" But she took the phone and held it to her ear. "Hello, this is Sheila at the Regal Inn. Who's this? Oh. Oh!" Her eyebrows lifted, then she turned away and had a hurried but hushed conversation.

Jake waited patiently. After a minute Sheila turned back, her face red. "Paul wants to talk to you."

Jake took the phone back.

"Jake, I'm really sorry about your car," Paul said. "Sheila's my aunt, and she thought you were a reporter. My family hates the media. If I knew you were going down there I could have given them a heads-up."

"It's going to slow me down a bit."

"Sheila's son Lenny is going to fix the tires for you."

The least he can do, Jake thought. "How's Linda doing?"

"Anxious. We thought you were going to talk to Miller yesterday. We were hoping for a call but didn't want to bother you. What are you doing down there? Did he say something to—"

Jake broke in. Now wasn't the time. "I'll call you later this morning when I have a few minutes." *And some privacy.*

"Okay," Paul said. Linda's voice sounded in the background.

"Linda says to tell you thank you. And we both mean it. And again, sorry about the car."

"No problem, Paul."

They hung up and Jake stepped up to the counter, where Sheila was now talking on her landline. She continued in a quiet but forceful tone for another minute, then turned back to the counter.

"Okay. I straightened things out." Her eyes stayed off Jake's. "Thank you for not... you know, hurting my boys last night."

"Sure."

But what if it had gone the other way? Jake wondered. *How far would her boys have gone?*

He glanced outside and back to Sheila. "Your son's going to fix my tires?"

"Lenny's on his way over with the flatbed and something for you to drive. If you'll leave your keys, we'll get that done for you right away."

Jake gave the Mustang's key fob to Sheila, then sat in one of the chairs and waited for Lenny. He considered locking the Glock in the Mustang's glove box, but decided to keep it on him. Even with "the boys" off his back, it was better to stay prepared for whatever else this town might throw at him.

17

Jake's phone buzzed in his pocket—a text from Chief Bell: *Murder book is offsite. It will be here in a week.*

Jake doubted that was true. More likely Bell just didn't want some out-of-towner second-guessing the decisions he'd made during the heat and pressure of the active investigation. But he still thanked Chief Bell for his time and for requesting the book.

A few minutes later a flatbed truck with *Siebert Towing* on the door pulled into the lot. Jake watched through the window as Sheila ran out and handed Jake's car key to the driver. The man took it, gave Jake a long look through the office window, then nodded. Jake didn't return the gesture.

The truck's engine roared as the flatbed pulled into a three-point turn to align with the Mustang's rear bumper. A burly man climbed down from the passenger side. He wore boots, jeans, and a flannel shirt. Operating the hydraulic controls mounted behind his door, he lowered the truck's bed. When the edge hit the pavement, he stretched a cable over and bent to reach under the Mustang to hook it to the rear axle. He stopped with a jerk, a hand groping his lower back.

Jake smiled. That was probably the guy he'd flipped.

An early seventies Chevy C10 pickup pulled off Tenth and

parked in front of the office. A younger man jumped out. He had that now-familiar jawline and wide-shouldered build of a Siebert. He glanced at Jake, handed the truck's keys to Sheila, pecked her on the cheek, and jogged over to the flatbed where he took over hooking up the Mustang. The older guy stood back up but kept rubbing his back.

"How's the other one?" Jake asked Sheila when she stepped back into the lobby.

"He'll be fine. Just a little gravel rash." She handed him the keys to the pickup. "No charge for the room."

Jake nodded and left her there watching her boys.

* * *

Wayne Nelson, the man who'd handled the David Smith prosecution as ASA seven years before, now owned a law firm named Nelson and Associates. Jake found it in a stucco building with white pillars on the northeast corner of Tenth and Main, across the street from the courthouse. A photography studio with a Main Street entrance occupied the first floor, and the law firm sat above it with its entrance under a green awning around the corner on Tenth. Jake parked the pickup in an empty spot along the curb and went inside, climbing a set of squeaky wood stairs to a comfortable reception area rimmed with black leather couches and lit by large windows. Two groups of people held down opposite ends of the space.

A woman in a white blouse sporting an oversized bow at the neck sat behind a small desk guarding a door into the offices themselves. She pulled her hands off her keyboard and pasted on a smile as Jake approached.

"I'd like to see Mr. Nelson," Jake said.

"He *is* in this morning, but he's terribly busy." Her eyes darted toward the people waiting, then swept over him, probably evaluating his clothing for a hint of how much the firm could charge him. Small firms had flexible pricing. She lowered her voice to a flat whisper. "Can I tell him what this is about? Divorce? DUI? If it's city business you'll have to go to City Hall to make an appointment."

Jake handed her a card. Her eyebrows rose, then she bounced up from her desk and disappeared through the door.

She was back within two minutes. She waved for him to follow her through the door and into a warren of cubicles on the other side. Every desk was cluttered with files and legal pads, but Jake saw no people. Nelson's army of associates was probably handling morning court calls while the big man signed up new clients.

The receptionist led Jake to a pair of doors in the south wall. She swung open the right-hand door and waved Jake through.

"Here he is, Mr. Nelson."

"Thank you, Barbara."

Jake stepped into a wide room that spanned the entire front of the building.

"You're lucky to have caught me, Detective Houser." Nelson stood up from his big leather chair, Jake's business card in his hand. He was a large man of about sixty, muscle marbling into fat, gray hair swept back, his tie too red and too long. "I'm in court most mornings. A courtesy call from Weston's mayor or your chief would have been nice."

Nelson's opening move put Jake on the defensive. It was a politician's play. "Thank you for seeing me anyway."

"Have a seat." Nelson sat heavily back in his chair.

As Jake sat, he took a moment to scan the room in order to get a feel for the man. A pair of large multi-paned windows behind the desk looked over Main Street and the courthouse beyond. The furniture was old and heavy, the wood stained dark but polished to a gleam. Photos and certificates covered the east wall and diplomas the west. Nelson's desk held nothing but a legal pad, a phone, and a souvenir coffee mug from Las Vegas full of pens.

Ego-driven.

"Chief Bell called—as mayor he works for me, you know—and said Paul asked you to look at his son's case."

"That's right. Good police work led to a confession and no appeal. You buttoned it up very nicely. Textbook." Politicians loved to have their egos stroked.

"Damn right." Nelson relaxed back into his chair. "Linda is probably the force behind your visit, and that's fine. My niece was in her class, so we hear how she's been struggling. But why a local cop and not a private detective? Tell me that."

Nelson wanted to tell Jake about his perfect case, but he still needed a reason to do so that made sense to him.

"Friendship," Jake said. "Debts owed." Nelson probably traded in favors all day long.

Nelson sighed loudly through his nose. "I see."

"I knew you'd understand."

Nelson nodded and jumped right into a smooth tale that breezed quickly through the weeks of investigation to get to Smith. "Then David Smith got arrested for public intoxication and we cracked him like a walnut."

Got arrested. A slick way to remove Officer Brakur from the narrative. "You and…"

"Detective Greer. We gave Smith the old rope-a-dope and he spilled it. And the rest is history." Nelson spread his hands wide as if the Siebert case had led him to his current success. And maybe it had.

"Why did the state's attorney let you have the case?"

"Let me? Shit, he *made* me. He was scared of that case. Those Sieberts can throw a hell of a lot of weight around, and he didn't want to get buried by them if things went to shit. Like they started to. I saved his career getting that confession." Nelson shook his head. "Bastard's still in office, although not for much longer if I can help it."

"Being mayor not enough?"

Nelson waved his hand again. "We have a city council government—all the real power is with them and the city manager. Mayor's just a tiebreaker at meetings, the city cheerleader." He caught Jake's eye and swallowed. "Don't get me wrong. It's an amazing honor. But I feel I can do more for the people of my city, and our county, as state's attorney."

Politicians were always campaigning.

"So you pulled the confession out of Smith," Jake said, playing along. "How did Smith convince you it was true?"

"You think it wasn't?" Nelson's voice rose, blotchy red flashing across his pale face.

"Not at all, Mayor. But—"

"That was a solid confession. He knew things that only the abductor could have known. And he never recanted. Not when he sobered up. Not even after he got a public defender. Never. And don't forget the allocution. He told it to the judge and the judge accepted it. Buttoned up, like you said." Nelson leaned back, the chair's springs shrieking in protest.

"What things did he know?"

"I don't have the authority to tell you that." Nelson smiled.

"Chief Bell told me the murder book is off-site and it'll take a week to get it back." Jake needed to see that book.

"I'm sure that's right."

Jake didn't like the smirk—or the fact that Nelson didn't try to hide it. The man felt completely in control. Mayor and master of his own destiny.

"I think the book's right there in his office, and you and Bell are hiding something," Jake said. "If you are, I will find it. Just remember I gave you this chance to come clean."

He left the man grinding his teeth so hard the sound carried into the outer room.

18

Back outside Jake found a piece of paper flapping under the truck's wiper blade. It was a note on a blank receipt from Siebert Auto that said his car would be ready by ten thirty. It was almost ten now, so Jake decided to retrieve the Mustang before heading out to the prison. He scanned the street for a place to get a cup of coffee and was surprised to find nothing within view. A coffee shop next to the courthouse was as American as apple pie.

He hoisted himself into the truck and fired it up. The address for Siebert Auto was circled in red ink: north Tenth Street. As he headed that way, he kept his eyes peeled for a coffee shop. When the road tightened into a tree-tunneled lane, he resigned himself to not getting a second cup of coffee that morning, but then he rounded a curve and found a Casey's General Store.

He parked on the side of the store by the ice chests and went inside. It was the smallest Casey's he'd ever been in, the aisles narrow and packed tight with merchandise, the burnt grease smell of the hotdogs rotating on the cooker filling the place. He found the coffee near the register, poured himself a sixteen-ouncer, paid, then went back out to the truck. As he sat there sipping the coffee, he called Paul back, as he'd promised.

Paul answered before Jake even heard a ring. "Jake, I am so, *so* sorry. Aunt Sheila just now told me about what happened last night, on top of the tires this morning. I can't apologize enough. I promise you her boys—those are my cousins—wouldn't have hurt you. They just thought they were scaring off a reporter. You can't imagine how much those anniversary follow-up articles hurt Linda."

"It's okay, Paul. I'm fine."

"I'm glad to hear it. What are you doing down there, Jake? We thought you were just going to talk to Miller."

"I started with Miller, but he was gone. The landlord said he'll be back in a couple days." Jake didn't tell Paul about the call from the prison. Not until he knew more about what it meant.

"So you're, what... talking to the police down there?"

"Yes. I decided to come down and talk to the people involved back then."

"What did they tell you?"

"Paul, an investigation has a lot of false starts and empty leads. For now I'm just talking to people, and most of that will mean nothing. Some of it might mean something, but I won't know which is what until I get the work done and see if it takes me anywhere."

"And you don't want us pestering you while you're at it," Paul said.

"I'll let you know when I have something concrete."

"Got it, Jake. And thank you."

Jake found Siebert Auto Repair and Service a few curves up the road, a steel-sided building set far back from the road behind a large gravel yard. The Mustang sat directly in front of the building, a pair of young men working off a coat of wax with strong circular rubs of dingy towels.

Jake pulled the C10 to the open garage door on the side of the building. The man who'd ridden along in the flatbed that morning stepped through the door and waved for Jake to park it right there. Jake did, then got out, tossing the empty coffee cup in a barrel between the doors.

"My mom—Sheila—told me what's going on," the man said. He leaned against the front of the Chevy. "I'm Lenny."

Jake tossed the keys, and Lenny snatched them out of the air.

Lenny patted the hood. "The truck treat you okay?"

"Just fine, thank you. How well connected are you in this town, Lenny?"

"Very."

"And in the county?"

"Mount Logan *is* the county. Ain't another town of more than five hundred people in the rest of the county." Lenny crossed his arms. "What do you need?"

"Think you can get Detective Greer to talk to me?"

Lenny shook his head. "I'll try, but he's a hard case."

"How about connections with the police department? I'd like to see the file on Mark's case, but Chief Bell says it's stored off-site."

"Yeah, we got kin there at the station. I can find out about that."

"Let me know."

Jake collected his car, thanking the men taking the final few swabs at the wax. The car looked great inside and out: vacuumed, windows washed, even an air freshener hanging from the rearview mirror. Jake pulled it hard, breaking the string looped around the mirror, and handed it out the window to one of the men. Then he started up the Mustang and headed south.

He passed back through downtown and a few minutes later escaped the commercial district. After another half mile of scattered houses, the road crossed over Highway 64 and he was in the country. A green sign told him it was eleven miles to Rend Lake College, which Sheila had said was near the prison.

He spent the short drive letting his brain spin through what he knew about David Smith. The problem was, he knew almost nothing. Officer Brakur had told him everything he knew, the newspaper stories said almost nothing about the man's background, the name was too common for Levi to find anything, and the murder book was out of his reach.

For now.

Soon a fat water tower rose from the plain ahead of him, then a scatter of blue guard towers appeared above a wide sprawl of two- and three-story buildings surrounded by a tall perimeter fence, itself circled by high light poles. Jake slowed and followed the signs to the visitor lot. As he parked, his heartbeat kicked up a notch. If he could crack Smith open, he would soon know how he was connected to Miller and what Smith was getting from the con.

* * *

Benchley took another hit from the bottle of antacid. The thick chalky liquid brought instant relief to his churning gut.

The deal he'd made the night before would eliminate his downstate vulnerability, but he still needed to get his files back. And he needed to make sure Thomas and Andy kept their damn mouths shut. What he should do was sell them so far down the chain they'd never have a chance to talk to anyone ever again. Or better yet, he could just silence them himself after a few hours of fun in the basement.

He nibbled at his mustache. Twenty-four hours and still nothing from Reznik. His operative must be stuck down in Mount Logan. Hell, maybe he wasn't even there yet. But that might be for the best. If Benchley got the files back without Reznik's help, it would be easier to exclude the congressman going forward. Benchley would recruit new boys and this time sell them off before their brains could shake off what he'd done to them. By seventeen, just to be absolutely sure.

And if Reznik tried to worm in on the action, Benchley would simply pull out the file he'd put together on the man.

Worth considering.

Benchley called Seth.

"Hey, boss."

"Thomas show up?"

"I said I'd call you."

"Yes, you did."

Benchley closed his eyes and thought about everything that could go wrong with Seth up there all alone. The boy had done well so far, but didn't have the attention span to go it alone much longer.

"Tell you what, Seth. I'm going to come up and hang out with you. Can't let you have all the fun."

19

———

Jake locked the Glock in the glove box and left his phone in the car —the Illinois Department of Corrections had strict rules for visitors. He joined the thin stream of people making their way from the parking lot to the visitors' entrance, weaving through them in his excitement to get at Smith.

He badged himself past the first two layers of security. He had to step around a woman throwing a fit because her stretch pants and cleavage-revealing top violated the DOC's dress code, and the guards wouldn't let her in. The metal detector lit up as Jake stepped through, but wanding revealed it was only his watch and his badge, and he was waved on.

Past that hurdle, he stepped up to a Dutch door with the top swung open and a sign that said ATTORNEYS AND LAW ENFORCEMENT CHECK IN HERE. A bored guard behind the door perked up as Jake approached.

"Good morning, Officer."

"How'd you know I'm not an attorney?" Jake said. Technically, he *was* an attorney. He had graduated from law school and kept his license current, paying the annual fee and taking the mandatory continuing education classes, even though he'd never practiced law and never planned to.

"You're not wearing a tie."

"Nice observation, Officer... Holmes." Jack smiled as he read the man's nametag. This Holmes looked nothing like the famous Baker Street detective. He was eighty pounds heavier and many shades darker. "I'm here to see David Smith."

"Someone called ahead, so we have him handy. But a couple things first." Holmes slid a clipboard onto the little counter affixed to the top of the half-door. "We need you to fill this out."

Jake filled in the form, identifying his purpose as a follow-up inquiry, then Holmes swung the door open and waved for Jake to follow him. They passed through several more locked doors, then into a grouping of small interview rooms apparently reserved for police officers and defense attorneys.

Holmes ushered Jake into a room with a metal table and three chairs. Jake turned to ask Holmes where Smith was, but the door had already clicked shut, leaving him alone. He grabbed the handle and found it locked.

Shit. He wiped a sudden sheen of sweat from his forehead and tried not to think about being locked in a concrete-block room deep inside a prison surrounded by layers of security and two thousand inmates. He wasn't claustrophobic, but he had to remind himself of that every time he made a prison visit. He took a couple of deep breaths without relief—the air was stale and smelled of sweat and unwashed bodies—then stepped across the room and back, grit on the concrete floor crunching under his shoes. When he realized he was pacing, he stopped and leaned against the wall. It solidity somehow grounded him, and he felt his pulse slowing and his breathing even out. Nothing to worry about.

He closed his eyes.

A few long minutes passed before the door handle rattled and a woman came in. Jake guessed her to be in her mid-fifties, although she was so trim and fit she might have been older. She wore a dark blue skirt and matching jacket. Jake knew almost nothing about women's clothes, but something about the outfit gave the impression of high quality; maybe it was how she wore it.

A scent rode in with her, subtle and flowery, but strong enough to freshen the air. She carried a thin red file.

"Good morning, Detective Houser." She looked him over. "Shall we?" She gestured at the table and sat down, comfortable with the environment. At home.

Jake took the chair across from her, the metal cold through his pants.

"I'm Warden Stevenson. Your emergency request for an inmate visit hit my desk yesterday afternoon. I made a few calls. Your boss, Deputy Chief Braff, was a little vague about why you're here." She smiled.

Jake liked her smile. She was busting his balls, but not like she planned to get in his way. More fraternal. "I'll have to brief him when I get back," Jake said. Of course Braff had no idea where Jake was or what he was doing. And the deputy chief was a terrible liar.

"Paul and Linda live in Weston."

"Yes." First names again, like with Bell. Maybe everyone in Mount Logan had a personal connection to the Sieberts. "I'm here for them."

"They asked you to talk with Smith?"

"Linda wanted a last look at the case. Fresh eyes."

"Because they never found Mark's body?"

Jake nodded and left it at that.

The warden flipped open the file, scanned the top sheet, then closed it again. She gave Jake a slow once-over. "This morning I got a call from His Highness, the great Mayor Nelson. You made quite the impression on him. He told me not to let you talk to Smith if you came down here."

Jake smiled. The two must have history for Nelson to think he could tell her what to do.

"Do you think there was something 'off' about the case against Smith, Detective?"

"Why else would Nelson tell you to stop my visit?" Jake asked.

"Maybe just to see if he could."

"Can he?"

"No." She allowed herself another smile. "I'm from this county, Detective. My family has been here as long as the Sieberts. I've never mapped it out, but Paul Siebert and I are probably related through several lines of cousins."

"And the mayor's family?"

"Moved to town in eighth grade." She smiled again. "That's part of what attracted me to him. We dated in high school. It didn't end well."

Jake smiled back at her.

She flipped the file open again. "Let's talk for a few minutes, then I'll have Mr. Smith brought in."

Jake pulled out his notebook and opened it to a blank page, pen ready.

"When Smith filled out his BDS—biographical data sheet— he left his visitation list blank and wrote that he had 'no next of kin.'"

Old news. "Has he had any visitors?"

"No *personal* visitors." She flipped a couple pages. "But he recently accepted a visit from a church group, Christian Ministry for Lost Youths."

Prisons were flooded with requests from Christian groups wanting to lead prisoners to salvation. Jake wrote the ministry's name down. "Are you familiar with this group, Warden?"

She shook her head. "Not this one, no."

"Where's it located?"

She ran a finger down the page. "Rockford." She read off an address, and he wrote it down. Smith and Miller could be communicating through this outfit.

"How about phone calls? Has he made any?"

She flipped another few pages. "Not a single one."

"Could he have made a call from the prison library?"

The warden's gaze drifted as she thought about it. When her focus returned, there was a hardness that hadn't been there before. "Mr. Smith works in the library. He puts in a lot of hours there, soliciting books from libraries across the state. But he does that by mail. The library phone is locked in the director's office. Inmates can't use it."

"Someone used that phone to call a number in Weston yesterday morning. Maybe the director lets him use the phone to speed things up?"

The warden frowned. "I will look into that."

"Are those calls recorded?"

"No."

Jake fished a card out of his wallet and slid it across the table. "Please let me know what you find out."

She took the card and tapped it on the table. Her eyes met his, then dropped to the card. More tapping. Jake read her sudden reluctance to speak to mean she had something to tell him but wasn't sure she should.

He set his pen down.

She lowered her eyes to the file and the biological data sheet. "I encourage every inmate to meet with a psychologist once a quarter, minimum. Smith never did until a few days after that first ministry visit. I don't get reports on the substance of these meetings unless the inmate is a danger to himself or someone else. No troubles with Smith."

"But…"

"But word got out through our internal informant network that Smith has started talking in his sleep about his momma."

Momma. Like in Hawkeye's message to Miller.

"But he has no living kin," Jake said.

"That's what he put on his data sheet." She flicked at the edge of the folder. "The only proof we have that his name is even David Smith is his say-so." She flipped a couple more pages and put her finger on an entry. "No Social Security number, no driver's license number. No identification on him when he was arrested." She closed the file.

"What are you saying, Warden?" She was more familiar with Smith than a warden of two thousand men should be. Maybe because she was related, however distantly, to Mark Siebert.

She patted the file. "Everything we know about David Smith he told us himself, from the abduction all the way through what's on this data sheet. Not one single fact came from any investigative effort."

Jake nodded along with her observations. They were interesting, but the Mount Logan police would not have accepted Smith's confession unless he provided corroborating details, as Nelson claimed Smith had done. And all of that would be in the murder book.

He needed to see that book.

"Anything else you can tell me before I talk to Smith?"

"Yes, although it is not unique to him. According to the summary report from the psychologist, Smith was abused as a child. Physically, emotionally, and sexually. By a close relative or someone else important to him. Repeatedly and persistently. Like the vast majority of our inmates."

20

———————

Drill always made his own travel arrangements in country. He liked to control his personal security and keep his actual home base a secret. As far as the agency knew, he lived near Denver, and that was as far as they could backtrack him if they made the effort. They would not connect him to the flight up from Phoenix.

Arizona was private.

The passenger compartment of this commercial flight was packed with people, their chatter, and their smells. His last-second ticket purchase had stuck him in the middle seat, wedged between a college-aged kid who kept his face pressed to the window and a fat businessman who kept stretching his feet into the aisle and tripping people. Drill was not convinced these tripping incidents were all accidents. The guy was a bit of a dick.

Drill had put in a pair of earbuds but didn't pump any music through them. Distracting yourself from your environment was a good way to get killed.

He shifted in the seat, pressing his back against the lumbar support. He'd started his hike this morning before the sun had fully broken over the mountains, and in the dark he'd tripped on a small barrel cactus and wrenched his back. It was already sensitive

—had been ever since he fell out of his sniper's nest when an RPG hit it a glancing blow back in 2014.

He unzipped an outside pocket of his small duffel bag, popped a painkiller, and swallowed it with a slosh of bottled water.

He didn't like how this op was starting. With most rush jobs Spec flooded him with information as if to compensate for the timetable, but not this one. In fact Spec had loaded so little information on the board that Drill was sure he could google a random resident of Mount Logan, Illinois, and find out more about that person than Spec had delivered on Roman Greer. But he had enough to find the man.

Greer was retired and a widower. He ate his dinner at the Red Lion Café every night, hung out at the courthouse every weekday, and lived alone at a rural route address southeast of town. Drill would find Greer at one of those three places, then he'd do it fast and make it look unprofessional, as ordered. He'd smack Greer over the head with whatever was handy, rob him, and get out, job done.

He'd done exactly that, or something like it, many times over the years.

From there he was to head north to a Chicago suburb to recover a file containing sensitive classified information. *More intel to come.*

It better be a hell of a lot more.

He pulled his tablet out of his bag, tapped into the plane's Wi-Fi, and opened a satellite-mapping tool to study his destination. Memorizing the locale had saved his ass many times. He took mental note of the roads in and out of Mount Logan, then circled in on Greer's house and the diner. The house was out in the country, on a big lot near the end of a dead-end road. He zoomed in for the street view. The neighborhood was deteriorating—most of the houses looked to be in need of a new roof and a coat of paint. Not a place a burglar would go looking for a score.

The diner was a better choice. It was out by the highway and set back from the road behind a large parking lot. Towering light poles covered the entire lot. That made it trickier, but it was far more believable.

His satellite phone buzzed inside his bag, and he pulled it out. A text from Spec: *Change of plans and additional intel. Check the board.*

Drill put the phone away and accessed the message board using the tablet.

Unconfirmed intelligence says Weston police detective Jake Houser is in Mount Logan. Driving a personal vehicle. Mustang. Report says he's trying to set up a meeting with Greer. Do NOT allow this meeting to occur.

Drill didn't like unconfirmed intelligence. It meant it came from someone outside the intelligence community. An amateur. But it still might be true. And if it *was* true, it was bad news. Killing a guy a cop was trying to talk to would generate a lot of attention.

But Spec had made it clear.

That meeting was not to take place.

21

Jake's conversation with the warden had raised his confidence level. Although Smith had always refused to talk in the past, things were different now: Smith had accepted a visit from a prison ministry, he was worried about his momma—which meant she was alive—and he had called Miller.

But Jake's confidence faded along with the warden's fragrance only a few minutes after she'd left the room. Smith had been inside for seven long years. Over two thousand days. No matter how soft he'd been coming into this place, two thousand days and nights inside would have hardened him.

The door opened and slammed against the wall, and a pair of guards walked Smith into the room.

Smith was a small, slight man with pale skin and messy brown hair. His orange jumpsuit looked faded and dull next to the shiny blue polyester of the guards' uniforms. He kept his head down as the guards guided him by his elbows, his hands manacled in front of him. They pushed him into the same chair the warden had used, then hauled his hands onto the tabletop, chains clanking against the metal.

One of the guards gestured at the large eyebolt sticking out of the center of the table. "You want we should chain his hands to the table?"

"No, thanks," Jake said. "I'll be fine."

"Suit yourself."

The guards left and closed the door behind them.

"My name is Jake Houser."

Smith raised his head, shot a quick look at the door, then sat taller. Jake knew Smith was approaching thirty, but he didn't look a day older than twenty-three. His face was a little puffy, probably from eating starchy prison food, and a wispy beard lined his jaw. His eyes were set close together. They jittered around the room, passing over Jake several times before locking on.

"The guard said you're a cop, but he didn't say what you want."

"I want to talk about what you're doing to your mother," Jake said.

Jake was taking a leap here, but he felt confident in it—the pieces fit. Miller's con, and Smith's involvement in it, had somehow put Smith's mother at risk. That was why Smith had called Miller. *What about my momma?*

Smith's eyes narrowed, and he scooted his chair forward, a raw scrape against the concrete floor. His hands clenched, the muscles in his forearms popping into relief. One forearm was marked by a dark bruise.

"You gotta tell Mr. B I remember our deal! I got no part in what Thomas is doing up there in Weston."

Jake let Smith stew as he unpacked what the little man had said. *Up there in Weston.* That clearly referred to Robert Miller. Which meant—as Levi had thought—Robert Miller was an alias for a man named Thomas. Whatever Thomas/Miller was doing in Weston was against this Mr. B's interest, and if Smith helped Thomas, that would violate a deal Smith had made with Mr. B. Which, according to the message Smith had left for Thomas, would put Smith's mom at risk.

Perhaps most interesting of all, Smith thought Jake was a cop on Mr. B's payroll.

Jake would use that mistake for as long as he could get away with it.

"What do you want me to tell Mr. B about what you and Thomas are doing up in Weston?" he asked.

"I'm *not* part of that! You gotta tell him. That's all Thomas!"

"If that's all Thomas, why did you call him from the library?"

Smith stood up, then shot a look at the door and sat back down, manacles clanging against the tabletop. He lowered his voice. "That guy that Thomas sent to see me..."

"The minister," Jake said, completing Smith's thought. A risky move if he was wrong, but Smith nodded.

"What that guy told me?" Smith scooted his chair forward until he was tight up to the table. He reached for Jake's hands, but Jake pulled them away. "It's not true, right?"

Jake kept his face still. For Smith to be asking Jake whether "it" was true, the "it" had to be something that Mr. B—and therefore Jake, as his agent here—would already know.

"What do you think?" Jake said.

"I just don't know anymore. Things are all twisted around. I was so sure, but now..." He shook his head.

Whatever the minister had told Smith seemed to have scrambled his reality.

"David, what aren't you sure of?"

"About me being the one who—" Smith's eyes bored into Jake's, and apparently he found something there he didn't like. He wagged his head back and forth, his expression suddenly wary. "I thought... Who are you really?"

"I already told you."

"No you didn't." Smith crossed his arms. "You just said your name and I... I made a mistake about who you are. Let me see your badge. I can see it, right?"

Shit. Jake realized his mistake. He'd called the man David, but if he worked for Mr. B, he would know this man's real name. He should have stayed the hell away from using any name, but using a subject's name was so ingrained in his technique it had just slipped out.

"Where did you meet Thomas?"

Smith shook his head and reached across the desk. "Badge."

Jake pulled his badge off his belt and showed it to Smith. Smith looked close.

"Weston." He leaned back, chains dragging on the steel. "I can't help you."

"Your mom doesn't think you belong in here. She wants you home." Jake kept his face still.

Smith shook his head. "Liar."

"I'm not the liar here." Jake lowered his voice. "You're the one who said your name is David Smith. You said your mom is dead." He stopped there, unsure what else was true and what was a lie.

"I'm done talking to you. I know my rights."

"I've read the statement you made in court to corroborate your confession. I'm starting to doubt every word of that story." No reaction from Smith. "But maybe this is where you belong anyway. Damaged kids like you tend to carry on the family tradition."

"Don't you talk about my family." Smith crossed his arms, then went still.

"Did you kill Mark Siebert?"

Jake had finally asked the question that had brought him here, but it was too late—Smith was done talking. The man turned away, his mouth clamped tight.

Jake asked the question two more times, even promising to help Smith get out of jail if someone else had killed Mark, but Smith still said nothing. Giving up, Jake rapped his knuckles on the window set into the door.

"Last chance," he said. "If there's anything you can tell me, this is it." Nothing. "Maybe something you'd like me to relay to Mark Siebert's parents?"

A tight shake of Smith's head.

Then the door opened and a guard escorted Jake back through the security gates to the entry lobby.

The sun had burned off the morning chill and Jake left his windbreaker unzipped as he walked out to the Mustang.

The drive back to Mount Logan went quickly, his foot heavy on the pedal. Even though Smith didn't answer the ultimate question, it had been a productive trip. He'd learned about this other player —Mr. B— who apparently had the clout to send a dirty cop to see Smith. And he'd confirmed the connection between Smith and Miller. A connection Smith did not want Mr. B to think was a partnership. If Smith and Miller were partners, then Smith should have had Miller's cell phone number, and the impact of the con on Smith's mother would have been worked out beforehand. So maybe Smith was just another victim of Miller's con. Or maybe their relationship was too complicated for Jake to decipher without more information.

He hoped the quiet time in the long drive back to Weston would free the explanation he felt bubbling away at the edge of his consciousness.

* * *

Benchley cruised past the address where Thomas was staying, a big rundown house on the end of Main Street. The detached garage that had been converted to an apartment sat behind it, its driveway clogged with mid-level sedans that all looked alike, except for the Chevy Impala that Thomas had taken. Between the house and garage a worn lawn held a scattering of lawn chairs and a picnic table. Seth's wide-shouldered form held down one side of the table and two scrawny guys sat across from him.

Benchley pulled to the curb half a block down and across the street, and called Seth. Seth got up from the table and stepped a few feet away before answering.

"Hey."

"Thomas has shown up?" Benchley asked.

"About a half hour ago." Seth's head swung back and forth,

stopping when he spotted the Mercury. "Figured you'd be driving, so I didn't call. Is that you?" Seth nodded toward the car.

"That's me. Did Thomas see you?"

"Barely looked our way. I kept my hood up."

"How about telling those boys you gotta go, then come join me?"

"Will do, but I'll head off the other way and circle around the block and back to you."

"Good."

Benchley watched Seth bump fists and head off to the west. As he waited for the boy to work his way around, his phone vibrated with a call—Reznik.

The congressman started ranting as soon as Benchley answered. "That goddamn tweeter says he's going to give the location where the parties happen!"

"How can he know the address?"

"It has to be Thomas."

"I told you he was in the basement when those first tweets came out."

"Yeah, well I found out you can schedule them in advance through some other service."

"You're saying he planned on being locked in my basement, so he scheduled the tweets for then? Thomas didn't even know where those parties were. I worked him hard on that."

"Damn it, Stan. I have to do something!"

"Law enforcement can't go in there without a search warrant, and that requires probable cause of a crime. A tweet isn't probable cause."

"People who have been there will panic, Stan. Washington politicians are not stand-up guys. They're blamers. Finger-pointers. Deflectors."

Like you, Benchley thought. He needed to be free of this man. But not until he had the files back.

"When's the operative going to be here?" he asked.

Reznik sighed loudly. "I'll call you when I know something.

Right now I have to do something about the house. I *own* that damn house. Not directly, but it can be traced back to me. I have to do like you did out there. Sanitize the place."

"That took a lot of time."

"I'll do it faster." Reznik hung up.

Faster? What the hell did Reznik mean by that? Benchley feared it was another disaster in the making, but at least it would keep the focus on DC.

The passenger door opened and Seth slid onto the leather, bringing the cold and the pungent smell of pot with him.

"They have no idea," the boy said, nodding toward the young men sitting around the picnic table. His voice held an excited quaver.

"You enjoying yourself?" Benchley asked.

"I've never done something like this before, so it's kind of neat."

Benchley couldn't help smiling. "How long those boys going to be there?"

"Hard to say, boss. They don't much like it inside. Their rooms are crummy and don't have Wi-Fi, and the guy who runs the place controls the TV and he only watches talk shows and reality crap."

"Thomas have anyone with him when he came back?"

"He was alone." Seth slid down in the seat. "What now, boss?"

"We watch."

22

———

Jake acquired a tail as he slowed to enter the southern edge of Mount Logan. A truck looking a lot like the Chevy loaner he'd driven that morning was right on his bumper, giving him a clear view of the two flannel-clad men inside it. Lenny was driving, and his passenger also had the wide-shouldered bulk of the Siebert clan—along with a shiny red gravel rash on one side of his face.

Maybe they had some news for him. Or maybe they wanted round two.

It was past noon and he hadn't eaten, so Jake stopped for another meal at the gas station Burger King. He parked near the corner of the building by the restaurant entrance. The Chevy parked along his passenger side. Jake met the two men on the sidewalk.

"Hey Lenny, who's your friend?"

"My brother, Clint."

The gravel rash looked even worse close up. "Can I buy you guys lunch?"

They were okay with that, and when they all had their orders they took a booth along the front windows. Lenny lowered himself stiffly onto the bench seat, apparently still feeling the effects of his hard landing on the gravel.

Jake kept an eye on Clint, who still hadn't said a word. The big man took a gigantic bite of his burger. The gravel rash across his jaw and cheek glistened wetly as he chewed. A wound like that might make a guy a little mad.

"How's the burger?" Jake asked.

Clint held it up. "Good," he said around a mouthful. "Thanks."

Both men seemed willing to forget about their encounter the night before. Good.

"You seen that murdering peedo-file out there to the prison?" Lenny asked.

"I did."

"I gotta say, we don't understand why you're doing what you're doing," Lenny said. "I mean, we know it's for Paul and Linda, and that's good enough for us. It's just... seems like stirring it up'll make it worse, not better. Fresh again, I guess is what I'm saying."

Jake shrugged. "It's their call."

"Right." Lenny looked at his brother. "Clint here don't talk so much, but he's the one who got this information we want to give you."

Clint pointed to his full mouth.

"I guess I'll tell it," Lenny said. "But first, Clint and I both want to say we're sorry about last night, and we thank you for not reporting it."

Clint nodded and kept eating.

"Okay." Jake again wondered how far they would have taken things if he hadn't gotten away from them. "What's the information?"

"About that police file on Mark's case. Clint's wife, Roberta, has a sister, Rhonda, who's married to Big Steve. That's Steve Brakur, Senior. Rhonda's stepson, Steve Junior, was the one that arrested Smith. You talked to him last night. Over at the courthouse?"

Jake nodded along, the string of names meaningless until Lenny got to Brakur. He took a bite as he waited for the Lenny to get to the point.

"So since we're related, Clint went and talked to Little Steve and asked him about the file."

"And?"

"Chief Bell lied to you." Lenny took a bite of his chicken sandwich, then talked around it. "The whole dang box of evidence plus that book you want to see—it's all right there in the evidence room."

Just as Jake had thought. "Can you get the book for me?"

"Can't do that. But we *can* get you inside to look at it, just as soon as you're ready."

"Another shirttail relative?"

Lenny frowned. "I don't know about shirttail—either you're related or you're not."

"What about Greer? Any luck there?"

Lenny shook his head. "That man don't listen to anyone. And he's no relation of ours. Clint's son-in-law plays softball with Greer's son, but even that couldn't pry him open."

"Well, thanks for trying." The murder book was the key—it should tell him most of what he needed to know.

The three men finished their meals quickly and headed out to the parking lot.

"Let's take the truck," said Lenny. "That car of yours sticks out like a sore thumb."

Jake agreed. "But I want to leave it at the motel. I need to head out as soon as we're done."

The brothers followed Jake up to the motel. Before he changed vehicles, Jake held up a finger for the men to wait a minute as he checked his phone for email, texts, and voicemails. He hadn't checked since he'd left the prison, and they'd backed up on him.

A detective on the heroin task force was checking to see if Jake had any information to act on, because the brass was pushing hard for something to show the press. Erin said Deputy Chief Braff wanted him to know that when he flashed his badge he was working, not on vacation, and he should be working on crimes committed in the town that paid his salary. ASA McKay wanted to talk about the Storch case. And the last text message was from a number Jake didn't recognize, but which turned out to be Carl at the boarding house. Miller was back, and Carl had sent along the plate number on the car Miller was driving.

Jake added Carl's number to his contact list, then texted Miller's name and the plate number to Erin and asked her to find out everything she could about it—off-book. He'd kept Erin in the dark about the Miller part of what he was into, but he knew she'd do this without demanding an explanation, for now anyway.

Then he remembered the ministry and sent her another text asking her to look into that, too.

He hopped out of the Mustang and stepped up to the truck. "Guys, sorry to make you wait longer, but I need to run inside and pack. I've got to head north as soon as we're done."

The Sieberts looked to be in no rush. "No problem. We'll be right here."

Jake was in and out in five minutes, leaving the room key on the dresser. He locked his bag in his trunk before joining the brothers in the C10, riding between them with his knees pulled tight to his chest and his feet on the hump.

Lenny parked in a church parking lot across the street from the rear of the police station. He made a call, then gave Jake his instructions. Jack was to approach the back door, and when he was a few steps away it would open. He was then to take the first left and go into the first door on his right.

"Keep your head down and keep moving. And wear these." Lenny reached behind the seat and pulled out a brown barn coat and a green John Deere hat, both worn and faded. Jake adjusted the snap-back and pulled it on, then jumped out of the truck, skinned off his jacket, and pulled on the coat. It smelled faintly of hay and horse manure.

He strode quickly across the street and through the police department's back parking lot, straight for the metal door at the top of a short set of concrete steps. Just as he hit the bottom step the door swung inward, and he scampered inside, nodding to the uniformed officer who was holding it open for him. The officer, a twenty-something woman in tight polyester, diverted her eyes and walked away as soon as he was through the door, whispering, "You have an hour."

Jake checked his watch so he'd know when his time was getting short.

Following Lenny's instructions, he pushed through a solid gray door into a stark interview room. A cardboard box sat in the middle of the table, labeled in thick black marker with Mark Siebert's name, the date of his abduction, and a case number. In a square marked "Disposition," the word "Closed" was inscribed.

But not forgotten, Jake thought.

23

As Jake took the lid off the box, excitement thrummed through to his fingertips. And hope, for the Sieberts, that something in this box would convince him Mark was still alive.

The box held three plastic evidence bags and a thick binder—the murder book.

Jake started with the bags, turning and flipping each to examine the contents without opening them. The two larger bags held Smith's clothes: jeans, a Cubs T-shirt, white socks, plain white boxers, and a pair of worn Nikes. The third, smaller bag held a few bills folded together, a quarter, two dimes, and a penny. And that was it. Like the warden said, there were no personal effects. No wallet, no car keys, no driver's license. You could stop a thousand people on the street and every one of them would be carrying more than this.

Jake put the bags back in the box and pulled out the murder book. The book should contain the complete story of the investigation, from the initial report through the arrest and beyond. It was heavy and bulged with paper and plastic sleeves.

He sat down and got started, the ticking clock like an itch on his scalp.

Greer had laid out the day of Mark's disappearance in a grid, everything cross-referenced with interviews. Mark was home for breakfast before going into town to hang out with his friends. He pitched pennies behind The Locker with two classmates, then went to the video arcade alone. He came home around noon and had lunch with his mom. He told his mom he'd met a new kid at the arcade; a cross-referenced interview indicated the arcade manager remembered seeing Mark, but saw no one with him. Mark then folded newspapers on the front porch before setting out on his paper route. There were four people, all cross-referenced, who saw or spoke to him along the way.

And then he was gone.

Jake flipped through the book to Greer's typed narrative summary and scanned it for any information on this "new kid" Mark had met. Greer chased the lead but found nothing; none of Mark's classmates knew about a new kid, and neither the public schools nor utility companies had a record of any new residents with boys near Mark's age. Since it was the Fourth of July holiday, the kid was most likely an out-of-town visitor. Jake considered whether Smith could be this new kid, but quickly discarded the idea; even seven years ago no one could have mistakenly thought Smith was eleven, Mark's age at the time.

Jake read the rest of the narrative summary. Paul and Linda reported their son's disappearance when he didn't come home from delivering his newspapers. They gave Greer the names of the people who'd complained about not getting the paper, a list of Mark's friends, and a loose schedule of his day. Greer got the subscription list for Mark's route from the newspaper's editor and walked the route with a neighbor—Melinda Sayers—who knew the order in which Mark delivered the papers. With her help, Greer was able to determine the last house to receive a paper, which gave them a focal point for a door-to-door canvas. The murder book contained a map in a plastic sleeve showing Mark's route marked in red, with a circle around the last confirmed delivery.

Greer called in Lenny and his hunting dogs and they found the wagon Mark used to haul the papers hidden under a bush two houses down from his last delivery. Instead of taking the wagon into evidence to check for prints of whoever had hidden it, Greer let Melanie finish the boy's paper route and return the wagon to the Sieberts' garage.

Lenny's dogs followed Mark's scent a few hundred feet into an alley, where it disappeared. The police went over the alley carefully but found nothing helpful, and no one saw anything suspicious in or around the alley that day.

Greer and the rest of the detective division then spread over the town, interviewing neighbors and friends and classmates and teachers and people along the paper route. A picture emerged of a kind, sensitive boy who never gave a hint he would run away.

Over the second week, the police efforts spread out to include hotels and campgrounds and out-of-town visitors staying with families or friends for the Fourth of July holiday. Then Greer started re-interviewing the tier-one people—parents, neighbors, and friends—and his summary reflected his frustration at finding nothing new.

Jake sympathized; he had lived that feeling.

Sixteen days after Mark disappeared, Greer sent an email to the local FBI office asking for help. The FBI replied, saying it would need a formal request from Chief Bell. Greer's response was the most explicit internal finger-pointing Jake had ever seen in an official file:

Chief Bell refused to submit the case to the FBI just as he refused my requests for roadblocks and state police support on day one. Chief Bell insists that Mark Siebert was gay and ran away to be free of his family's expectations.

And then, a bit later: *... though the subject was effeminate and spent a lot of time in solitary activities, there is no evidence to support the chief's theory.*

No wonder Bell didn't want Jake to see this book.

Jake flipped to the Smith portion of Greer's narrative. ASA Nelson sent Officer Brakur away immediately after he'd brought

Smith into the station. Smith declined both the breathalyzer and the urine test, then refused to write up his own confession. Greer wrote it himself, his handwriting a cramped cursive, but Smith initialed every page of that statement and then signed the typed-up version.

Jake scoured the confession for the details that had convinced Greer and Nelson that the confession was legit—details that had not been contained in any of the media reports. He found two possibilities. First, in describing the boy he abducted, Smith said he had a birthmark on his left hip spreading onto his buttock. Second, Smith offered up three details of Mark's personal and family life: where they ate Thanksgiving dinner, where they vacationed, and that they opened one present on Christmas Eve. Paul had confirmed all to be true.

Jake tapped his finger on the page. Miller had told Linda Siebert one other family tidbit not listed here: that they ate Swedish sausage with applesauce. So Miller's inside information did not come from this file—or at least not *only* from this file.

There wasn't a lot more to the narrative. Greer did get around to interviewing people at the bars, but not until almost three weeks after the arrest, and by then, like Brakur had, Greer found a lot of people who claimed to have seen Smith. Greer even mentioned that "a patrol officer already made this inquiry" at several bars along Ninth Street.

A noise in the hallway. He checked his watch. His hour had ended long before. When the door didn't open, Jake got back to the file.

Greer had devoted a single page to his work trying to confirm Smith's identity. Smith had refused to offer any information about his background other than that he was from California, he was twenty-one, and his birthdate was January first. But no David Smith born on that date existed in any California database. Greer ran Smith's fingerprints and got no hits. And all Smith said about his July visit to Mount Logan was that he'd been driving a borrowed van; he wouldn't say who owned it or where it was now.

In short, David Smith was a ghost. He'd created a fake identity with so few details it couldn't be defeated.

Smith wouldn't say how he got to Mount Logan on the day he ran into Officer Brakur, other than to say a friend dropped him off. And he wouldn't explain why he came back except to say he'd felt he needed to.

The killer returning to the scene of the crime.

Greer was just as unsuccessful in getting details on what Smith did with Mark after abducting him. Smith said they drove and camped and enjoyed each other's company, and then Smith killed the boy. He wouldn't say how or where or why. He did say he buried the body in the Shawnee National Forest, but although they marched Smith back and forth across it, he couldn't lead them to the grave. Greer brought in Lenny and his dogs, and they found nothing.

Jake turned to the tab for forensic evidence. All it held was a report on the things in the evidence bags. Smith refused blood tests, so there were no such reports. Greer didn't get a warrant to compel the tests, probably because he had the confession.

Jake flipped to the end of the book for any follow-up, but found only the sentencing record and a brief handwritten report in Greer's scrawl. Greer wrote that after signing the confession, Smith stopped talking, other than to enter his guilty plea in court. All further attempts to verify his story failed.

"The important thing to remember," Greer wrote, was the crime was solved and the perpetrator was being punished. And although "our civilized society" would like to know where this monster came from and why he picked "our town and this little boy," those answers were not necessary for the criminal justice system.

Almost philosophical.

Jake had gotten all he could. He finished the notes he'd been making, then put the binder back in the box and closed the lid. He held his ear to the door, and when the hallway went quiet, he retraced his steps and exited through the back door.

The sun had dropped significantly while he'd been inside, and was now in his eyes as he walked west toward where the Sieberts had dropped him off. He squinted against the brightness and slowed as he neared the street. The Siebert brothers and their CIO were still there and Jake hopped in. Clint squeezed into the middle with his knees under his chin. Lenny pulled out of the lot and they drove south toward the motel.

"Didn't expect you to be in there so long," Lenny said. "How'd it look?"

"Greer did a competent job." Not perfect, but solid.

"People say if he'd-a got the FBI involved maybe Mark would still be alive."

"No way to know if that would have made a difference." There'd been no signs of foul play. No suspicious people or vehicles reported in town even after the story hit the news. On its face, Chief Bell's position on not involving the feds wasn't completely wrong.

"So that's what you're telling Paul? You dropping it?" Clint's worried eyes swung on Jake.

"Not yet. I still have a few rocks to look under."

They wanted to know what rocks and could they help turning them over, but Jake refused. He was doing this for Paul and Linda, and if they wanted to share information, that was their decision. So when they got to the motel, he gave Lenny back the barn coat and Deere hat and thanked him for getting him access to the murder book, and the two men left.

The Mustang felt like home after all the time Jake spent closed up in the interrogation room at the prison and the little interview room at the police station. He went north on Tenth, then left at the courthouse, and within minutes he was back on 57 cruising north on a wide-open highway.

Time to think.

He'd be back in Weston in four hours and was looking forward to a conversation with Robert Miller.

Or was his name Thomas?

24

Jake cruised north, the traffic light, the Mustang eating up the miles.

Because Chief Bell lied about the murder book being off-site, Jake had expected to find a sloppy job—but the book documented a competent investigation. Maybe Bell had lied because he was worried Jake would second-guess his decision not to involve the FBI. But Jake couldn't imagine what the feds would have added. They might even have gotten in the way. And with no signs of foul play or ransom demands, the feds might have declined to get involved even if Bell had asked.

It was more likely Bell was worried about the Sieberts finding out he'd thought Mark was gay and ran away because his family wouldn't, or didn't, accept him.

Jake wasn't going to share that with them.

Wind buffeted the car as he passed a massive semi, and Jake put both hands on the wheel to fight the vibrating stutter. Back in smooth air, his thoughts returned to the confession. It did look as solid as both Bell and Nelson claimed. The personal and family details Smith provided, and Paul confirmed, could only have come from Mark.

But the warden was right about Smith's identity. Greer had

gotten nowhere confirming it, so all the personal information the man had given, even his name, had probably been a lie.

But why?

Jake's phone vibrated with a call. He answered it hoping for progress.

"Houser."

Erin jumped past conversational niceties. "The car Robert Miller is driving is owned by a leasing company, so that's the only name on the title."

Jake smiled. She had to be burning with curiosity about what he was doing on his PTO time, but still she got right to the work. "Did you find out who they leased it to?"

"I was able to convince the VP there to talk to me off the record. They leased it to Accord Services, LLC. The VP said the payments are up to date and come in automatically. His system couldn't give me any more than that."

"Where is Accord Services?"

"Springfield. I found a filing at the Illinois Secretary of State website. Accord Services LLC is an active company. Its registered agent is a big law firm in Springfield, and one of its partners is also the listed manager of the LLC. The LLC's legal address is a box at a storefront in Springfield a block from the lawyer's office."

"Is Accord Services a real company? One that does business publicly?" Lots of people created simple LLCs for small family businesses, like to own a rental property.

"It's real. It handles commercial insurance. Has an office and a website."

"How about the ministry?"

"It's a legit not-for-profit entity, but there's nothing on its website about prisons. It's all about getting teens get off the street —homeless and prostitutes—and helping them find a future. That's the tagline on the website. Finding your Future."

"Who's the minister there? The face man?"

"A guy named Lowell Carr. He's a former runaway street kid slash prostitute who straightened himself out."

"Interesting." Jake would need to talk to this guy.

"Also, I pulled Levi in to dig deeper into Accord—who owns it and all that," Erin said. "If you stop by on the way in he might have something for you."

"Okay, I will." Jake changed lanes to get around a giant motorhome towing a Jeep.

"By the way, Deputy Chief Braff wasn't happy about the calls he got from the mayor down there and from the warden at the prison. You'll probably get an earful when you get back."

"Yeah, I figured. Thanks for the heads-up." Jake would come up with a story for Braff later.

Erin hung up, and Jake was alone once again. Billy Currington came on the radio, and Jake turned it up. One song led to another, and he ended up giving his brain a break, letting the case bubble away in his subconscious.

* * *

Drill twisted his torso right and left, stretching his lower back. The Suburban's cloth seats were too soft for a stakeout. He'd driven a lot of cars in a lot of countries, and he'd learned that leather seats were always the way to go. He pumped up the lumbar support to its max, then refocused. He had a job to do.

He had planned to hit Greer outside the diner as the more believable spot for an assault to occur, but it was too well lit and too busy. So he'd driven out to the man's house and found a good surveillance spot. Greer's street ended in a circle with driveways leading off it like spokes on a wheel. A scattering of newspapers at the foot of one driveway, along with a row of foot-tall weeds sprouting in the crack in front of the garage door, told Drill that particular house was empty. He backed the Suburban up the driveway and parked it where a row of overgrown bushes screened it from the street. Through winter-bared branches he had a decent view of Greer's house a hundred yards back up the dead-end road.

The seat wasn't the only problem with this vehicle. The shiny black Suburban practically screamed, *Look at me, I'm a fed*. When he first saw it waiting at the airport Drill assumed Spec had done his homework and chosen a vehicle that would fit in here, but it didn't. It was too new, too shiny, and wasn't what people drove in this town. He needed a pickup truck, a big American road car, or a beater Japanese econo-box. He'd considered stealing a more appropriate ride, but the risk wasn't worth it. He just needed to get in and out.

Night fell, and the street went deep dark. There were no streetlights out here in the boonies, and a dense roil of clouds had spread over the sky, blotting out the moon. The only light was what spilled from a few windows along the street, plus one porch light five hundred yards back up the road.

According to the intel, Greer was supposed to be home and in front of the television by now. Spec's team had clearly missed something: a bowling league, a card game, maybe a high school sporting event. It was what, basketball season? A two-hour game starting at seven with some jawboning afterwards would still put the guy home by ten at the latest.

Drill would wait.

He reached for the satellite phone to send a text message and found one waiting for him from Spec: *Weston detective is headed home.*

Good.

He typed in his own message: *Waiting. Subject a no-show. Staying put.*

25

———

Paget County Cleaners was in a strip mall a mile off the tollway. Jake pulled into a spot two rows from the front door and got out. It was dark now, and the wind had kicked up, so he zipped up his windbreaker as he hustled across the parking lot.

The cleaners' was empty except for Levi, perched on his stool behind the high counter, black T-shirt hanging loose on his slender frame, his trusty laptop open. When the bell over the door announced Jake's entrance, Levi's face lit up before he even turned his head. Everyone got the Levi charm.

"Detective Houser! I have a lot to show you." He waved Jake to the extra stool.

As soon as Jake sat, Levi jumped into his report.

"Erin called me with the new information. Accord Financial, LLC, Attorney Dirk Mandan, Springfield." He clicked through a dozen open windows —they appeared to show results for searches, using different combinations of these words and the name "Robert Miller." "Are you ready?"

Jake pulled out his notebook. "Bring it."

Levi's presentation was clear and quick. Accord Services, LLC, was a commercial insurance agency. Although its LLC listing used a law firm to disguise its ownership, archived news articles revealed it had been started by a man named Oscar Benchley. Recent news and society reporting said the current owner was Stanley Benchley. Stanley had been an academic superstar at the University of Illinois before disappearing for twenty years, even from the reach of the Internet. He reappeared only when he returned to take over the agency after his parents died in a car accident.

"I called over to the agency and pretended I was interested in meeting with Benchley about a policy. The receptionist told me he only comes in on Mondays, but they had two other people who could meet with me. I chatted her up, and she eventually told me Benchley rarely comes into the office at all. He mostly goes to Chamber of Commerce events and golf outings and such. Leaves the business alone."

"So the business is a face for him while he does... what?"

"Socializes, apparently. As a respected businessman he's invited to all the big political shindigs in Springfield. He goes to a lot of them. I found tons of pictures of him shaking hands and slapping backs."

"A player," Jake said. "Did you find his address and phone number?"

"I have his address in a neighborhood of ten-acre ranchettes out on the edge of Springfield. A neighbor told me he lives there alone except for a younger guy who takes care of the place."

"Did Miller's name come up in connection with Benchley or Accord?"

"No. I even slipped the name in when I was talking to the receptionist, and she didn't know it. I also checked to see if the state has issued an insurance license to anyone with that name in Springfield. They haven't."

Benchley, Jake thought. *Could that be the "Mr. B" that Smith referred to?*

"I learned that Miller's real name might be Thomas," he said. "I don't have a last name. Did a Thomas come up in your searches?"

"No, sorry."

"I'd like you to look at another guy. Lowell Carr. He runs the Christian Ministry for Lost Youths in Rockford. Erin did some work on him, but can you do one of your deeper dives?"

"I'll get right on it."

* * *

As the evening wore on, Benchley shivered against the cold seeping into the car. Seth had fallen asleep and hadn't moved in hours. Benchley didn't need help watching a closed door, so he let the boy sleep. Bored, he repeatedly checked his phone for messages, even though it hadn't buzzed or beeped.

He started the car and turned on the heat. But the chill had settled in his bones, and it was hard to shake off.

The group around the picnic table had grown to four, and one of them had pulled a metal fire pit out from behind the garage and filled it with branches the group gathered up from the yard, along with some logs they stole from a pile behind their neighbor's house. Some of the wood must have been wet, because the fire was kicking out a dense white smoke that swirled with the breeze, and the men had to keep moving around the pit to stay out of the cloud. Two of them passed a bottle back and forth while the other two passed a joint. Probably one Benchley had paid for. Seth was generous.

Benchley glanced up and down the street. It wasn't late, but the area was quiet. Was it too quiet? He didn't know this town or its people, so he couldn't judge. He didn't like being so far from home, in a town where no one owed him anything and he had no power over anyone. He'd rather be in his chair, at his desk, in his office.

He pulled out his phone and dialed through to check for messages off his home answering machine. There were three updates from the agency that were too routine to worry about, then a message from a source that shriveled his ball sack.

"Um... well, a woman from the Weston Police Department—

not a cop. A civilian investigator, whatever that is. Anyway, she called in asking a bunch of questions about the corporate filings on your insurance company. She already had what's on the web and I didn't give her anything more than that. She was interested in who owned the agency. In you, basically. Bye."

Shit.

The Weston cops must have run the plates on the car Thomas took, then found their way past the leasing company to Accord Services. *Which leads straight to me.* Maybe he should have reported it stolen. But if he had, Thomas would have been arrested when the Weston PD ran the plate, and who knows what would have happened to the files then.

He had to get out of here.

He reached to put his car in drive, but he still had the phone in his hand, and as he fumbled the shifter he dropped the phone.

"Damn it." He felt around the grit-covered carpet to pick it up.

"Boss?" Seth's voice was lazy with sleep. "Thomas come out?"

"No." Benchley's voice was sharp, and Seth sat up straight. "What is it?"

"Nothing," Benchley said. His pulse pounded, and despite the chill, sweat was beading on his forehead and he could already feel some trickling down his chest to pool on the shelf of his belly.

Pull yourself together, man. You got this.

He shut off the heater, then lowered his window to let the cool night air flood through. He took a few deep breaths, feeling his body relaxing. The sounds from the backyard gathering were louder now, and he could hear the men arguing about the Bears' new quarterback. A tendril of smoke wafted past the car, and he had to hold back a cough.

As soon as those losers went inside, he would go in and get the damn files himself.

Thomas is mine.

26

Jake found the boarding house yard busy; the mild night had brought a cluster of residents out to the picnic table on the worn-out lawn. He parked the Mustang across the street and watched them. Just four men with nothing better to do than tend a small fire and pass around a bottle. Miller wasn't with them, but both little windows in the side of the garage glowed with light so he was probably in there.

As Jake got out of the car, he decided his promise to the Sieberts had to bend. He'd already waved his badge around in Mount Logan, and he was going to wave it around here, too. The badge cut through the bullshit.

A Chevy Impala with the license plate Carl had texted to Jake was parked in the driveway, its back end hanging over the sidewalk. It was brown, not green as Paul's boys had said. As Jake walked past it, he gave it a quick once-over, glancing through the windows and trying the door, but it was locked. He continued on.

Wood smoke scented the air, mixed with the powerful reek of marijuana. As Jake walked up the driveway, the men in the yard went silent and one of them flicked something into the fire. Jake nodded to them, but said nothing.

In front of Miller's door, he stood for a moment, listening to a monotone drone from inside. The TV news, maybe. He gave the door a hard triple rap. The drone stopped, and a few seconds later the door opened.

Robert Miller stood just under six feet and was slender. He wore one of the flannel shirts that had been in the closet on Jake's first visit, faded jeans, and white socks that were baggy at the toes.

"Yes?" Miller held the door half open, leaning a shoulder on it, blocking Jake's view inside. His skin was so smooth and unlined he could pass for a teenager.

Jake pulled out his badge. "Detective Jake Houser. May I come in?"

Miller looked at the badge, then stepped back. "Do I have a choice?"

Jake stepped inside and closed the door. The place looked the same as on his first visit except for a pair of black work boots by the door and a leather jacket hanging on the bathroom doorknob.

Miller edged around Jake and took a seat behind the kitchen table. A defensive position. Jake took the other chair.

Miller's chair squeaked as he adjusted himself, and Jake almost smiled. Body movement and imbalance were good indicators of deception, but they were sometimes hard to observe. The squeaky chair would help magnify both.

"What do you want, Officer?"

"It's Detective," Jake said. "Why do you think I'm here?"

Miller's hands came together and his thumbs circled each other. "I don't have any idea." He licked his lips.

Deception. Miller knew exactly why Jake was here.

"I'm here about your visit to Linda Siebert," Jake said.

"I visited Mrs. Siebert, but that's not a crime." Miller licked his lips again and his eyes shifted away. His chair squeaked.

"Fraud is a crime." Jake pulled out his notebook and pretended to read from it before flipping to a blank page, his gaze lifting to rest on Miller. "Mrs. Siebert told me your story."

More shifting and lip-licking. Then: "I didn't ask her for a penny, so there's no fraud."

"Not yet. But why else come back here after taking the other boys somewhere else?"

Miller swallowed, but didn't answer.

"I've arrested enough con men to recognize one." Jake held out his hand. "Driver's license."

Miller pulled out his wallet and handed over his license. It was a real license with the hologram of the state seal and an address in Cherry Valley. But it had been issued only three weeks before, and it said Miller was twenty-one. He looked closer to seventeen.

Jake pulled out his phone and took a picture of the license, then handed it back.

Miller's eyebrows arched. He put his wallet away, then sat up straighter at the table. "Are you even a real cop or are you just some friend of theirs?"

Miller had sensed something off in Jake's approach. Probably because anyone who watched cop shows on TV knew that a cop working a case would have called the license in to check for outstanding warrants.

Jake went on the offensive to get Miller off that. "I'm also here about the phone message David Smith left for you on Carl's phone."

Miller blanched, and looked away.

"You're thinking I got lucky with Smith. You're thinking I don't know about Lowell Carr visiting him, or about Accord Services."

Sweat beaded on Miller's upper lip. "You ran the plates on my car."

"Which led me to Accord, and to Mr. B." If Miller accepted that, then Benchley and Mr. B were the same person.

Miller said nothing, but his hands shook and sweat ran down his temples. He wiped his face and sat up straighter. Then his gaze shot to the closet. Jake almost turned to see what he was looking at, but then Miller's shoulders bunched and he pulled his feet underneath him.

"You shouldn't have done that," Miller said. His voice was low, his eyes dark.

"This is about what *you've* done."

"Did you... have you talked to David?"

Jake considered lying—the policeman's privilege—but decided the truth would shake Miller harder. "This morning."

Miller's mouth pulled into a tight, flat line. Then he stood, his chair shooting from behind him to bang up against the fridge. Jake popped up just as quickly, his hands rising in a defensive stance as he moved to close on Miller and drop him. But as Jake pulled his right hand back and twisted his torso to load his shoulder for a throat shot, he realized Miller wasn't even looking at him. The kid was merely pacing, his face taut with worry.

Jake shook the tension out of his shoulders. His breathing and pulse had both kicked up, his system pumping him full of adrenaline. He took a few long slow breaths, and his heart slowed. He took a step back to give Miller more space.

"You shouldn't have stirred them up." Miller faced Jake, his eyes fierce, his hands clenching. "That's not good for any of us."

"Who is *us*?"

"Us is... " Miller locked eyes with Jake, then he nodded gently. He grabbed his chair from against the fridge and sat back down at the table. Jake remained on his feet.

I just reminded him of something important, Jake thought. *About the other men in this with him.*

"Smith told me about his deal with Benchley."

Miller looked past him at the closet again, then met Jake's eye.

"Smith also told me your real name is Thomas."

Miller jumped up again, and Jake stepped back. But Miller simply went to the door and opened it. "You've said your piece, now leave."

"Fine." Jake strode to the doorway, then turned. "Stay away from the Sieberts or I'll run you in." He continued outside, the door closing behind him.

It had been a good interview. He'd confirmed that the three men—Miller, Benchley, and Smith—were connected. Each to the other. Connected, but not working together. Each of them with his own agenda. Mr. B was Benchley, the scary man in the shadows. But Miller was the key to this thing and Jake had shaken him hard. Hopefully hard enough to induce him to do something revealing.

On the way back to his car Jake pulled out his phone and scrolled through his contacts for Officer Sean Grady's number. He'd promised Linda he wouldn't involve the department, but Grady would work off-book if he was available.

Jake was in luck—Grady had the night off and was all in. He said he could be there in less than ten minutes. He'd keep an eye on Miller.

And if Miller tried to go to the Sieberts' house, Grady would stop him.

27

———————

Benchley's knees shook, and he pressed them together to stop it. "You're sure that guy was a cop?"

"He showed Thomas something before he went in there. I think it was a badge."

"Why's he just sitting in his car? Why doesn't he leave?"

"I don't know, boss."

Things were going to shit. If the files weren't in the room or the car, then Thomas had either hid them somewhere or Andy had them, wherever the hell he was. Benchley needed to do something before it got any worse. But first, one last attempt at getting Reznik's professional to handle it.

The congressman answered on the first ring. "What is it?"

"Where's the guy you're sending? I've found Thomas holed up here in Weston, and a cop was just talking to him!"

"Does he drive a Mustang?"

The guy inside *was* a cop. "That's right. How'd you know?"

"He was poking around down in Mount Logan earlier today. But he got nowhere."

"You need to get that asset up here. I—"

"He's going to handle my issue down south first, then he'll come straight to you."

"When?"

"As soon as he's done. He needs to find his opportunity."

"That sounds like I'm on my own."

"You're not on your own. He'll be up there tomorrow. Maybe even later tonight. Wait for him," Reznik's deep voice commanded.

"He's got *your* file, too," Benchley said. Time to spit out his hole card.

"My file? What the hell are you—you made a *file* on me? God damn it, Benchley! I don't suppose you made a file on yourself?"

"We're all at risk." Benchley *did* have a file on himself, not filled with compromising photos, but with his personal papers. Thomas had taken that file too. And if law enforcement found it with the others, Benchley was screwed. He *had* to recover those files.

Reznik was silent, then came the grinding of his molars. "When he's finished downstate, I'll send my asset to you."

Benchley's hole card had failed. Reznik simply did not change his mind.

"I might not be able to wait," Benchley said.

"You'll wait, God damn it! I'll—"

Benchley ended the call.

Reznik was a disaster in the making, but at least everything he did focused attention on DC. It was here in Weston that everything pointed at Benchley, and he had to act. Now. Maybe Thomas did have the files in there, and the boys who searched the room simply sucked at it. And if not?

He would take Thomas and *force* the files out of him.

Whatever it took.

A white Volkswagen crept by, then swerved to the curb in front of the cop's Mustang. The Mustang started with a rumble, flashed its headlights, and sped away.

Damn it! The cop had called someone to watch Thomas.

Benchley ground his teeth, thinking. Then he turned to Seth. "You see that white car?"

"The Jetta?"

"It's another cop."

Seth nodded.

"When the bozos around the fire go inside, we'll give the cop a chance to fall asleep, then we'll go in."

"And what if he doesn't fall asleep?"

"We take him out."

28

It was a short drive home: through downtown, over the river, and past Weston Settlement, a historical village containing old buildings moved there from across the city. Jake pulled into his garage with his mind still working on the Smith-Miller-Benchley connections.

Smith had said he wasn't part of what Miller was doing in Weston, and he badly wanted Jake to tell that to Mr. B—Benchley. Smith feared that by helping Miller, he would violate some deal he had made with Benchley, which apparently would have dire consequences for Smith's mother.

So then, why had Smith called Miller?

Because whatever the minister, Carr, said to Smith had shaken the man very deeply and he thought Miller could tell him whether it was true. Smith had called Carl's landline because he didn't have Miller's cell number—which meant Miller hadn't expected Smith to call him. And once Miller had gotten what he wanted from Smith—the family secrets he then used to convince the Sieberts that Mark was alive—he was done with him.

Miller was afraid of Benchley too. That much was clear. Maybe he'd also violated a deal with "Mr. B," and had somehow drawn an unwitting Smith into it.

Jake pulled out his phone and sent the photo of Miller's driver's license to Erin, along with a text message asking her to verify it was a real license, and a reminder to keep it off book. He had the feeling the license was real—Miller didn't hesitate showing it—but it didn't hurt to check.

He got out of the car, closed the overhead garage door, and went inside. He shrugged his jacket off, draped it over the back of a folding chair at the card table in the kitchen, and just stood there for a moment at the edge of the big space. The emptiness pressed on him; the quiet was an indictment of his lifestyle. He crossed the bare plywood, his footsteps echoing in the hollowness, and turned on the stereo. It was tuned to a country station, and the strong strumming rhythms filled the room, reverberating against the blank walls and bare floor.

Better.

After his wife was killed, Jake had taken to being alone. It was better than people fussing over him, better than being out in the community seeing other couples and families enjoying a life he had been robbed of. Moving back to Weston had been, in part, an attempt to shake himself out of that solitude by coming home to the people and places he knew so well. But the effort had clearly failed—mostly because by the time he made the move, he'd grown to *like* being alone. It let him devote himself to the job. And his memories.

"Your job is what matters, Houser. It's where you make a difference."

His words echoed in the silence as a song ended, then were blasted away by a commercial for a jewelry store. He turned the stereo down.

If he was meant to have more, to be more, it would happen.

He shook his head at his pathetic, fatalistic musings. A person made his own life; he didn't wait for it to happen to him.

What he needed was to get out of this empty house.

He considered joining Grady on the stakeout, but that would give the impression he didn't trust the man. So he decided to go for a run instead. He put on his gear, adding a reflective vest because of the late hour, then stretched in the breezeway, getting used to the cold air on his face. When he was warmed up, he jogged north at a comfortable pace.

The moon was high and nearly full, so he could see clearly. He sped up when he made it to the Riverwalk, dodged a rowdy group of high school kids near Centennial Beach, and crossed the river on the Jefferson Avenue Bridge before cutting north on the Paget River Bike Trail. The trail took him under the railroad tracks, up and down the hills against the river, and beneath Ogden Avenue. There he took the tight left and looped up onto the sidewalk to run east along the street, through town, and back to the house. The entire run was smooth and easy.

Back home, he stretched and recovered in his breezeway, letting the night air cool him. Then he went inside, showered, and put on a pair of sweats.

At the kitchen table, he spent a minute bundling up the materials from the Storch case to take back to the station. Those poor girls. Used and abused by a man they trusted, then pulled into the system and promised justice. But that justice came with a price—one that the victims themselves had to pay. And without their sacrifice, justice died.

He pulled out his phone and found the earlier text from ASA McKay: *I want to talk about Storch.*

But talking wouldn't put Storch in jail. They needed a new plan, which Jake didn't have—not yet anyway. And he didn't want to tell McKay that. So he put the phone down and pulled out his Siebert notes.

He started by writing up everything he knew about Mark Siebert's disappearance in a new document on his laptop. There was no official book to keep, but writing things down helped Jake make sense of the facts he knew and expose both what he didn't know and what he thought he knew but couldn't explain clearly enough to write down.

His cell phone buzzed, skittering across the table. Grady.

"Is he up to something?" Jake asked.

"He's been busy. But I called to tell you I've been called in to cover for Hudson. His wife's gone into labor."

"That's fine. I appreciate your help. What's our man been busy with?"

"At nine thirty-one he came outside, looking around like he expected to be jumped. He had something blocky under his jacket. Held it tight to his belly with his forearm. He got in his car and took off. I followed him, but all he did was drive over and park in the Van Buren Street garage. I parked my car, too, and followed him from there on foot. He just walked back to his room."

"All with the thing under his jacket?"

"He left that in the car."

"Does he have a permit for overnight parking?" The garage was for shoppers and diners but allowed overnight parking for some downtown-area apartment dwellers.

"No, but he probably won't be towed. Downtown patrols don't go through the garage more than once a week unless something shows on a security camera."

"Thanks, Grady."

"Also, I think he's expecting someone to come at him. When he got back here he scooped up a bunch of loose gravel from the driveway and scattered it across that little wood porch in front of his door. Then he walked over it a few times—testing it, I think— and that gravel crunching on the wood made a lot of noise. Like an alarm if someone stepped on the porch."

So, Miller was expecting company. Jake had a good idea who. *Benchley.*

"What's going on with the guys in the yard with the fire?" Jake asked. A bunch of witnesses right outside the door should keep Benchley away.

"A strange little guy with wild hair came out of the house and told them to put it out. They were all inside before Miller came out."

"Thanks again."

With Grady taking off, and the guys cleared out of the yard, Miller was now on his own to handle whatever it was he was expecting from Benchley. He called Coogan, hoping his fresh perspective would help Jake see it all more clearly.

"Hey, Jake. Figure out that Siebert mess yet? Need my immense brain power to clear away the rubble and lead you to the truth?"

"That's why I called. You have a few minutes to wade through this with me?"

"Sure. Judy's busy watching one of those reality shows with the singers. Or maybe it's dancers."

Jake took him through what he had, then waited while Coogan's big brain churned.

"Tell me again how you're sure Benchley's connected to Miller?"

"Benchley owns the company that holds the lease on the car Miller's driving. Miller panicked when I mentioned Benchley. Smith mentioned a deal with a 'Mr. B,' and when I floated Benchley as the guy Smith had a deal with, Miller let it stand."

"Yeah, that's plenty. But Smith denied he was working with Miller."

"And I think he was telling the truth. The con is all Miller's. I'm guessing he conned Smith too, to get the details he needed to convince Linda Siebert that her son is still alive."

"And Smith has a deal with Benchley. Do you think that's something to do with his confession?"

Jake's thoughts had been running in that exact direction. "The deal being that Smith took the rap for someone else in exchange for something."

Mark was dead, but Smith didn't kill him, and Miller was a con man.

"So let's assume for a minute that Smith took the rap for someone. From what you've told me about the murder book, the case was basically stalled. So why would Smith, or anyone, have to confess?"

That was a very good question. Greer had tracked down every

lead, had questioned everyone who might know something, and had run out of ideas. Jake understood how that was; he'd had his share of cases like that, where the trail went cold and he treaded water re-interviewing people until something broke it open. *The flat spot.*

But sometimes... sometimes the only flat spot was in the book. Sometimes he was working something he didn't want to document because it was so far out he didn't want to have to explain it to his boss. What if Greer had been doing that in *his* flat spot?

"I need to talk to Greer."

"What are you thinking?"

"That Greer was working something that wasn't in the book. Something he didn't want to make a record of it unless it panned out."

"And whatever he was working on triggered Smith's arrival and confession?"

"Exactly. And with the confession, Greer dropped whatever he'd been digging into."

"Not whatever, *who*ever. And that person convinced Smith to take the rap in exchange for something for his momma. Or simply a promise to leave her alone."

Coogan had that exactly right, Jake thought. Smith's deal with Benchley was all about his mother. He'd taken the rap either to protect her, or to provide for her.

But there was more to it than that. Smith had been awfully confused in Jake's conversation with him at the prison. *I just don't know anymore,* the man had said. *Things are all twisted around. I was so sure, but now...*

It sounded like Smith had actually believed that he had killed Mark Siebert. Until the visit from the prison ministry.

"Let's keep running this down," Jake said. "Let's say the thing Greer was chasing off-book was what brought Smith to town. If that's the case, the patrol officer, Brakur, didn't get lucky. His encounter with Smith was staged."

"Makes sense."

"French fries."

Coogan laughed. "You hungry? You've never been a fry guy."

"Brakur said Smith burped, and it smelled like french fries. But if he was as drunk as he looked to Brakur, as drunk as he smelled, his burps would have smelled like booze."

"So Smith wasn't drunk. He was just trying to get arrested so he could 'let it slip' that he killed Mark Siebert."

"Exactly."

"But wasn't there a breathalyzer?"

"Smith refused both the breathalyzer and the urine test."

Coogan was quiet for a minute that stretched to two. But the men were comfortable with each other's silences, and Jake waited patiently.

"I'm sorry it shook out that way," Coog said at last. "I had hoped Mark Siebert was still alive."

"Yeah. Me too." He'd expected this result, but there was always room for hope. Until there wasn't.

"What now?" Coogan said.

"I go talk to Greer, and then to Smith again." Jake needed more than speculation before he told the Sieberts that not only was their son indeed dead, but his real killer had escaped punishment.

"What about Miller?"

"I'll take another run at Miller right now." Running at Miller with this new theory that Smith made a deal with Benchley to take the rap for Mark's real killer, might shake something loose.

"And then down to Mount Logan again?"

"Of course."

Jake had to be who he was. No one else would do it.

29

———

Benchley reached across the center console and tapped Seth's shoulder.

The boy opened his eyes, then stretched with a low groan. "What?"

"That cop just left again. Probably to recover his Jetta from wherever he left it when he followed Thomas before."

"What about Thomas?"

"He's still inside."

For a while there, Benchley had been afraid they'd lost him. When Thomas came out earlier and drove away in the Impala, followed by Jetta Cop, Benchley had reluctantly stayed put, fearing a three-car string would be too obvious to both Thomas *and* the cop. But Thomas walked back less than ten minutes later, Jetta Cop following on foot. Thomas had probably just moved his car somewhere in the hopes the cop in the Mustang would think he'd left.

But now Mustang Cop was gone, Jetta Cop was gone, and Thomas was alone. This was Benchley's chance. They would grab Thomas, get the files back, and Benchley would rebuild his operation with new boys. And without Reznik.

"We're going in and taking Thomas." Benchley's voice shook with the sudden dump of adrenaline into his system.

"Then what, boss?"

"He gives me what's mine."

Benchley felt the energy surge pushing aside the anxiety built up through the long hours of waiting.

Action beat inaction every time.

* * *

Drill opened the car door and slipped out into the night. Sitting too long had made his legs numb, which could slow him down and get him killed. He put a hand on the back of the SUV and did some squats and stretches and got his blood pumping. The cool air was heavy with humidity and the smell of plowed dirt—Middle-America farm country.

He walked to the end of the driveway and looked up the length of the street. Dead still and almost silent, just the faint whistle of wind through the bare branches of the neighborhood trees. The one porch light was still on at the head of the street, and the light of a TV flickered in a window across from Greer's place. But still no sign of Greer.

The luminescent hands on Drill's watch showed almost eleven; Greer must be having a sleepover with some other geriatric.

It was time for Drill to go in and figure out where Greer might be.

He walked behind the house where he'd parked, then crept from shadow to shadow and house to house until he was behind the house next-door to Greer's. He paused there, letting several minutes pass before making a slow circuit around Greer's house. Not a single light was on, and all the doors and windows were locked. He stopped at the sliding glass door at the back of the house, set his feet, lifted the door high enough for the latch to clear the strike plate, then moved it over an inch and set it back down. He slid the door open and stepped inside. He wore thin leather gloves to avoid fingerprints, but he wasn't worried about trace or DNA. Even if he took Greer out here in his own house, it was very unlikely that a backwater burg like this had the resources to search for, or analyze, either.

He turned on the lights as he walked through the house; shining a flashlight around was a surefire way to alert neighbors that something was up. The place was cleaner than he'd expected for an old widower's house: magazines were stacked neatly, laundry was in the hamper, the kitchen floor was crumb-free. In the largest bedroom he found a single drawer filled with a woman's white cotton underwear, and in the bathroom a pink toothbrush stood next to a blue one in a holder by the sink. Greer had a steady girl who sometimes spent the night. He probably kept the place clean for her. Or maybe she kept it clean for him. But tonight the old man must be sleeping over at her place, wherever that was.

A second bedroom was decorated with sports trophies, team photos, and model cars. A boy's room, the boy long since moved out. A third bedroom held a bare mattress on a box spring piled with boxes and an exercise bike with dust on the seat.

Drill went through the kitchen cabinets and every drawer and closet in the house. He was surprised not to find any guns; that was odd, both for a retired cop and for a guy living out here in deer-hunting country. But what he wanted to find was something to indicate where Greer's woman lived. He found a photo of her stuck to the fridge in a tiny frame shaped like a heart—she was a pleasant-looking woman with a nice smile, sitting with Greer on metal bleachers at what looked like a high school football game— but there was no name written on the back.

A cluster of plastic medicine bottles, many empty, were stashed in a cabinet by the kitchen sink. Apparently Greer was on two medications. One was labeled as an anti-inflammatory using 5-aminosalicylate, and the other was a steroid. Both prescriptions carried unlimited ninety-pill refills. It seemed Greer had a chronic immune system problem. There were no medications for the woman.

Drill sighed. He'd found nothing to indicate where Greer was. Which meant he'd have to wait the old man out. Drill went back through the house, shutting off the lights, then left the same way he'd come in. He left the sliding door unlocked so he could slip right back in if he needed to.

He'd only been back in the car for a few minutes when the satellite phone rattled with a call.

"Drill," he said.

"Update?"

Update? Spec knew better than to bother him with such nonsense during an op. "Not done."

"I figured, but when do…"

Spec's words were drowned out by a loud voice droning on behind him. A voice that shouldn't be there. Spec always talked to Drill alone —that was one of many protocols designed to keep who knew what to a minimum. Spec responded to the voice, but he must have put his hand over the phone because the exchange was muffled, voices rising and overlapping in an argument that couldn't mean anything good.

Drill waited.

Finally Spec came back on the line, his voice resigned.

"I've got someone here with me who's read in on this op and has some questions."

"Spec, I don't—"

"Operative?" A deep smooth voice. "Are you there?"

Drill considered hanging up, but something about the voice kept him on the phone. It was familiar, but it wasn't Spec's boss; Drill knew how that stuffed shirt sounded. Maybe this was the next suit up the chain? But anyone in the chain of command knew better than to get on this call. Which meant something had gone sideways—or this guy wasn't in the chain of command.

Or both.

"Yes. Who are you?"

"Don't tell him." Spec in the background.

"Did you put me on speakerphone?" Drill asked.

"The room's secure, Drill," said Spec. "Just listen to... uh... Mr. Red, for a minute."

"Mr. Red?"

"Yes. Just answer his questions."

"Should I call him by his name?" asked Mr. Red. His voice was deep and sweet as dripping honey.

"Call him Drill," said Spec.

"Is that his name?"

Drill shook his head. This guy was an idiot.

"Mr. Drill?"

"Go ahead, Mr. Red."

"How is the... what terminology do you utilize... the operation?"

Utilize? That was a politician's word. "Not done."

"When will it be done?"

"Unknown. The intelligence was thin. I still haven't made contact."

"Mr. Drill, this operation has two parts, and the second part is heating up."

"Please advise. Abort here and head north or complete then proceed?"

"God damn it, you need to work faster!"

The deep shrillness tipped an image into Drill's memory. A long curve of desk with a bunch of middle-aged white men behind it badgering some civil service employee about... something. Some kind of congressional hearing.

"Spec?" he said. "Finish here or abort and head north?"

"One min—" Spec's voice cut off as the phone went to mute.

Drill used the time to focus on the voice and the memory it had called up, trying to pull it into focus. The subject of the men's energetic attacks had been a woman...

He had it. They'd been badgering the former head of the State

Department about a security lapse every informed American knew had been caused by Republican budget cuts. And—

"Drill?"

"Yes, Spec?"

"Finish there, then contact me and I'll send you the rest of the information on phase two."

"Understood."

Drill terminated the call and pushed thoughts about Mr. Red from his mind. He'd have plenty of time later—after the op—to think about why Spec let a politician enter the operation. Right now, he needed a clear head, or he would fail.

Drill didn't fail.

30

Jake pulled on a pair of jeans and a sweatshirt, jumped in the Mustang, and drove to Miller's boarding house. He parked at the curb and headed for the door of Miller's room. Halfway up the driveway he noticed light spilling into the yard. Miller's door was open.

Had Benchley arrived?

Jake crept forward. The night was silent but for the skittering of wind-blown leaves down the street. The fire pit glowed, and a tendril of smoke wound up and was whisked away.

Moving diagonally out into the yard to get a better angle on the door, Jake spotted a bulky shape low in the doorway. A moment later he realized it was Carl, sitting on a kitchen chair futzing with the doorknob. If there had been any danger, it was long gone.

"Carl?"

Carl startled, the chair legs squeaking against the floor. He wore green flannel pajamas under his thick brown robe, and the same leather slippers he had on the day before.

"Christ's sake! Scared the crap out of me." He leaned back and looked at Jake through his coke-bottle glasses. "What are you doing here?"

"What happened to the door?" The wood around the knob was splintered, bright pine showing.

"Mr. Miller forgot his key and had to kick the door in."

"When did this happen?" Grady had only been gone for a little over half an hour.

"I just found it. Heard a noise out here but didn't come out right away because I was watching my show. When I came out, I found this." He gestured at the door.

"Wide open like that?"

"It was mostly closed, but I could tell something was wrong about it. Some light was coming through by the knob here." He pointed at the splintered mess.

"But you talked to Miller?"

"No." Carl turned back to poking at the knob with a screwdriver. A shoe print showed above the knob, a hard heel denting a crescent into the wood.

"Then how do you know he forgot his key?"

"He left a note." Carl pointed inside.

"Can I go in?" Jake asked. Consent would preserve anything he found.

"Sure. I don't know what it has to do with housing ordinances, though."

Jake crossed the little wood porch, gravel crunching under his feet, and slipped past Carl.

On the kitchen table, beside a half-empty six-pack of Corona, lay the square lid of a pizza box. A message had been printed on the soft cardboard in careful block letters with a pencil. In the note Miller apologized for kicking in the door and said he hoped two hundred would cover it.

"He left you two hundred dollars?"

"Yep. To fix the door."

Maybe Miller was okay.

Jake looked around. He remembered his conversation with Miller, and how his eyes had darted to the closet. Whatever he'd hidden there had probably been the same thing he'd stuffed under his jacket when Grady followed him, but it was still worth a look.

Jake pulled the string to turn on the closet light. *Empty.* Nothing on the hangers and nothing on the shelves.

He reached for the string to turn off the light and noticed the access panel cut into the ceiling. It had dirty handprints on it.

"When's the last time you went up through that access panel?"

Carl came over to look. "Don't think I ever have."

Jake grabbed the other kitchen chair and put it inside the closet, then stood on it to reach the panel. He pressed the panel upward, and it gave way with a rasping screech. He stretched and felt around the opening but encountered nothing but insulation and dust.

"Sit on the chair, will you? So it doesn't tip over on me."

Carl sat down on the edge of the chair. Jake put his hands on the wall to steady himself, then put his right foot on the chair's back and lifted himself slowly until his head rose above the lip of the opening. A string brushed against his face; he yanked it, and a bare bulb popped on, illuminating a low-ceilinged attic space. No flooring though, just insulation.

He scanned the area around the opening and spotted a square-shaped dent in the insulation, as if a heavy object had lain there. This must have been where Miller hid whatever Grady saw him sneak out to his car under his coat.

Jake turned off the light, closed the hatch, and jumped off the chair.

"Carl, you can go back to your TV while I look around."

"Trust me, there's nothing else left in here." Carl's hand covered the pocket of his robe.

"Let me see what you found."

Carl frowned, sighed, then pulled a cell phone out of the baggy pocket. It was a flip model. "It rang a bit ago but I didn't answer it."

Jake took it and opened it—it had power—then stuck it in his own pocket.

"Anything else?"

Carl shook his head.

"Where did you find the phone?"

Carl pointed to the six-pack on the table. "It was in one of those square pocket things, where the bottles go? I went to take the beer and felt something bounce around and looked, and there it was."

"Go on inside, Carl. I'll make sure this door is closed when I leave. You can fix it tomorrow."

"I can't have you—"

"Go, Carl."

Carl frowned and shook his head, but he went, taking the beer with him.

Jake sat in the wingback to consider. Had he scared the con man off, just as he'd planned? Doubtful. Miller hadn't run after the boys around the picnic table told him a cop had been here— he just moved his friends. He wasn't afraid of a cop. He didn't flee until Jake confronted him about Smith and Benchley. It was clearly Benchley who scared Miller, not Jake.

Jake again considered bringing in the forensics team, but he had nothing concrete to indicate foul play other than the door, and the note explained that. If it was a lie, the note was genius. *And if it was a lie,* then Jake's investigation had brought Benchley to town—exactly as Miller had feared. *What have you done,* Miller had asked him.

Jake examined the phone Carl had found. Phone's like it— burners—were available at every drugstore and discount retailer in the country and came with pre-paid minutes loaded right on them. Basically untraceable.

Jake opened the call log. Only one incoming number was listed, for a call received twenty minutes earlier. Nothing on the outgoing log. Miller probably cleared the log after every call.

Jake didn't recognize the area code on the incoming call, but new ones sprouted up every month. He considered calling the number, but decided to wait until he knew more. He might not get two cracks at speaking to whoever was on the other end. Instead he pulled out his own phone and sent Levi a text asking him to try and find out who owned both numbers: the number for the burner and the number that had called into it.

In response, his phone buzzed with an incoming call.

"Hey, Levi."

"Hey, Jake. Got your text, and I'm on it. But I've also got a bunch of info on Lowell Carr, the man who runs the ministry. You want to hear it?"

"Shoot."

In his usual long-winded way, Levi explained that after confirming Erin's information, he'd dived into Carr's background. Carr had run away from an abusive family and lived on the streets for a decade, selling his body to fund his heroin addiction, before a near-death overdose completely changed his life. He kicked the habit, became a minister, and started a ministry to help teens transition away from the streets by helping them see that they could have a future and helping them find it.

"A noble cause," Jake said.

"Yeah. Guy seems legit."

"Can you track down Carr's cell phone number for me too?"

"You got it."

Jake called Grady next. He told him about the door and the note on the pizza box.

"Can't have happened long ago. I didn't leave till ten fifteen."

"Someone might have known you were watching, waited until you left. Do you know the patrol officer covering this beat right now?"

"Cooper? Sure. I know him pretty well."

"Can you ask him to canvass the neighbors for a disturbance? Find out anything the neighbors saw between when you left and when I got here."

"He owes me from... well, never mind, but yeah."

"Thanks, Grady. Do that, and I got the rest."

Jake hung up. It was time to go back to Mount Logan.

Because now he had enough to crack Smith wide open.

31

Benchley backed the car into the garage and turned it off. It was late—after two. He was so exhausted that even the anticipation of having Thomas strapped into the chair in the basement didn't energize him.

The long drive back to Springfield in separate cars had been a tense trip, made worse when Thomas came to and started banging around in the trunk. Benchley's pulse had wound up until he thought he was going to pass out. Then Thomas suddenly went quiet and Benchley spent the rest of the drive worried that his best shot at finding the files—which had not been in the apartment— might have died on him.

"Boss?"

Benchley's eyes popped open. It was dark, and he was cold.

"Boss? You okay?"

Seth's voice. A tapping.

Benchley turned toward the sound and found Seth looking through the car window, his breath fogging it.

"Yeah," he said, gathering his wits. He was home, and Thomas was in the trunk.

Seth opened the door and Benchley unbuckled and got out. He stood and stretched, getting his blood flowing again. "Let's see how he looks." He felt his pocket for the keys, but they were still in the ignition. He reached into the car and pulled them out, then handed them to Seth.

Seth opened the trunk. The inside light came on.

"He looks asleep."

"Or dead," said Benchley.

The left side of Thomas's face was swollen, and there was a dark crust of dried blood around his eye. Seth had a big fist and had hit him hard—maybe too hard.

Benchley put a hand to Thomas's cheek. It was warm. He pried open one of his eyes, and Thomas didn't react. He was alive, but out. He'd been out for nearly three hours, other than that brief period where he'd thrashed around in the trunk. That was a long time to be unconscious. They might never get him back.

"How's your hand?"

Seth held it out and flexed it a few times. "Just a little sore."

"Carry him down to the basement and strap him into the chair. Be careful with his head."

"Will do, boss." Seth scooped Thomas out of the trunk and set off.

Benchley stretched out on the leather couch. He never slept in a bed when he was on a mission. Pulling the comforter off the back of the couch, he curled up on his side and covered himself.

He needed what was locked in that boy's brain, and he had the tools and experience to get the job done.

In the morning, he'd crack the boy open.

32

Jake's return trip to Mount Logan started smoothly, the traffic thinning to almost nothing as the Chicago metro area fell behind him. He sped south in his tunnel of light, his mind buzzing like a bass guitar string. He was pulled over as he flew through Kankakee, but a flash of his badge and professional courtesy had him on his way ticketless in minutes.

As he sped past Champaign his phone dinged with a message. Grady reporting that Cooper's canvass didn't turn up anything and that Miller's car was still in the parking garage.

Did leaving the car behind mean he'd been abducted? Maybe he suspected that Jake had tagged it with a tracker.

Jake gassed up outside Mattoon. He bought a large coffee, bitter from too much time on the burner, and got back on the road. His foot was heavy, and the squat muscle car flew through the night.

He set Miller aside and thought back to the original victim: Mark Siebert. Someone had killed that boy, and it wasn't David Smith. Benchley made the deal for Smith to take the rap, so the killer had to be someone close to Benchley, or the man himself. Someone Greer had been getting a bead on. Jake needed to know what the detective had been working on off-book during the flat spot in his case.

So he had both Greer and Smith to work. Between the two of them, he would finally know who had killed Mark Siebert, and who had covered it up.

If he couldn't deliver Mark alive to his parents, at least he could deliver the truth.

Then he would make the killer and his accomplices pay.

He exited the highway at Mount Logan, then slowed all the way down to the speed limit as he drove through town. Mount Logan was closed for the night; all the streetlights were flashing yellow and the only activity was a pair of squad cars pulled next to each other in a 7-Eleven parking lot. He rolled up to the Royal Inn at twenty minutes to four. The light was on in the manager's office but the door was locked. He hit the buzzer, and within a couple of minutes Sheila came through the door behind the counter, still belting her robe.

She smiled. It surprised Jake, but he found it comforting after the long drive. She unlocked the outer door and pushed it open a crack.

"Welcome back, Detective."

He tugged the door open and followed her into the lobby.

She stepped behind the counter. "How about we put you back in the same room and worry about the paperwork later?"

"Sounds good. Thanks, Sheila."

She gave him a little white envelope with his old room number scribbled on it. He went back outside, grabbed his overnight bag, and left the car where it was.

The room hadn't changed. He turned on the lights and the radio and set his bag on the far bed. He vibrated with caffeine and eagerness to get at Greer and Smith. He checked his cell phone and found a text he'd missed from Levi: *The burner was bought at a Walmart and can't be traced beyond that. The area code it called belongs to an internet service like Skype that allows people to use a computer as if it's a phone. Impossible for me to crack. Maybe with a warrant.*

But Jake couldn't get a warrant without opening a case.

He took out the burner and pulled up the call log. It was time to dial the number listed. It was four in the morning, but what the hell.

The line rang six times without going to voicemail, and Jake was about to hang up when the sixth ring cut off.

"Thomas?" A hesitant, breathy voice.

"Who's this?" Jake asked.

No response, just soft breaths coming closer together.

"I'm worried about Thomas," Jake said. "I'm a friend of the Sieberts."

Still nothing. Then the line went dead.

Like Smith, whoever was at the other end of the line called Miller by the name Thomas. His real name, Jake assumed.

He pulled his laptop out of his bag and sent Erin a short email asking her to put him down for time off for the rest of the week. Then he opened the document he'd started about the Siebert case. He entered his idea about Greer's off-book efforts, his latest thoughts about Smith being the fall guy for the real killer, and Miller's real name.

He then went back through his searches about Mark Siebert's abduction looking for anything an investigative reporter might have dug up about Smith that didn't make it to the murder book. He found nothing new.

He clicked back onto the missing children website where he'd found the Mark Siebert listing. The website allowed searches by date and location. Jake put in a search for the ten-year period before Mark's disappearance. He got 588 hits.

Jesus!

He scrolled through them, clicking on a few as he went. In most cases the little picture in the scroll was an artist-rendered age progression. Clicking an entry opened a larger listing, but the information provided was so minimal that he began copying names and pasting them into Google. That provided more interesting results. In some cases local police believed they had solved the case and identified the perpetrator but couldn't prove it, often because no body was ever found. Many of the cases were of non-custodial parents snatching up their own children. But that left hundreds of flat-out disappearances.

He kept scrolling, the faces becoming almost a blur as his eyes grew tired. He thought about stretching out for a few hours' sleep.

Wait.

Who was that?

He scrolled back to the face that had caught his attention. He looked at it more closely, then clicked on the listing to see the expanded photo. He stared at it—but whatever he'd seen, he wasn't seeing it now.

He clicked on a thumbnail photo inset in the bottom corner of the picture, and it enlarged, showing a photo from the time the boy went missing. *Now* recognition flashed across Jake's tired brain.

This boy was David Smith.

His real name was Tracy James.

Jake read the entry.

Tracy James disappeared while on his newspaper route in University Heights, Iowa, in 2001. Tracy's photo is shown age-progressed to 28 years. His eyes are set close together, he has a gap between his front teeth, a birthmark on his left forearm, and a horseshoe-shaped scar on his left kneecap.

Iowa. Sports teams for the University of Iowa were called Hawkeyes, the name Smith used in his phone message. And Jake remembered the birthmark; he'd thought it was a bruise.

He typed the name into Google and found dozens of hits. It appeared the boy was still missing and his mother wasn't dead, though she had moved away from University Heights. Jake copied a couple of links, emailed them to Levi, and asked him to find Tracy James's mother immediately. Knowing Smith's real name *might* unlock the man—but finding his momma surely would.

Greer and Smith. He'd shake the truth loose from both of them in a few hours.

He stretched out on the bed, his body finally loose. Finding Smith's real identity had released his brain from its anxiety and sleep poured in.

33

———

Jake's phone clattered against the nightstand when the alarm went off at eight, but he was already in the shower. He'd slept for a solid three hours before a passing truck rattled his window and woke him. Instead of rolling over, he hopped up and got moving. It was going to be a big day.

He dressed in gray pants with a white shirt and his black blazer—his standard work attire, because today he was solving a murder. He checked his phone and had three texts. McKay asked whether he had any thoughts on Storch. The answer was no, he'd been too busy with the Siebert case to even think about it, but she deserved a more helpful response from him than that. He texted her back. *He's dealing. The task force will find its way to him.*

Erin's text said Miller's driver's license was legit and the address was to a storefront mail drop. If Miller knew someone with the power to get a real license in a fake name, he had connections.

The third text was from Levi with a cell phone number for Lowell Carr.

Jake dialed it.

The phone was answered by a deep voice. "Carr."

"Mr. Carr, my name is Jake Houser. Paul and Linda Siebert have asked me to look into their son's disappearance."

"You're a cop."

It was more accusation than statement of fact.

"I visited David Smith, just like you did. The news you gave him disturbed him."

"I work with runaways and child prostitutes. I generally don't have good news for people."

"What did you tell him?'

"I deal in truth. I told him some." Carr was good at the runaround.

"What truth did—"

"You're not helping anyone. You need to back the hell off."

"Tell me how I *can* help."

"By staying the hell out of it."

"What is the *it* you want me to stay out of?"

Silence.

"Don't you think Mark's killer should be punished?"

"Screw the past," Carr said. "All that looking back and pointing fingers at parents and teachers and Uncle Whoever only perpetuates the condition."

"What condition?"

"The condition these teens are in. Believing they have no future. Hiding from themselves by keeping their minds clouded by drugs and booze. Living on the streets. Selling their bodies."

"What kind of future can you help Tracy James have? He has another twenty-three years to go."

Carr said nothing.

"What about Robert Miller? He lives in Cherry Valley, which is right next door to you there in Rockford, right? Also goes by Thomas?"

"You need to drop it."

The line went dead.

Jake sat for a moment thinking through the call. Carr's philosophy about focusing on the future made good sense for the people he wanted to help. But Jake's work focused on finding the truth about the past to avenge victims and punish people for what they'd done.

He headed to the front desk to settle up with Sheila.

"Too bad we don't charge by the hour. You'd save money." Sheila was dressed and sipping coffee.

She offered Jake a to-go cup, and he accepted with thanks. He sipped the scalding coffee while she ran his credit card.

"Who are you talking to today?" she asked. "Gonna pester Chief Bell again? Or our mayor?"

"No. Just a few loose strings to tie up."

"You didn't drive through the night to tie up loose strings." She handed his card back. "More likely you'll be yanking someone's string."

He laughed because her metaphor was more accurate. "Thanks for the coffee."

He pushed through the door and hopped in the Mustang. Greer lived out in the country south and east of town. Jake typed the address into the GPS map on his phone and followed the line it drew for him, sipping the coffee as he drove. South on Tenth Street to Highway 142 and then to Lynchburg Road, a narrow two-lane blacktop running east with crumbling shoulders and a high crown. Farm fields stretched north from the road while the south side was mostly woods. A mile in, short roads started poking off like teeth on a comb. Greer's street was one of these, and Jake turned down it and slowed.

The neighborhood was mostly small single-story homes, each with an attached one-car garage and a front porch. Some of the houses were well cared for, but most were not. Greer's place was the lone blue house on the east side of the road. His lawn was neat, the gravel drive clear of weeds, and the porch roof straight. Jake parked in the driveway.

On his way to the front door he stopped and peeked through the row of windows set in the garage door. No car. Greer might be out.

He climbed the steps and crossed the porch, the boards squeaking loud in the country stillness. He raised a fist to knock on the door.

"Hello?"

The loud warbly voice came from a small bent woman crossing the grass from the house to the south. She wore a faded pink robe and fuzzy green slippers, and her head bobbed as she walked. She raised a hand and waved for Jake to come to her.

"Morning, ma'am." Jake stepped down off the porch and flipped his badge open. The woman's pinched face relaxed and lost a few wrinkles. "I'm looking for Detective Greer about an old case."

"Well, I expect you missed him—if he even came home at all last night." She smiled. "He's got himself a lady friend."

A nosy neighbor. The policeman's friend. "Where would I find him?"

She squinted up at him, her giant eyeglasses blurring her eyes with their curvature. "He'll be over to the courthouse by now."

"The courthouse?"

"He's one of those whatcha-ma-call-ems?" She waved her hand in the air, then pointed toward town. "What, that hang around and watch all the trials."

"Trial junkie?"

She cracked a wide smile that showed a lot of gold. "That's it. That's where he'll be." She pointed back toward town. "Big case going to trial today. Was in the paper."

Jake thanked her and got moving.

34

———

Drill spent the night watching Greer's house, but the man never came home. He dozed on and off, but whenever he was awake he thought about Mr. Red. He still couldn't place the voice. It definitely belonged to one of those men behind the raised table looking down on the Secretary of State. A self-righteous politician.

He was chewing an energy bar when a Mustang pulled into Greer's driveway. Drill didn't have a photo of the Weston detective, but intel said he drove a Mustang. Of course, the intel *also* said the detective was back home in Weston. Spec's intel on this operation was for shit.

Drill rolled his window down and heard the neighborhood busybody selling out Greer with her bullhorn voice. The old man would be at the courthouse.

Shit.

Since 9/11, every courthouse in America had security: sheriff deputies, metal detectors, and cameras. Once Greer got inside the courthouse, Drill's options would be limited. As he fired up the Suburban, Houser hustled back to his car and took off.

Double shit.

Drill dropped the transmission into gear, goosed the pedal, and flew by the old woman now absorbed in climbing her front stoop. If he was going to prevent a meeting between Greer and the Weston cop as ordered, he had to act now. And he only had one play: force Houser off the road.

The Mustang beat the Suburban to the main road by three hundred yards. Drill came up onto the crowned asphalt and floored it, the Suburban rushing into the Mustang's wake. The Mustang pulled ahead and Drill pushed his boxy vehicle to keep up.

The road jogged north and quickly back west, and the Suburban's high suspension couldn't handle it. It tilted up on two tires, then banged down. Drill fought it back under control, gripped the steering wheel tighter, and floored it again. The engine roared, the transmission dropped into the passing gear, and the vehicle surged forward again.

"Let's go," Drill said, urging the SUV on.

He caught an orange blur in his rearview mirror, then it slid out of view. Another orange flash, this time in his in his driver's-side mirror, was followed by the loud whine of a machine ramping up. Drill pulled his eyes off Houser's car and glanced left to see an orange pickup veering toward him.

Whack!

The back end of the Suburban slewed sideways as the impact broke its grip on the road.

Drill fought the steering wheel, turning into the skid, but he over-corrected. He spun the wheel back the other way and then he was out of control. The SUV plunged into the shallow ditch and bounced up into a plowed field, dirt clods exploding off the tires. He fought the big SUV to a stop in a cloud of dust and dirt.

What the hell!

Drill sat still as the dirt settled, the air clearing around him, the big engine coughing out. The SUV was pointed back the way he'd come. Through the passenger window he saw the orange pickup truck stopped on the road. Its wheels were huge, and a giant block of aluminum stuck out of the hood, with a pair of carburetors on top. Two flannel-clad hillbillies stood next to it, watching him, one talking into a cell phone.

No security team would drive around in a hot-rodded pickup with a blower-inducted engine. These boys and their truck were local. Something separate from Houser, or at least that Houser didn't know about, otherwise he would have stopped to see what this was all about. And Drill would have seen them if they'd been watching Greer. So they must have been following Houser.

Protecting him? Because they knew someone like Drill was coming to town?

He didn't have enough information to answer those questions.

As he eyed the two men leaning on their ridiculous truck, anger built inside him. How did these two yahoos get the drop on him? He'd been too focused. And too confident.

That wouldn't happen again.

The man with the phone slapped the other man on the back, then flipped Drill off.

Heat rose up the back of Drill's neck and around to his face, but he took a calming breath and pushed it down. He didn't have time for revenge, but he couldn't leave the hicks mobile. They might interfere again.

He started the SUV back up, put it in gear, and took his foot off the brake. The Suburban bumped forward across the furrowed field, away from the two hicks, the undercarriage scraping on the stubs of harvested corn stalks poking from the soil. He flicked the wipers on to clear the dust from the windshield.

"You better run, asshole!" the hillbilly shouted, his words booming across the field.

When Drill was lined up properly, he stopped, shifted the SUV into reverse, spun the wheel, and gave it some gas. The big vehicle picked up speed as he bounced over the plowed ground, aiming directly for the men leaning against the truck's front fender. He twisted in his seat to confirm his aim, then he floored it, hanging tight to the wheel.

The men dove away just before he popped onto the road and

slammed into their truck. He dropped the transmission into drive and pulled away.

He looked back. The orange truck's front fender was flattened against the engine compartment, and one wheel had come off and lay by itself on the road. They wouldn't be following him. But they had a phone.

He drove east. Away from Houser and the courthouse.

For now.

35
____

Jake sped down the crown of the rural road, the Mustang floating on its suspension over the bumps. It was approaching nine, so he was cutting it close. When he got to the highway he punched it, and within minutes he was on Tenth, cruising north for the courthouse. As he pulled into a spot along the curb he saw a cluster of people hanging out near the doors, waiting to get inside.

He'd made it.

His phone buzzed as he climbed out of the car. Levi. He decided to answer; information about Tracy James might help crack Greer open.

"What did you learn, Levi?" Jake stepped around his car and stood by the hood, scanning the small crowd of people in front of the doors. An old-timer in jeans and a barn coat tugged on one of the doors and it rattled but didn't open. A second cluster stood twenty feet south of the doors, smoking. A group of gray-hairs sat off by themselves on the low concrete wall along the sidewalk, laughing and shooting the shit. They looked like Greer's people.

"Is Tracy James your David Smith?" Levi asked. His voice had an excited lilt.

"I think so."

"Well, I found his mother."

"Excellent." That would definitely help.

One of the courthouse doors opened and a man in uniform stuck his head out and said something Jake couldn't hear—probably announcing that a judge had taken the bench, or that a trial was starting. The smokers flicked their butts and started moving toward the doors.

"I'll call you back." Jake put away his phone and ran forward, calling out to the group of old-timers. "Greer!"

One of them broke off the pack and stepped toward Jake, cocking his head. Greer was a few inches shorter than Jake, stocky with a bit of belly, and wore khakis and a golf shirt under a leather bomber jacket.

"My name's Jake Houser."

Greer's expectant smile flipped into a frown. "What are you doing here?" He swept a hand through his thick gray hair and shot his gaze past Jake and around the square. "I told you I don't know anything that isn't in the file."

"Then why would Brakur tell me you left something out?" Brakur hadn't, but the lie might prompt a response.

Greer squinted into the rising sun, then stepped around Jake to put the sun at his back. "Brakur couldn't have told you that."

A deflection instead of a denial. Greer *had* left something out, but it wasn't something Brakur could identify.

Jake's phone buzzed again in his pocket. Levi would have to wait.

"I had a chance to read through the murder book since we last talked."

"No way Bell'd let an out-of-towner see that book." Greer snorted in disgust. "Those damn Sieberts throwing their weight around."

"Why did they have to?"

"What're you after?" Greer suddenly grabbed his stomach and winced. He shuffled back over to the low concrete wall that separated the sidewalk from a row of squat bushes and desiccated perennials, and sat down gently, his face pale.

Jake sat down near Greer. "The murder book showed your efforts to find Mark. A lot of good work there. Nothing to be ashamed of in that file."

Greer eyed Jake, not buying the flattery, rubbing the side of his belly.

"But there's little in there covering the few weeks leading up to Smith's confession."

"There it is," Greer said. "Big-shot city dick using his twenty-twenty hindsight to tell me what I did wrong."

"That's not what I—"

"Why are you here?" Greer winced again. He gritted his teeth and shook his head. "You shitting on my work just for fun? Make the bumpkin look bad? That your thing?"

"No. I think you kept working the case in that flat spot but didn't write it up because whatever you were chasing was too far out there. Then Smith confessed, and you never put all that work in the book because there was no point."

Greer's grimace relaxed and he probed his belly with one hand, his cheeks puffing out with a captured burp. He released it like he was blowing a smoke ring. "What are you getting at?"

Jake had led Greer far enough that he should see the point, but the pain in his gut must be clouding his thinking. "What if this far-out thing you chased off-book is what brought Smith to town to confess?"

Greer shook his head violently, another burp shaking loose. "I confirmed that goddamn confession." He sucked air between his teeth, one leg shooting out straight with a spasm. "He... *hssst...* knew a lot of inside dope."

"You okay?" Jake asked.

"Peachy."

Jake didn't need to be a detective to see that was a lie. The man was in serious pain.

Jake pressed. "If Smith was taking a fall for the real killer, he *would* know inside dope."

"He'd know..." Greer went still. His focus faded off and away.

Jake waited, watching Greer's eyes as realization dawned and took hold. Greer would either get mad, or he would shut down and refuse to acknowledge what he could have, and maybe should have, seen way back then.

"Jesus H. Christ." Greer looked away.

Mad. Good. Jake would get the missing parts of the story.

"Take your time, Detective Greer."

Greer's face reddened, and sweat popped on his upper lip. "I was at a dead end, like you said. I'd talked to everyone who'd ever met that kid. Most of them twice. I was getting ready to accept what Bell and Nelson had been pushing—that the boy ran away. Then I got drunk one night. Off the shit for more'n five years now." A smile, before his face tightened. "Had a dream—a nightmare, really, that put me in mind of something that happened when I was on patrol way back, long before the boy disappeared."

Jake waited as Greer worked through how to explain it. This was the key to the whole thing.

"We had a string of vandalism in the forest preserves, and I was working my way through them one night. Preserves close at dark, so anyone in there after that is trespassing. I found a parked car and thought I might have caught 'em, but then I saw the windows were fogged up so it was just some kids necking. I was bored, so thought I'd sneak up and scare 'em." He shrugged. "Probably hoped to catch a peek."

Greer went silent for a minute, remembering. His lips pursing in distaste. "So I come up on the window and shine my light in there and see a head bobbing up and down in this teenager's lap. He startles, but the head stays at it. I'm thinking she must have her eyes closed or something. The guy pushes her away, and then I see the head bobber's not a girl but another guy."

Greer's cheeks puffed again, and he rubbed his belly while he swallowed. "An older guy. And I recognized him."

Jake's pulse quickened, but he held still, letting Greer get to it.

"It was Blake Reznik."

The name took Jake by surprise. "The US congressman from

Illinois? *That* Blake Reznik?" He had known Reznik was a down-state product but didn't remember him being from Mount Logan. Now he was a Washington establishment big shot. Had a sound bite nearly every time Jake turned on the news.

"Back then he was just Blake. An attorney here in town and on the city council. Anyway, I wasn't going to bust him for... you know, what they were doing. I got a nephew like that. The boy getting the, uh... servicing, was of age—didn't look like it, but I checked his license and he was. He said he wanted to be there, so I never even wrote it up. Never even told anyone."

Reznik's name was a bomb dropped from so high Jake never saw it coming. "And after Mark disappeared?"

"I was out of things to chase, but I needed to keep moving. Keep talking to people. Hoping something would shake loose."

Jake followed the same investigative principle: just keep working.

"Bell was pushing the gay thing, and I remembered Reznik. I know a gay guy and a pedophile are two different things. But I was at a dead end—I had nothing to do and I had to do something. So I figured to ask him a few questions. Just to keep moving."

"Was he cooperative?"

Greer nodded. "He remembered me and that I hadn't, you know, told anyone about him. So he met with me even though he was already a state senator and was campaigning for US Congress. A big deal. He was visiting us back home here and I pushed him hard. Way harder than I should have, because I had nothing on him other than his secret. But he had an alibi. Said he'd been at an important government meeting in Springfield and had to get clearance before he could give me the names. Said it would take a few days and he'd let me know when it was done."

Greer went silent.

"You talked to Reznik, then Smith showed up."

Greer nodded, his face twisting as Jake's words sank in, the cause and effect suddenly clear. A slick sheen spread across his face, and his cheeks reddened.

"Did he ever give you that alibi?"

"Sent me a list of names—people I'd heard of—and even photos of him at some meeting." Greer turned back to Jake. "I didn't confirm it, but those names weren't people who'd lie for him."

"Which only proves he didn't do it himself."

"What now?" Greer asked.

Indeed, Jake thought. Greer's story was good circumstantial evidence that Blake Reznik was somehow connected to Mark Siebert's murder, but alone it proved nothing.

"I go talk to Smith," Jake said.

And he left Greer sitting there, his face pale and slick with sweat.

36

When Benchley woke, he set up the coffee maker, then went to go splash water on his face. The machine had finished by the time he returned, so he filled a travel mug, grabbed two bottles of orange Gatorade and his kit from the fridge, and went to the basement. His hands full, he descended the creaking wood stairs slowly, one elbow pressed to the wall for balance.

The stairs ended in space that had once been the boys' dormitory; now it was an empty concrete expanse with a line of bare bulbs down the center. Benchley crossed the gritty floor to the closed door in the middle of the concrete block wall on the other side. He set the Gatorade bottles on the floor and opened the wood door into a short vestibule with an insulated steel door on the opposite wall. When he opened *that* door, the sour stench of vomit wafted over him.

Bare concrete with two chairs, a steel table, and a high-powered lamp on a steel base. Thomas sat duct-taped to the chair bolted to the floor, the light shining on his bowed head. Seth sat in the other chair, his shoulders and head against the wall.

Seth bounced up. "Sorry about the smell, boss. I cleaned it up best I could."

Thomas's head jerked; he wasn't dead. A good start.

"You did good," Benchley said. "I left two Gatorades on the floor outside."

"I'll get 'em." Seth dragged his chair in front of Thomas then went for the drinks.

"Leave the doors open."

Benchley put his coffee and the kit on the table, then sat down in front of Thomas. He put his palm on the boy's forehead and tilted his head back, thumbing open an eyelid.

Thomas twisted out from under Benchley's hand, and both eyes opened.

"Good morning," Benchley said. Seth came back with the Gatorade. "You're dehydrated. I'm going to help you drink this down." Benchley held one of the bottles in front of Thomas and twisted the cap off, the clacking rip of the plastic seal clear in the quiet room. He put it to Thomas's lips and helped him drink it, slowly, until the boy got it all down.

"There." Benchley tossed the empty bottle to Seth, then pulled his chair closer. For interrogations he liked to get right in there, his face in the subject's face, inhaling each other's exhalations. Occasionally he would get up and work from behind, moving back and forth and in and out of the subject's peripheral vision. Talking non-stop, then going quiet. Establish a pattern, then break it. All enhanced by his truth formula that he had tested on over three hundred subjects during his time with the program.

That program had been shut down when a new director came on board—a lawyer, his thinking corrupted by admissibility concerns. He didn't understand that such concerns didn't apply because the information being extracted never saw a courtroom. The program was its own court, its own judge, its own jury.

Justice delivered swiftly.

In this room, Benchley had all of that back.

"I need you to tell me where the files are, Thomas. Tell me now and we don't have to get to the rest of it. To what's in that syringe or to what you know Seth can do."

Thomas's eyes opened wide. His pupils were the same size, so even if he had a concussion, it probably wouldn't kill him.

Benchley leaned in. "Where are the files?"

Thomas pulled his head back, blinking as if trying to focus. His mouth opened and a string of drool spilled out.

"Seth," Benchley said, "help him drink down this other bottle and then let him sleep. Right there in that chair. Then come get me in three hours."

"Want me to soften him up before I come get you?" Seth flexed his big hands.

"Not before."

37

While Jake was talking with Greer, Lenny's pickup had pulled up across the street from the courthouse. Lenny now waved Jake over, and his burly brother Clint hopped out and motioned for Jake to get in.

Jake stood next to Clint. He didn't have time for a drive. "I'm good right here,"

Lenny leaned over and spoke out through the door. "When you left Greer's a little bit ago? A guy driving a black SUV tried to follow you. One of our boys ran him off the road. But he turned tables on them and rammed them, then took off. I was following our tow truck out there just now, but I saw your car and I'm glad I caught ya."

"This all happened right behind me?" Jake hadn't seen anyone behind him, but he'd been focused on getting to the courthouse and cracking Greer open.

Lenny laughed. "I'm not surprised you didn't notice. The boys said you were driving like an idiot."

"Why were your guys there?"

"Followed you." Lenny shrugged. "We look out for ours."

"How'd they know the SUV was following me?"

"Came shooting out of Greer's street after you. Fast as hell. And the SUV don't belong there, we know that."

"Just one guy in it? Not a local?"

"Right."

"Did the driver identify himself?" Feds drove big black SUVs. Or was Jake just being paranoid because of hearing Reznik's name?

"He wasn't a cop. He rammed them like I said, then turned tail and took off east toward Evansville. Boys scared the crap out of him. He won't be back." Lenny gestured toward the courthouse with his chin. "Greer tell you what you need to know?"

"Some of it. Now I'm headed out to the prison to pry loose a little more."

"Clint and me'll follow you out there. Just to be sure."

Jake started to shake his head, then decided it couldn't hurt. He got in his Mustang, pulled a U-turn, and drove south.

He'd gone less than a block when his phone vibrated with a call.

"Houser."

"It's me," said Coogan. "When you couldn't talk, Levi called me about what he'd found. Couldn't wait to tell somebody."

This sounded promising. "Let's hear it."

"He confirmed what you sent him about Tracy James. Abducted and never found, et cetera. We both looked at the website's photos and compared them with the newspaper photos of Smith and his picture on the Illinois Offender Database. It's him; there's no doubt. Plus the database says Smith has a scar above his left kneecap; the missing children's website says the same thing about Tracy James."

"Good. I'm headed to see him now."

"Levi also tracked down Tracy James's mom. She's alive and lives in Keokuk, Iowa. Levi called her pretending to be a telemarketer selling college bonds, and she told him she didn't need bonds because her son was taken. Told him all about it. Levi's sure she has no idea her boy is alive. Said she couldn't afford any bonds anyway. All she has coming in is a payment on a reverse mortgage. He's checking into that now."

"This is great. Be sure to thank Levi for me. I've made progress here too." Jake told Coogan about Congressman Reznik and then about the SUV.

"Jake... Reznik is vice chairman of the House Select Committee on Intelligence. That means he has access to the black ops agents of all the shadow agencies that don't even have names. The guy in the SUV could be extremely dangerous."

"I'll keep my eyes open." If the man in the SUV *was* an operative from one of the shadow agencies, that would explain why he'd left the scene of his altercation with the Sieberts. "I have a local escort following me out to the prison, then I'm heading home."

"Maybe you should leave this one alone."

"No way. With what Greer told me and Levi's news, I now have a good shot at cracking Smith open and getting to the truth. Then I can roll up Benchley. If I can break Benchley, I can get to Reznik."

"Because you think he started the whole ball rolling," Coogan said.

"Very likely."

After the call, Jake thought through his approach with Smith. He decided to start by revealing he'd learned his real name, and Mr. B's. From there he'd bring up Smith's mother. That would shake him. And then they'd discuss his taking the fall to protect Reznik.

Jake parked in the prison's visitor lot, and Lenny pulled in next to him. Jake asked Lenny to put out the word to the Siebert network to keep on the lookout for the SUV, but to stay away from it. He didn't explain why.

As Jake walked through the parking lot, his phone buzzed with another text. McKay, responding to his text about the task force eventually getting to Storch: *I hope you're right.*

He'd been a cop too long to believe in hope.

Action made things happen. Not thoughts or prayers.

As he approached the entrance, he saw that something was

different. Last time he'd been here a thin stream of people had snaked up the sidewalk to line up for visitor entry. But now clusters of people stood bunched up at the base of the sidewalk, their voices combining into an excited babble.

A young woman's voice rose about the fray. "Five-hour drive and they won't even let us in? I drive all the way here for some lockdown shit?"

Jake's stomach roiled, and he sped up. Prisons locked down many reasons, but he didn't believe in coincidences. A politician like Reznik would have favors to collect all over Illinois.

Hustling around the throng, he walked straight up to the double glass doors, where a guard stood on the other side. Jake pulled out his badge and pressed it to the glass.

"I'm here to see the warden." He shouted to be heard through the glass. If the lockdown was about Smith, the warden would want to talk to him. If it wasn't about Smith, then she was his only hope of getting inside while it was on.

The guard came up to the glass, read Jake's badge, and spoke into his shoulder microphone.

Jake waited.

"They letting you in?" A shout from the crowd back down the sidewalk.

"It doesn't look like it," Jake shouted back.

They turned away and went back to their conversations. Some people broke off and headed for their cars.

The door rattled. "Step in quickly, Detective Houser."

The prison's sour air engulfed Jake as he stepped inside.

38

———

The door closed behind Jake, muffling the chorus of shouts from the crowd wanting to get in. A voice over an outside loudspeaker reverberated through the glass, instructing the crowd to step back.

"Officer Holmes, right?" Jake said. It was the same portly guard who'd signed him in on his previous visit.

"Good memory. The warden does want to see you, Detective." Holmes's face was a mask. "Follow me."

Holmes led the way through a metal detector into what looked like a middle-management cubicle farm with narrow offices lined up against the north-facing windows. Most of the desks were empty, the employees standing around in groups of four or five talking quietly, their faces grim. Holmes proceeded to a heavy wood door fronted by a secretary post manned by a slender Latina. Holmes motioned toward her, then left Jake to make it the rest of the way on his own.

"Good morning." The woman pointed to a chair against the wall. "Please have a seat, Detective Houser. It'll only be a few minutes."

Jake sat. "What caused the lockdown?" he asked.

"The warden will explain." She turned away and started typing.

"Can you tell me what level it is?" Illinois had five lockdown levels, rising in severity from one to five.

"The warden will be with you shortly." She didn't even look at him.

He waited, the flight of time thrumming against his skull. The lockdown didn't *have* to be about Smith. The warden might want to see him about the library phone calls or the ministry that had visited Smith. But his gut said something had happened to Smith.

The door opened and a twenty-something man with a weak goatee and wrinkled clothes backed out, thanking the warden for something obscured by his mumble. Jake jumped up and squeezed past the man into the warden's office.

Warden Stevenson sat at a small conference table, a laptop open in front of her. She waved him over. "I need to show you some video." Her face was hard and pale.

Jake sat with her at the table. "Something happened to Smith."

"He was killed this morning."

Jake's stomach burned. "What happened?"

The warden angled the computer toward him. "The video is queued up."

The screen showed the inmate cafeteria from a high corner angle. It was a large space of hexagonal stainless steel tables with attached stools. Most occupied. The warden punched a button and the scene broke into motion, people eating and gesturing. There was no sound, but the picture quality was good.

The warden pointed out Smith. His table was full, the men bent over their trays shoveling it in. One of them suddenly stood up and poked the guy next to him, and the poke went around the table until they had all stood up and drifted away—except for Smith, who kept eating. A few seconds later Smith looked up from his food and around the table, then his back straightened and his head whipped around. His butt had just left his stool when another inmate who'd entered the right edge of the screen reached him, wrapped his left arm around Smith's neck from behind, then punched at his back ten or twelve times before releasing him and stepping away.

The warden stopped the video.

Jake fought down a slug of bile. "Who is that?"

She manipulated the mouse, and a photo popped up. "Dex Mutton. In for life on a triple murder he pulled for his gang. He's from St Louis."

Jake pointed. "What's that on his neck?"

"He's an Eastie. It's a pair of dice showing eleven."

"Did he say why he did it?" Jake asked. But he knew the answer. Reznik had put out a hit.

"Mr. Mutton said it was a lover's quarrel." She closed the laptop. "He was already doing life without parole. We threw him in solitary, where we'll keep him until the ACLU screams. David Smith certainly deserved better than that."

"His name is Tracy James." Jake rubbed his face with both hands. "I'll send you an email with his mom's information when I can. Give me your card."

"Tracy James." The warden said the name softly, but didn't ask him how he knew it. She went to her desk and grabbed a file. "I looked into the phone calls and the ministry visit." As she sat back down, she slid her business card across the table, then opened the file. "The library manager did let Smith—James—use the phone to solicit donations from libraries around Illinois. It's a breach of protocol, and I'm disciplining her. She said he'd been using the phone for almost two years without a problem. Donations are up almost one thousand percent."

She pulled a stapled sheaf of pages out of the file and flipped through them until she got to a yellow sticky note. "On the day you said the library called the number in Weston, he was working the phone for donations. I had the numbers checked, and all the numbers are to libraries except this bunch here."

She turned the pages around and pushed them toward Jake. Five numbers were highlighted in yellow. The first four calls all lasted less than a half minute—wrong numbers—but the last call lasted almost four minutes. Smith had been calling around looking for Miller, and finally found him when he dialed the phone in Carl's kitchen.

Jake pulled out his notebook to write the numbers down, but the warden slid the page across the table. "You can keep this. And here's a surveillance photo of the man who visited with Mr. Smith from the ministry." The photo she pulled from her file showed a man in his thirties with wide eyes and a thin face. His hair was shaved up the sides and floppy on top. "His name is Lowell Carr. Before his visit we did confirm the organization is legit. It's registered and has a nonprofit designation with the IRS."

Jake appreciated the photo, but he already had the rest of the information from Erin. He folded the papers and slipped them into the inside pocket of his windbreaker.

"Did Carr meet with a lot of inmates?"

"Only David Smith."

Of course. "I'm sorry I didn't get you Smith's real name before this... happened."

The warden sighed. "What would it have changed?"

39

The SUV's back end shimmied and tracked unevenly as Drill drove east, away from the hillbillies. When he was out of their sight, he pulled over to inspect the damage. It was significant, but the gas tank wasn't ruptured and the bumper wasn't dragging. Hell, the dirt and damage even helped the SUV fit in.

But a few minutes farther down the road, he heard a sharp metal clang and the shimmy turned into a shake that vibrated all the way through the big vehicle. Drill swore. The damage was his own damn fault. He'd been so distracted with trying to figure out who Mr. Red was, that he hadn't spotted the hillbillies.

But if it hadn't been the hillbillies, it would have been something else. No matter how well an op was planned, something always went to shit. No exceptions. A good operator improvised— and the better he was at it, the longer he lived.

After bouncing over a railroad crossing he cut north and then west, working his way back to Mount Logan, heading for the mall he'd seen on the satellite map out near the highway. He would ditch the Suburban in its acres of parked cars and pick up something new. He drove slowly in the right lane, holding the wiggling steering wheel loose in his hands. The shake getting worse.

When he got to the mall, he took the turn slowly, struggling with the wheel now, the back end almost bouncing. He found an empty parking spot and backed the Suburban in to hide the rear end damage. He wiped it down, just in case, took his duffel bag with him, and looked for his new vehicle. He chose an old silver Accord. It was second only to a rusty pickup for the perfect vehicle to blend in with the locals.

Then he took a slow drive past the courthouse, though he knew it was a waste of time. Houser had already beaten him to Greer. Drill's only remaining task was to eliminate the retired cop.

He drove back to Greer's house. The orange truck was gone and Greer's street was as quiet as it had been the night before. He backed the Accord into his old spot in the driveway at the end of the street, pulled out the satellite phone, and sent a text to Spec: *Houser showed up here and has likely met with Greer. Proceeding with primary task.*

He didn't mention the hillbillies. Spec didn't have the stomach for operational hiccups, so Drill always kept them to himself. Shit happened. You moved on.

He stuffed the sat phone back in his bag, put on his leather gloves, strapped his small go-bag around his waist, then got out of the car. It was an hour until noon, the sun bright, so he again went through the back yards, stepping from bush to shadow to building. At Greer's house he slid open the patio door and stepped inside.

He cleared the house first, then went to the kitchen. His earlier recognizance of the house had given him an idea that would help reduce any police interest in Greer's death. He found a pad of paper and a pen by the phone and put it on the table. Then he sat, waiting.

Less than twenty minutes later the garage door groaned and squeaked in its tracks. Greer was home for lunch. A stroke of luck. Drill got up and stood close to the door from the garage. It opened, and there was Greer.

"Who the hell are—"

Drill punched Greer in the gut. The old man folded around his fist, then started to collapse, but Drill held him up and guided him to a chair at the kitchen table. He pulled his own chair over and sat facing Greer, waiting for him to get his breath back. It took a lot longer than it should have; pain passed over the man's face in continual waves for several minutes before he finally straightened up, both hands holding his belly tight, his face pale and shiny with sweat.

"What do you want?" he gasped.

Drill patted the pad of paper. "Write out a list with the heading, 'Things I regret.'"

Greer leaned back and eyed Drill. "Suicide? Why would anyone believe that?"

"Retired guy. Living alone. Has a medical problem." Drill gestured at the man's gut.

Greer picked up the pen, then put it down. "Or what? You're here to kill me anyway, right? Note or no note."

Greer's words made Drill pause. What the hell had Houser told this guy to make him expect this hit? Something from the classified files? What could they contain to make this retired cop in bumble-butt farm country expect to be taken out? Great questions, but questions were for Spec to answer *before* launching an operation. Once an operation was launched, Drill followed his orders.

"You're right, Mr. Greer. But if you don't cooperate, I'll take your lack of cooperation out on that nice lady you spent the night with. Or on your son. Maybe both. Cooperate, and you save them. You're a hero. Only you'll know it, but that means something, doesn't it?"

Greer burped, and the stench of sour rot wafted past Drill's face. The old man rubbed his belly, then his face calmed and he bent over the pad and started writing. A tear dropped onto the note and blurred the ink, but Greer ignored it.

Drill stood up and got behind the man, waiting for him to finish. The list grew to a second page before Greer pushed the pad and pen away.

He wiped his eyes. "That's it," he said. His shoulders dropped and his knees splayed an inch, then two, as tension left him. Resigned to his fate.

Drill pulled a syringe loaded with M98 out of his go-bag, jabbed it into Greer's neck, and plunged in the paralytic. Greer tensed and his arms started to come up, but the drug took him quickly and he slumped, sliding out of the chair. Drill guided him gently to the floor.

Then he went out to the garage and sealed up the gaps around the big garage door with rags. He came back for Greer, hauled him out, and manhandled him into the driver's seat of his car. He started the engine. It was a single-stall garage and would fill with carbon monoxide in minutes.

Back inside, Drill read the suicide note to make sure Greer hadn't mentioned him. He ran his eyes down the two pages of bullet points. Some were general: *That I wasn't more generous to the church.* And some were specific: *That in seventh grade I didn't have the guts to ask out Missy Sorenson.* In the middle of the second page a line caught Drill by the balls so hard he startled: *That I didn't write up Reznik way back when I caught him sucking that boy's cock.*

That was who owned the voice on the phone with Spec. Mr. Red was Illinois Congressman Blake Reznik. Reznik was a member of the House Select Committee on Intelligence—the committee that oversaw Drill's agency. He was also the chairman of an ad hoc investigative committee that had three separate intelligence failures in congressional hearings. A powerful politician with authority over the entire intelligence community.

God damn that Spec. Was this op nothing more than cleanup for a politician? The agency didn't do that. Hell, as far as Drill knew, *no* agency did that. Even if someone was concerned that Reznik was vulnerable to blackmail, that would be more easily handled by eliminating the congressman himself. There had to be more going on here.

And why was Drill's agency the one chosen? He was too far outside the Washington system to know. What he did know was that Washington meant politics in everything: relationships, deals, favors. Maybe his agency owed Reznik a favor. Or wanted Reznik to owe *it* a favor.

Maybe something in those files up in Weston would shine a light on what was going on.

But first he had to finish this. He held his breath and checked his work.

Perfect.

He left the car running and exited through the sliding glass door—gone like smoke whisked away in the cold clear air.

He left behind the suicide note.

The hell with Mr. Red.

40

Jake shook his head as he exited the prison. With Smith dead, figuring out—and proving—who really killed Mark Siebert had just gotten a lot harder. Benchley and Reznik were too seasoned to talk and Jake didn't yet know enough to corner them with their lies. But Miller might know something.

As he stepped outside the prison, Jake pulled in a deep breath that felt fresh and clean after the dead, stale air inside the prison. He took a moment to let the feeling flow through him, flexing and rolling his shoulders to help dispel the tension that had built up from being locked inside that steel and concrete labyrinth.

The crowd on the sidewalk had broken up, leaving small clusters scattered among the few cars left in the lot. A few people looked at him as he walked back to his car, but he kept moving. He had nothing to tell them.

Lenny had backed his truck in next to the Mustang. Jake came around the front and stood at Lenny's open window.

"What's wrong? You get some bad news in there?"

"Smith was killed this morning."

Lenny shrugged, his face suggesting Smith deserved it.

"I'm heading back to Weston. Remember, if one of your people sees the Suburban, just get a plate number or a photo. Don't engage with him. He's too dangerous."

"You think he had something to do with Smith?"

"Not directly." But the two events *were* related. Reznik was cleaning up after himself, but how was he connected to the Easties?

"Maybe we should call Chief Bell about what happened with the Suburban."

"Bad idea," Jake said. "Your boys ran him off the road and he hit back. Everything else is guesswork."

Lenny frowned. "You want we should follow you home?"

Jake smiled. "Thanks for the offer, but a Suburban has no chance of keeping up with the Mustang." He got in his car and took off with a squeal of his tires.

When he got to Ina he went west, picked up the highway, and became a northbound blur.

As he passed the exit to Salem, the phone Carl had found rang in the cup holder where Jake had left it. He flipped it open and saw the call was from the same number he called earlier.

"Are you ready to talk?" Jake asked.

"Why do you have Thomas's phone?" A gentle voice.

"He left it behind."

"That's not..."

Jake held his breath, waiting for something more, but heard only silence. Silence didn't help. He needed this guy to trust him. Maybe if he met him somewhere safe.

"I'm headed home," Jake said. "How about you come see me at my house?" He recited his address, then repeated it more slowly.

Still nothing.

"I came down to Mount Logan again."

Silence.

"I just left the prison, and Smith—Tracy James—was killed this morning. Less than an hour ago. With your help I can make the killer pay."

A sharp intake of breath, followed by something verbal—a curse, maybe, or a sob. Then the line went dead.

Jake put the phone back in the cup holder and stared at it. Why *did* he have Thomas's phone? Thomas had left it behind, but he hadn't forgotten it in a six-pack carton. He must have left it in that strange place as a signal.

He *had* been abducted.

As Jake sped north he kept an eye on his rearview mirror, but he saw nothing suspicious among the receding forms of the vehicles he flew past. Certainly no big SUV driven by a black ops hit man.

His own phone buzzed with a call. Jake checked the screen: Paul Siebert. Today's developments just raised more questions. When Jake had the full truth, he would take the call.

But maybe...

He declined the call, then found the photo he'd taken of Smoke's CI card and called him.

"Talk to me."

"It's Houser."

"Christ's sake, man," Smoke whined. "We just talked two-three days ago. I got nothing new for you and I'm in some shit right now."

"I need something from you, Smoke. One of your brothers down at Big Rend killed another inmate this morning. Someone bought that hit and I need to know who."

"Can't do it. No way. That'll get me dead."

"I just need the name so I know I'm on the right track. No one will ever know where I got it. This'll stay between me and you."

Smoke went silent for a minute. In the background, the wind blew and voices rose in an angry spatter. "My shit's happening now."

"And?"

"I'll make some calls. I know a guy who's tight with that chapter."

Chapter. Like they're the Knights Of Columbus. "I'll be there by four." Jake hung up before Smoke could complain about the deadline.

Jake gassed up in Effingham, grabbing a twenty-four-ounce Diet Mountain Dew and a bag of nuts. He got the car back up to cruising speed and settled back into his thoughts as he crunched down the nuts.

Smith wasn't killed in a lover's spat. Reznik got nervous when Jake started digging into Mark Siebert's abduction, so he sent a man to stop Jake from talking to Greer, and he cashed in a favor to have Smith shut up for good.

Jake dropped his speed as he entered the Kankakee region. While he was between the exits he realized he had part of that wrong. He hoped it wasn't too late.

He called Greer, but there was no answer. *Shit!*

He voice-dialed another new contact.

"Lenny."

"That SUV wasn't after me," Jake said. "It was after Greer. It was following me to him."

Greer was the threat to Reznik, not Jake. Jake could do nothing without proof. Greer and Smith had the proof. And Smith was already dead.

"He'll either be at home or at the courthouse," Lenny said. "I'll drop Clint off at the courthouse and go out to the house myself."

* * *

Jake passed Weston, then dropped off the tollway at the Lake Street exit in Kirwin and drove south into the city. Kirwin was Weston's slightly larger and much grittier big brother to the west. It had been the first city in America to have streetlights, and had been a thriving urban center for many decades before its industry went into a long slow decline that still continued today. The city had recently grabbed the brass ring of legalized gambling and pumped the profits into revamping its downtown, but it might have been too late.

Jake's phone buzzed with a text from Lenny. *Call me.*

Jake pulled into the lot at Northgate Mall and made the call.

"Greer is dead. He didn't answer the door, but I heard his car running in the garage. I busted in but it was too late. Called Bell and they come out, a bunch of 'em, and said it was a suicide. Note on the kitchen table."

Jake's stomach churned, and he fought down an acidic bubble trying to rise.

"Did you see the note?"

"No. I shut off the car, then waited outside."

Greer had been angry when Jake pointed out his mistake with Reznik. Anger didn't lead to suicide. Despair did. Jake's questions had incited Reznik to protect himself: first with Smith, now with Greer. Loose ends, tidied up.

The truth was getting further away.

Jake thanked Lenny, hung up, and continued on. Cursing himself. If he had recognized the danger earlier, both men might still be alive.

Lake Street took him all the way into downtown Kirwin, where he turned east on New York Street, crossed the Wolf River, and threaded his way to the park where he'd found Smoke on Monday. He cruised around it and the surrounding blocks until he spotted Smoke walking backwards in front of a shapely Latina who was shaking her head and laughing. Smoke's crew was watching from the corner, hooting and carrying on loud enough for Jake to hear it through closed windows. But the woman shot Smoke down, and he rejoined his squad.

Jake pulled to the curb down the street and dialed Smoke's number. The banger pulled out his phone and looked at the screen. He waved to his boys that he needed to take the call, then he stepped away from them. A smile bloomed as he answered.

"Hello, my friend."

"By that smile on your face I'm guessing you got my answer."

Smoke's eyes came up slowly and he turned in place, sweeping his gaze over the area, no reaction when he found Jake. "You gonna be happy. Order came down through the Springfield chapter. Paid for by some old white dude."

Reznik had been a state congressman in Springfield before being elected to national office. But the world was still run by old white dudes, so he needed more. "Name?"

"Couldn't get the name, but they said it was an old faggot lives in Springfield that buys product from us every couple months. Faggoty party drugs and psychedelics."

The congressman's secret was locked up so tight there was no way East St. Louis bangers knew about it. So some other old white guy had bought the drugs. And the hit. Maybe Benchley: hived in Springfield and had a deal with Smith to keep quiet that he might have been worried about.

"Okay," Jake said. Smoke's shoulders relaxed. "I need something else."

It took some convincing—Smoke at first denying that he could even get his hands on any of "that shit," but fifteen minutes later Jake had it and was on his way home. He pulled into the Wolf Valley Mall parking lot and locked it away in the glove box. While he had it open he put the Glock in the pocket of his windbreaker.

Then he called Chief Bell.

41

Benchley stepped into the concrete-block room. The acidic vomit stench had dissipated and Thomas sat straighter now, his head swiveling to watch Benchley enter. Benchley sat on the chair in front of Thomas and scooted it up close so their knees wove together like the teeth of a zipper. Thomas looked better, his eyes clear and his face less pale. His breathing sounded normal.

He was ready.

Benchley pointed at the kit laid open on the table, the syringe clearly visible. "Tell me where the files are, Thomas, and that stays on the table. Once I have the files, you and Andy will be free to go anywhere you want to go. To be whoever it is you think you can be."

"I don't trust you," Thomas replied, his voice rasping.

Benchley shrugged. "Last chance."

He waited a few seconds, then gestured to Seth, who brought over the syringe. Thomas leaned his head back, tracking the syringe in the corner of his eye.

Benchley took the syringe, plunged it into Thomas's neck, then watched the drug take hold of him. The drug slowed men down and opened them up. Thomas would accept what he heard as the truth, and he would tell only truth. If he spoke. The drug couldn't make him talk.

Thomas's eyes dulled and his breathing slowed.

Now.

"Where are my files, Thomas?" Benchley spoke softly and slowly, giving Thomas time to absorb the words.

Thomas's head lifted. "They don't... I can't..."

"Did you give the files to that cop?"

"I... don't think he even cared."

That wasn't an answer. "Did you give the cop my files?"

"I don't... I just can't... My head's too foggy."

Seth's punch had done too much damage.

"Maybe just ask him about Andy," Seth said.

Worth a shot.

"Where is Andy?"

"Place in Sycamore."

Sycamore was only three hours away. "What place?"

"I don't know the address."

"His license says Cherry Valley," said Seth. He handed it to Benchley. It was a real license, in the fake name, complete with the state seal hologram. Thomas must have used the file Benchley had on his man at the DMV.

"What's this address?" Benchley asked Thomas.

"That's just a mailbox place."

Benchley's phone buzzed. Reznik. He turned away and answered.

"I sanitized the house last night," Reznik said. "About killed myself doing it but it had to be done."

"What *exactly* did you do?" Reznik was not good at doing things. The last time the man had done something operational, he'd ruined everything.

"I took care of it."

"Any collateral damage?"

"Just my goddamn hand. And my man is headed your way now."

A day late. "We have Thomas back home now."

"And the files? *My* file?"

"They weren't with him," Benchley admitted. He might need Reznik's help getting them after all. "They're either with the other one—Thomas says he's in Sycamore—or with the cop."

"The cop?" Reznik's voice vibrated with hysteria. "The one who drives the Mustang?"

"Yes. I'll keep working on Thomas."

"Get him to tell you, for Christ's sake."

"I'm working him, but he's... damaged."

"You work him. I'll send my man to work the cop in Weston." Reznik hung up.

Work the cop! Reznik was losing it. Benchley needed to beat Reznik to the files so he would have the leverage to keep the man's mouth shut.

He sat back down and made his voice soft. "Thomas, I'd like to take you to Andy so we can work this through together. You need to remember the address."

"I'll have to show you," Thomas said.

"I'll get the map, boss." Seth darted away. Thomas's eyes followed him, then his head drooped. A few minutes later Seth returned with the Illinois atlas from the study.

"I'm going to show you a map," Benchley said. He found the right page and held it open in front of Thomas. "You point to where we're going."

"Can't." Thomas shrugged his shoulders against the tape binding them.

A pencil poked the page, gripped tight in Seth's big hand. "Left or right or up or down?"

"I'll tell you, but..." Thomas's voice faded into nothing.

"You aren't in a position to bargain, son."

"We give and you go," Thomas said. "Like you said. We're done with each other."

"Agreed."

Thomas looked at the pencil. "Up."

Within a minute they'd pinpointed a location west of Sycamore. Benchley told Seth to fetch his laptop, then he opened a satellite map of the area and zoomed in on the spot Thomas had indicated. It was a house on a gravel road that served several confinement pig operations. He switched to the 3D view and rotated the image. A long low ranch house behind a stand of evergreens.

"Who owns this place?"

"Andy's man, Daniel."

"State Senator Daniel Lenzo?" He was a long-term client from Sycamore.

"Andy was out there before and knew Daniel was out of town."

Benchley told Seth to help Thomas drink another bottle of Gatorade, then they gagged him and Seth carried him out to the garage and put him in the trunk. This time they put a pillow under his head to avoid doing more damage to his brain just in case they needed something more out of him.

Benchley would still leverage the congressman's help. He'd let Reznik's man finish things and clean it all up. But not until Benchley had the files.

He would keep those for himself.

42

The woman who answered the phone at the Mount Logan PD
agreed to put Jake through to Chief Bell when he told her he was
calling about Greer. Jake gazed around the mall parking lot as he
waited for Bell to come on the line, watching the shoppers hustle
back and forth. Christmas shopping.

"What is it, Houser?" Chief Bell said.

"I just heard about Detective Greer. I talked to him this morning. I—"

"How did you get him to talk to you?"

"I surprised him at the courthouse."

Bell was quiet, likely wondering what Greer had said. But he
didn't ask.

"Are you sure it was a suicide?" Jake asked. "When I talked to
him this morning he didn't seem—"

"Detective Houser." Bell's voice rumbled with anger, but then
he took an audible breath and continued in a softer tone. "Listen,
just because Greer killed himself soon after that doesn't mean you
caused it. It was clearly a suicide. The people he was close to—his
lady friend and his adult son—both said he was struggling with
retirement. The girlfriend says he was sick but wouldn't talk about
it, and there's a boatload of prescription medications here, so that

checks out. Nothing at the scene is inconsistent with suicide. And he left a note that's definitely in his handwriting—there were comparisons right on the table."

Jake understood Bell's approach: the dead man's state of mind, his health problems, no inconsistent facts, and the note. Powerful circumstantial evidence. Telling Bell about Reznik and about Smith's murder might get Bell to rethink that conclusion, but would also pull Jake back down to Mount Logan to explain in person, and he had work to do up here. He needed to find Miller.

"Anything interesting in the note?" Jake asked.

"He didn't mention *you*, if that's what you're getting at."

"But he named other people?"

"Not you."

"Can you send me a copy of the note?"

"No way, Houser. Privacy."

Jake wondered if the Sieberts could get it. "Anything in it raise any flags?"

"What are you getting at, Houser?"

A damn good question. If Greer had been murdered, his killer surely wouldn't allow the note to contain anything helpful. Jake was stirring Bell up for nothing. "I'm sorry for your loss, Chief."

"Are you done messing around down here about Mark Siebert?"

"No promises." Jake ended the call.

Maybe Greer *had* killed himself. Jake barely knew the man so couldn't say it was impossible. Maybe his medical issue had been bigger than a sour gut. Combine that with finding out Reznik had played him and gotten away with whatever his role had been in Mark Siebert's murder, and that could have put Greer over the edge.

Jake got back on the road. He had just crossed Route 59 when he got a call from Levi.

"I have some interesting information."

"I'll swing by in a few minutes."

Levi hung up without a goodbye, which reminded Jake he also

hadn't said hello. That was very uncharacteristic; the young man had been raised with a textbook sense of courtesy. Whatever Levi found must have shaken him deeply.

Jake took a left at the next light, wound through a series of interconnected parking lots in the sprawl of retail buildings around the mall, then drove north on 59. He was at Levi's shop in minutes.

He found Levi finishing a transaction for a large bundle of dress shirts while sharing pop-culture news with a woman working a giant wad of chewing gum. Levi's Uncle Dave was just coming in from the back room, a wave of humidity pulsing through the door with him. Jake exchanged nods with Dave, and they both hung back until the customer left.

As soon as the door closed behind her, Levi waved Jake over to the counter.

"Uncle Dave," Levi said. "Can you give us a few minutes?"

"You bet, Skippy. Hit the buzzer when you're ready to leave and I'll take over."

Levi started in before Jake's butt hit the guest stool. "The reverse mortgage on Mrs. James's house is held by Stanley Benchley. Not directly, but through a company called Middle America Reverse. It's a DBA Benchley's insurance agency registered that has since lapsed. She receives five hundred dollars every month."

That was how Benchley was paying for Smith's silence.

"You sure about this? Could it be a legitimate deal?" Jake normally avoided compound questions, but Levi's excitement was contagious. He pulled out his notebook and pen and started scribbling away.

"I'm sure, and I don't think it's a legitimate mortgage. Her house is only worth seventy-one thousand dollars, and less than that when the mortgage began. I found a reverse mortgage calculator that says the payment should have been under three hundred dollars."

Levi's eyes still held the light of a discovery not shared.

"What else?"

"A woman named Nancy Birch in northern Iowa had a son named Tommy who went missing ten years ago. She got a lot of press. Picketed politicians for tougher laws on pedophiles and had her son's case profiled on TV news shows. She created a website about her son's case and other boys in the Midwest who disappeared. The website is long gone, but the Way Back Machine had some screen captures. And I found two things."

"Benchley?" Jake asked, but Levi shook off the prompt.

"First look at this from the old website." Levi opened a window on his screen, showing a fuzzy screenshot of a webpage displaying the photo of a young boy. Jake leaned in, but nothing about the boy was familiar, and the text around it was too blurry to read.

Levi opened a different window. "And now look at this. Here's an age progression showing what her son might look like now. He would be twenty-one."

The pen fell from Jake's hand and clattered on the tile floor. "That's Robert Miller."

"And the case is still open. Tommy Birch was never found."

Until now.

"Maybe she did find him and that's why she took her website down," Jake said. "How does this connect to Benchley?"

"It doesn't connect by name, but her website claimed two people—who she did name—told her Tommy was abducted by a pedophile ring that provided underage boys for sex parties attended by big-shot businessmen and politicians in Springfield and St. Louis. And Benchley is a Springfield businessman who likes to hang out with politicians."

Jake opened his mouth to say something, but Levi held up a hand. "There's more. The ring was run by a man known only as 'the Colonel.' Shortly before Nancy Birch's webpage was taken down, she said she was going to publish the Colonel's real name and the names of the men who used the boys—just as soon as she contacted each man for a response. She never did publish those names, because like I said, she took her webpage down not long after."

"She accused politicians of being pedophiles and the story immediately died?" That sounded too juicy not to have been picked up by the politician-hating conspiracy theorists of the Internet.

Levi sat back on his stool. "When her webpage was deleted, that was the end of it. Like that was proof she'd lied about all of it. She refused to talk to anyone after that."

"This is good stuff, Levi."

"I have the names of the two people who gave Mrs. Birch her information, but they're ghosts on the Internet."

"Text them to Erin and tell her what they claimed. She knows some people downstate." She knew people everywhere. "Tell her I said we need to keep it unofficial."

"Okay." Levi's hands were a spidery blur on his smartphone. "Anything else?"

"Yeah," Jake said, then paused. Reznik was too dangerous for Levi to stay involved in this case. "I need you to drop this right now."

Levi's gaze swung up to Jake's face. "How come? What is it? One of these politicians? I'm not scared of them. I have rights."

Jake frowned. The kid was too damn eager, and Jake's warning was too vague to be anything more than a challenge to him. He'd have to tell Levi more. "The man who oversees the intelligence community—the NSA and all the rest of it—is on the edge of this thing."

Levi's eyes widened, and he quickly closed his laptop. "Understood."

"You've done your part, Levi. The rest is on me."

43

Drill sent Spec a message when he finished with Greer, then drove north, fighting doubts about the whole damn operation. He couldn't imagine a scenario where the retired cop intersected with national security. He'd seen nothing in Greer's house to indicate the man was anything but a retired small-town cop with a girlfriend. Nothing to justify the operation or explain why Greer had to die. Nothing beyond what the man had written in his suicide note about Reznik liking teenage boys.

Was this whole operation a personal vendetta?

And where does that leave me?

But he knew the answer. He was a weapon. Weapons hit what they're aimed at and they don't ask questions.

He seethed some more, but forced himself to shake it off. Doubts would slow him down and get him killed. When this was over, he could indulge in as many questions as he wanted.

As he turned onto the westbound tollway toward Weston, he received a text from Spec saying the files he was chasing might now be with the Weston cop, Houser. Another cop? What the hell was in those files?

A follow-up text gave him the cop's address. Drill punched it into the sat phone's GPS and followed the blue line off the tollway and into Weston, which was decked out in full-on holiday decorations. Every tree in the shopping district was draped in tiny white lights, giant candy canes were on every light pole, and all the store windows were painted with ornaments and fake snow. The ringing bells of Christmas carols even played on a hidden sound system. This town went overboard on Christmas.

The GPS led him a few blocks south to a small ranch on a corner lot where Main Street ended at a big graveyard. The house sat on the northeast corner with the front door facing west and a separate garage opening south onto the street that bordered the graveyard. A breezeway connected the garage and the house. Drill drove a hundred yards west before turning around and parking at the curb. His view of both the garage and the front of Houser's house was clear except for a few thin bushes at the corner of the yard.

He turned off the ignition and got comfortable, leaning the seat back a few notches. He'd been prepared to swap for a new car, but the Accord had run well on the long drive north, and he was far enough away from Mount Logan that he could keep it. He'd changed the license plates at a truck stop and felt invisible.

He was only there a few minutes before his sat phone vibrated with a call.

"Drill," he said.

"Are you at Houser's?"

That deep melodious voice again. Reznik was involved up here, too. "Mr. Red, is Spec there?"

"I'm here, Drill. Have you made contact with this subject?"

"I have not. No one is home."

"How can you be sure?" Mr. Red again.

"Reconnaissance." It was getting dark and all the lights in the house were off except for the obligatory-in-the-burbs living room light on a timer. *Has that ever deterred a burglar?* "Intel and instructions please."

"The files were in Weston in the possession of a young man, but my ally says he no longer has the files."

"What ally? Spec, if there's another player here I need details so we don't end up interfering with each other." People died that way.

"I'll respond, Mr. Spec." The congressman cleared his throat. "My ally will remain anonymous, but he took the young man and has left town. So there will be no interference there."

Drill waited for Spec to speak, but the man stayed silent, letting stand the congressman's response to Drill's operational question. A politician running an op. This was going to go bad, and Drill would be left hanging. He needed to start thinking about covering his own ass. And to do that successfully he needed more information.

"The files are with this cop? Houser?"

"Yes. And you must get them before he looks at them or shares them with anyone." Mr. Red's voice throbbed with the deep bass he used during television interviews—his selling voice.

"Because?" Drill asked. That question belonged to Spec, but he hadn't asked it, and didn't jump in now to shut Drill down as he should have.

There was nothing normal about this op.

The congressman blustered about national security and need-to-know, then spewed a long string of concept nouns and buzz-words—loyalty and duty and fealty. His ramble eventually circled back to national security before stumbling along to sensitive documents.

"Please describe these documents so I can identify the correct files."

"No. You don't have the clearance to look inside the files."

"What level of prejudice is authorized?"

"What do you mean?"

Drill didn't answer the congressman's question. The phone went to mute, and a minute passed before Spec came on the line, sounding like he was no longer on speaker.

"Drill, confirm your new target has the files, and find out

whether he has looked inside them or made copies. Then contact me about what level of force is authorized."

The line went dead.

Drill stared at the phone for a long minute. Spec's instruction made no sense. He didn't have time for phone calls in the middle of the action. This operation was screwed.

He massaged his legs and thighs, then settled back and got as comfortable as this situation allowed. He knew one thing for sure.

When he had those files, he would definitely look inside them.

44

Jake's stomach gurgled in response to the sweet odor of baked bread floating over from the Firehouse Subs on the other side of Radar Road. He went inside, the meaty tang from the steamers spiking his hunger, and ordered a turkey sandwich with double veggies. While he waited, he deliberately kept his mind blank to let things percolate in his subconscious. When his sandwich was ready, he took it to a back table. He walked himself through the narrative he was building while he ate.

Robert Miller's mom—Nancy Birch—claimed her son and other boys were abducted into a pedophile ring to be used by the rich and powerful. Boys like Mark Siebert. Benchley was a powerful businessman from Springfield, and Reznik had been a politician in Springfield at that time.

Then Mark Siebert was killed and Greer investigated. Right after Greer pressured Reznik, Smith showed up and confessed to the crime. Benchley paid Smith's mom five hundred dollars a month in return for that confession.

And that was how things stayed for seven years until Jake's investigation stirred things up. Now Smith had been killed by the Easties, doing a job for a "faggot" from Springfield who also bought party drugs from them. The man from Springfield had to be Benchley and he was working to protect Reznik.

Benchley and Reznik were involved in the pedophile ring back then, and they were working together again now to clean up their mess. One of them was the Colonel. Miller's fear of Benchley made Jake think the man from Springfield was the ring leader. The man who had abducted Miller as a child and forced him to service the perverted desires of his clients.

And it had to be Benchley who had taken Miller. The broken door, the note on the pizza box, the phone left behind... all those things implied an amateur, not a black ops pro.

Where had Benchley taken Miller?

And why take him? It couldn't be to shut him up because if Miller was going to talk, he would have done it already. It must be about whatever Miller had hidden in the attic and then carried out to his car. In fact, it might *still* be in the car.

Thinking about Benchley and what he'd done to these boys destroyed Jake's appetite, but he ate the rest of the sandwich anyway—the body needed fuel. Then he tossed his trash and hurried back across Radar Road to his Mustang. He needed to find Miller's car and whatever secrets the blocky shape might hold.

Jake drove straight to the Van Buren parking garage where Grady had said Miller left the car. He cruised in the south entrance, then slowly circled each level, the Mustang's sport-tuned exhaust rumbling musically against the concrete. He found the Impala on the fourth level.

He pulled into a slot a few spots away and rummaged through his glove box until he found his car rescue tool. On one end it had a slot with an internal blade for cutting seatbelts, and on the other was a pointed metal spike for breaking windows. Using it to break open the Impala meant anything he found inside the car couldn't be used as evidence, but finding Robert Miller before he suffered the same fate as Mark Siebert was more important than a possible prosecution, and Jake didn't have the time or probable cause to get a search warrant.

He got out of the Mustang and walked toward the Impala. The ceiling was low, the air dense with old exhaust, and the lights bright. A camera mounted twenty feet from Miller's car watched over the scene with a bulbous black lens. The feed went directly to dispatch, but Jake knew they had more cameras than screens so there was about an even chance no one was watching him live. If a complaint was made, the recorded footage would be reviewed, but he'd deal with that later. Right now, he just had to play his part for any tech who might be watching.

Jake raised his face to the camera and waved. He'd spent plenty of time in dispatch reviewing 911 calls and combing through archived video so the people there would recognize him and assume he was working.

After all, he was one of the good guys.

45

———————

Jake peered in the Impala's driver's side window and spotted a white plastic bag on the floor in front of the passenger seat. He stepped around to that side of the car, leaned against the car with his back to the camera to shield what he was about to do, then pressed the car rescue tool's pointed end against the bottom corner of the window. He slowly added his weight to the pressure until the window popped and shattered into tiny fragments. He reached in and unlocked the door, sat down on the pebbled glass covering the seat, and shut the door behind him.

The interior of the car was so clean it looked like it had been professionally detailed, right down to the shiny Armor All on the vinyl. Jake popped the glove compartment, hoping to find some clue as to where Benchley had taken Miller, but it was empty save for a plastic envelope holding the registration in the leasing company's name and an insurance card with the same address Jake already had for Accord Services. Jake then checked the trunk, but it was also empty. Nothing to indicate where Miller and Benchley might be.

Finally, Jake picked up the plastic shopping bag. It was heavier than it looked, a dense bulk, probably paper. He zipped it inside his jacket then got out and walked back to his car, his left hand in his coat pocket holding the bulk against his gut, his right hand waving to the camera.

He paused to brush the glass bits off the seat of his pants then got in the Mustang and got moving. If a dispatcher *was* watching the live camera feed and didn't recognize him, a patrol car would be on the way. Jake could talk his way out of it, but that would cost time he didn't have.

He circled down through the garage and out onto Van Buren, headed west, then pulled into a lot surrounding the three-story office building by the elementary school. He parked, turned on his dome light, and pulled the bag onto his lap.

Inside the bag was an accordion folder, about four inches thick, containing several dozen manila folders. Jake flicked his thumb over the staggered file tabs, each filled with tight writing. He bent a tab back to get more light on it, but still couldn't read what it said. He moved the bundle to the center console directly under the dome light.

The tabs held names in alphabetical order. Some were familiar from state politics. One was a big-shot real estate investor in Chicago.

And one was Blake Reznik.

He pulled the congressman's file out of the tight pack. Thanks to Levi's work, Jake had a good idea what he'd find and he didn't really want to see it. Seeing stuff like that carried a weight that stayed with you. But he couldn't just assume what the file contained.

He found exactly what he'd anticipated: photos of the congressman having sex with boys. Apparently over the course of years, judging by how the man's appearance changed—his hair graying, his body thickening. Jake went through them, focusing on the boys, all of them were of a similar type: slim builds, prominent cheekbones, and pouty lips. But none of the boys were Smith or Miller.

Jake closed the file. A bubble of bile rose into his mouth. He powered down the window and spit it out onto the parking lot. He found the water bottle on the passenger seat and washed the sour taste from his mouth.

Benchley had to be the Colonel. He ran a pedophile ring not just to entertain powerful men but also to get these pictures. This *leverage*. For political or business advantage, or maybe just for money.

These files were why Benchley was after Miller. Somehow Miller had gotten his hands on these powerful tools. Tools he was likely already using. It took power—or leverage over someone in power—to get a driver's license in a fake name.

Jake put the Reznik file back in with the others and was closing the flap when he spotted a blue folder at the back of the bundle. The tab was blank, and the file was thicker than the others. He pulled it out.

It contained Stanley Benchley's personal papers. Birth certificate, passport, deed for a house in Sangamon County. High school and college transcripts showing Benchley had been an excellent student. His ACT test results and the military equivalent, the ASVAB, were both at the ninety-ninth percentile. A letter from the Defense Finance and Accounting Service specified a pension payment from the Army of almost five thousand dollars a month. You had to be in for twenty years to get a pension, and that large of a payment meant Benchley had been an officer. Perhaps he really was a colonel.

An ID card with a magnetic strip had Benchley's name and photo. Jake held the ID up under the light. It looked like a corporate ID, but without the colorful logos and branding. It said "Stanley Benchley, SOD-SID." On the back, beneath the magnetic strip, was a printed notice. *If found, drop in any mailbox.* The address was a PO Box in Langley, Virginia.

Home of the CIA.

Jake pulled out his phone and scrolled through his contacts until he found the man he wanted to talk to. Mark Kotzan was an old high school friend who'd enlisted in the Army out of high school and had leveraged his benefits into a college education and law degree. He was now a major in the Judge Advocate General Corps at Fort Bragg.

He answered on the first ring. "Major Kotzan."

"Marcus, it's Jake."

"Did another one of us bite it?"

Jake had last seen Kotzan at the funeral for a good friend. "No. I've run across something I was hoping you could help me with. I need some background on an army officer, Stanley Benchley, who's on the periphery of a thing I'm working. You have access to records on retired guys, right?"

"Yes, but you don't."

"I understand that. I just want background, not specifics."

"Well, try me."

"Benchley has an old ID badge that says he was in SOD-SID. The return address on the ID—so if someone finds it they can mail it back—is a PO Box in Langley."

"Repeat that designation."

"S-O-D dash S-I-D."

The line was quiet.

"Marcus?"

"How peripheral is this guy to your case?"

"Well, it's not really a case. More like a favor for a friend."

"So nothing will be entered in any official databases?"

"Right."

"That designation was for the partnership between the Special Operations Division of the Chemical Corps of the Army and the CIA's Scientific Intelligence Division."

"A lot of words there, Marcus. What did this partnership do?"

"They were mindbenders, Jake. Drug-induced interrogations. Mind control."

"Are you saying… what, truth serums and brainwashing?"

"Exactly."

"We did that?"

"For a long time. Probably still do, but we don't talk about it. Jake, you should stay far away from this guy."

"Thanks, Marcus."

After the call Jake sat, frozen by indecision. He knew things now, important things, for which he had no admissible evidence. That Benchley and Reznik ran a pedophile ring. That Smith and Greer were murdered. That Miller was abducted. The photos of Reznik with the underage boys would get Chief Braff's attention, but they'd also make the brass scrutinize his evidence all the harder, for fear of crossing a man that powerful.

If he was going to save Miller, he had to do it on his own.

And the files would help him do that. Benchley wanted them back.

Which meant Jake could at least save this one boy. Thomas Birch. And reunite him with his mother.

Jake put the car in gear and drove for home. He needed to figure out where Benchley had gone with Miller. Surely not back to his own home in Springfield. Judging by how quickly Benchley grabbed Miller after Grady left his stakeout, Benchley had seen that Miller was being watched and would realize that the plates on Miller's car would lead almost straight to his own front door.

So where were they?

46

Jake flipped the deadbolt on the kitchen door and set the plastic bag on the card table and his overnight bag on the floor. He pulled off his windbreaker and put it on the back of a chair before sitting down heavily. Truth serums and brainwashing. Sounded like something straight out of a Cold War spy novel.

A sound in the house startled him and he stood up quickly, his head whipping around, his shoulders raised to his ears. *Relax, Houser. You know that sound.* It was the same long creaking groan across the ceiling that had started after he took out the fieldstone fireplace. Just the house settling around the new support beams he'd put in to compensate.

The ceiling groaned again, and a nervous charge shot up his spine. He walked to the front window, shaking the tension out of his shoulders and arms. *Two people are dead and one is missing. That's why you're jumpy.* And no one was investigating any of them. The Mount Logan police were convinced Greer had committed suicide, Smith's killer was caught, and Miller's disappearance was explained by a note. But that was all bullshit. Benchley and Reznik were cleaning up.

And they were doing it so smoothly Jake didn't even have

enough to open an investigation, much less launch a manhunt for Miller.

But no one is after you, *Houser.*

Unless Greer told his killer he'd already told his story to a cop. Would the man in the SUV come for Jake next?

His phone vibrated. Erin. Jake sat down at the card table and answered.

"I've got something on those two names Levi got from Birch's mom." The excitement in her voice made Jake sit straighter.

"Tell me."

"I met a woman at a civilian investigators' conference a few years ago who worked for the state's attorney down in Springfield." Erin always knew someone. "I called her and she remembered both names. They testified in front of a grand jury put together for an investigation into a purported sex trafficking slash pimping thing. Basically, sex parties for rich men and politicians. Supposedly the boys working the parties were all runaways."

They weren't *all* runaways, unless Chief Bell had been right about Mark. "Who was the ringleader?"

"She never knew the guy's real name. Said the whole thing was buttoned up tight because there were some big local players implicated."

"They had to use a name of some kind for running a grand jury."

"They called the case *State v. Individual 1.*"

"What happened?"

"The grand jury voted no because it came out that the teenage boy making the claims was actually a twenty-seven-year-old prostitute from Nebraska."

"And that was that?"

"No. The grand jury then pushed the ASA to indict the two for perjury, and he did. She doesn't remember what happened after that. I could find nothing explaining what happened to those indictments. Neither person is listed as an inmate in an Illinois prison. In fact, I couldn't find either one of them anywhere."

"But the two told their stories to a room full of people? Jurors, alternates, a court reporter, and an ASA. And no names ever leaked out to the media?"

"Right, although the basic story—perverted sex club for the rich and powerful—leaked, and a couple reporters nosed around. But once the grand jury indicted the two for perjury they dropped it. The perjury charges probably scared them off."

"Crazy," Jake said.

"One more thing. The ASA got drunk afterward and blamed the whole thing on one particular member of the grand jury. Thought he was bought."

"Did he pursue that?"

"Dropped it when he sobered up."

"Thanks, Erin." Jake ended the call.

The outrageous claims Mrs. Birch had made on her website had been corroborated at least enough that the state's attorney's office had taken them to a grand jury. But that's where the charges ended. One juror—possibly corrupted—derailed the case, and threats of criminal prosecution for perjury shut up the two witnesses.

Both of those actions were well within the combined powers of Reznik and Benchley.

The house groaned again and Jake sprang up from his chair, toppling it. He righted the chair, then got the Glock from his windbreaker's pocket. His hand was slippery with a sudden nervous sweat.

Jake made sure the outside doors were locked and bolted, then went through every room of the house, turning on all the lights and looking through every closet and under every piece of furniture. The house felt empty and foreign. When he finished clearing the first floor, he took the stairs into the basement, one big room since he'd gutted the mold-filled spaces the previous owner had boxed in down there. It, too, was empty.

His phone shook in his pocket. He pulled it out and stuck the gun in his waistband.

Levi.

"What is it, Levi?"

"I have something you need to hear."

"Damn it! I told you to drop it."

"I'm at a coffee shop with free Wi-Fi and no cameras, and I'm using a cloned computer with a masked IP."

Jake wasn't sure what all that meant, but whatever Levi had done, he'd already done it. "Tell me."

"So, when that guy was elected to the bigger office, he moved to where they meet, right?"

"Right."

"About a month ago a guy who describes himself as a citizen journalist started tweeting about similar parties going on in that city. The tweeter says he has visitor logs showing the entertainers —that's what he calls them—sometimes go to the offices of the people they entertain."

"Visitor logs means government officials," Jake said. "Politicians. Bureaucrats. But the tweeter hasn't given out any names?"

"Just hints. Like 'a Midwest congressman' or 'leading industrialist.' Like that. And get this: a reply to one of his early tweets said the whole thing started with MK-Ultra."

Levi emphasized the odd phrase like it was significant, but it didn't mean anything to Jake. "What is that?"

"It's the name of a supposedly canceled, but still classified, CIA experiment into mind control."

Benchley!

"And yesterday the guy tweeted that he was about to reveal the address of the place where the parties happened. An actual location owned by a person or entity that could be investigated."

"Has he?"

"He tweeted the address an hour ago but said it burned down last night."

Reznik cleaning up. "Thanks, Levi. But that's the end of it, okay?"

"You got it."

Jake hung up, dialed Kotzan again, and jumped right to it when the major answered.

"The name MK-Ultra popped up."

"Leave it alone."

"I can't."

"Of course you can't." Kotzan sighed. "I looked your guy up after you called before. He worked in the successor program to Ultra until he was asked to retire."

"Asked?"

"The men up the chain didn't like his methods."

"What was his rank when he retired?"

"Colonel."

* * *

Jake climbed back up the stairs and sat down at the kitchen table. Benchley *was* a colonel—and *the* Colonel who Birch had written about on her now-deleted website. And Reznik was involved as a client and maybe even as a partner. When Reznik moved to DC, the two took their pedophile show on the road. But they'd gotten away with it so easily in the backwater of Springfield that they were too open about it in DC, and a Twitter user—a citizen journalist—got onto it.

Jake felt the gun digging into his gut, and pulled it out and set it on the table. He slid the accordion folder out of its bag and squared it up in front of him. Turning to gaze around the big room, he shivered. The house was locked up tight and every light was on, but he still felt exposed. Vulnerable.

Snap.

Jake startled. That sound was the storm door slapping shut.

He snatched up the Glock and crossed the great room, stepping softly to avoid giving away his approach. His mind filled with the black ops hit man and the banger at Big Rend. He got behind the door and was just easing his head up to peek through the window when a loud knock sounded. A hit man wouldn't knock.

Jake lowered his gun hand to hide the weapon along his thigh, then pulled the door open.

Standing on his doorstep was a young man with the chiseled features of an underfed model and matching puffed lips. Like the many boys in photos with Reznik. But something else was familiar about him, too.

Something Jake couldn't quite place.

47

Benchley had no trouble finding the house Thomas had pointed to on the map. They drove down the gravel drive and parked in the back. A bright yard light bathed the area in its harsh, flat glow, and the air stank of raw dirt and animal shit.

He had Seth tear out the phone line where it dropped from a pole to the back of the house, then shoulder the door open.

They found Andy standing right in the middle of the kitchen, almost as if he'd been waiting for them. He gave up without a fight, and Seth stretched him out on the rug in the adjacent great room area and bound his hands and legs with duct tape. Benchley worked him for the location of the files, but the kid didn't even know they existed.

The interrogation wasn't a total waste though. Just as Benchley was about to slap Andy again, the boy blurted something that froze Benchley's hand in the air.

Michael.

* * *

Drill started the car every thirty or forty minutes to run the heat, and each time he stretched and flexed to keep from getting a cramp or going numb. His back felt surprisingly good considering he'd hauled Greer's dead weight out to the garage and wrestled it into the driver's seat.

The high school was hosting some kind of band event, and the parking lot filled, forcing latecomers to park along the street near Drill. People popped out of their cars and headed for the building in shiny shoes and wool overcoats, the teens toting hard-sided instrument cases. The concertgoers were too focused on their coming evening to give Drill even a passing glance.

Houser showed up in his Mustang a little later. Using the monocular, Drill saw that the man was carrying an overnight bag and a plastic grocery sack with a blocky shape in it. *The files.* He went in through the breezeway, and a minute later his shadow passed over the front window, then the rest of the lights in the house popped on, one by one. Light even spilled from the basement window wells.

Drill recognized the pattern. Houser was clearing the house, making sure he was alone. Drill doubted that was a normal behavior for the suburban cop, so something had spooked him. He'd probably heard about Greer and didn't buy the suicide. Perhaps because Greer had already spilled his Reznik secret to Houser.

Drill picked up the satellite phone to report his suspicion to Spec, but then set it back on the passenger seat. Spec would ask why he thought Houser doubted the suicide and Drill would have to reveal he'd read the suicide note himself and knew Mr. Red was Congressman Blake Reznik. Drill didn't want to give up that piece of information. Spec was guarding it, which meant it had value. Drill would keep the secret until he could use it.

And he might have to. The entire operation was twisted. It seemed that Spec, or more likely someone up the chain, had a relationship with the congressman where a favor was owed or desired.

But that didn't explain why Reznik himself was hands-on. Maybe Spec didn't like it any better than Drill so he'd flipped all the way over and agreed to let the congressman run the op himself, knowing the ass-covering revenge scheme would fall apart. Then the congressman would only have himself to blame.

And the field operative, of course.

Drill didn't like the conclusion, but he worked back through it several times and kept ending at the same place. Screw Spec, and screw Reznik. Drill would get the damn files and see what was in them, and that would tell him what was really going on.

And, maybe, give him the leverage he needed to protect himself.

Drill looked back at the house. He decided to wait for Houser to go to sleep, then sneak in and hit him with a dose of the M98. Drill needed to be more careful here than he'd been in Mount Logan. Weston was a much bigger town with a more capable police force and greater resources for mounting an investigation into anything hinky.

Twelve minutes later a light bloomed inside a '90s-era Bronco parked north of Houser's house on Main Street. Drill remembered the vehicle parking an hour or so before, but had thought the driver went into the high school for the band concert. He pulled his monocular out and glassed the Bronco, but there wasn't enough light to see anything more than a vague shape inside.

The Bronco rose on its springs as someone got out of it. Feet on the pavement under the SUV, a door closing, then a figure stepped from behind it walking fast toward Houser's house.

Who is this?

Maybe five foot six and slender, with the wide shoulders of a swimmer, wearing a hoodie and skinny jeans. The walk was almost slinky, but the lack of any meat in the hips and thighs said it was a man.

Hoodie opened Houser's storm door and raised a hand to knock, but then stopped. He stepped back and released the door, and it banged shut. That would freak Houser out.

A shadow crossed the front window. Hoodie pulled the storm

door open again, and this time knocked loud enough the sound carried all the way to Drill.

Houser opened the door and let Hoodie inside.

Was Hoodie's arrival a coincidence? Or was he part of whatever Reznik was into?

Drill grabbed his sat phone and sent a quick text: *Houser is here and now a young man who's short and slim just entered the house. I have not confirmed asset location.*

He set the phone back down.

"Let's see what Mr. Red thinks of that."

48

Jake studied the young man who stood in his unfinished great room. He wore a heavy gray sweatshirt with the hood pulled up and had a patchy beard on his thin face. His cheeks were flushed from the cold, and his eyes darted around the room as he pulled the hood back to reveal brown hair cut short on the sides and long and floppy on top.

Jake took a guess. "You're the man I talked to on the phone," he said. "Thomas's friend. I'm glad you came."

"Yes. I'm Michael." His voice was weak, tired. "I don't know what to do."

"Sit down," Jake said. But then he spotted the files still lying in plain sight on the card table. Sticking the gun back inside his waistband against his lower back, he hurried over to the table, stuffed the congressman's file back in the binder, and closed the flap.

"Thomas had that with him!" Michael said, his voice squeaking with sudden energy and rage. "Where did you get it? Did you take it from him?" He backed up, his head whipping around, eyes bright and wild.

"No. I'll explain. Just sit."

Jake sat down and waited while Michael took another look at

the bare floors, the unpainted walls, and the card table over the pipe stubs where the kitchen sink belonged. Nothing here could threaten him.

Finally his posture relaxed and he lowered himself into the chair across from Jake. He pulled the thick bundle of files across the table and circled it with his arms. His connection to Thomas.

"I went back to look for Thomas at the place we were staying, but Carl said he moved out. So I came to talk to you. But when I was waiting for you to get home, Andy called. Now I... I don't know what to do."

He looked up, and the sudden shift in shadow across his face brought Jake a stab of familiarity that he couldn't quite place. This young man looked like... someone.

And then recognition dawned, and heat spread through Jake's body.

"You're Mark Siebert!"

The young man's eyes skipped over Jake and back to the table. "I go by Michael Wilson now."

"But your name is Mark Siebert, right? The boy abducted from—"

"I ran away."

"You ran away." Jake couldn't help repeating the words. The boy had spoken them with complete confidence and no deception. It was his truth. But coercing children into leaving their families was standard molester practice. And Benchley was not just a standard molester; he was a CIA-trained brainwasher.

Mark Siebert.

Jake had been absolutely sure the boy was dead. And yet here he was.

"Your parents...." Jake couldn't even complete the thought, couldn't imagine how they'd feel.

Mark pulled the files to his chest and set his chin on the bundle. A tear rolled down his right cheek and then down his left. And they kept coming.

Jake went to get a box of tissues from the linen closet. In the hall he pulled out his phone to send Paul Siebert a text. He started typing in an explanation, but there was simply too much to say. He could go short and just text that Mark was there, but this news deserved more than that. He leaned back into the great room to check on Mark; the young man was still there, his head tilted back, rubbing his face.

The hell with it.

Jack deleted the long clumsy mess and sent a brief text with his address: *Come to my house. Now.*

He got an immediate response: *On my way.*

My way. It sounded like Linda wasn't coming.

When Jake handed the tissues to Mark, the boy held up a cell phone. "I bought a burner like the one Thomas had. When I was waiting for you I called Andy, and when we were talking something bad happened."

"Where is Andy? And who is Andy?"

"On a ranch out west of Sycamore that a friend of his owns." Mark wiped his eyes with a tissue, then balled it up in his fist. "Andy was a friend of Thomas's, from where he lived."

"And what was the bad thing that happened?"

"We were talking, then Andy yelled, 'They're here,' and the connection dropped."

"He said, 'They're here,' like you would know who he meant?

"Yeah. Mr. Benchley and Seth."

And Thomas, no doubt. "Who's Seth?"

"Thomas said he used to be one of them until he got too big. Now he's like the muscle for Mr. Benchley. Thomas said he's not exactly right." Mark tapped the side of his head.

Mark probably wasn't exactly right after seven years with Benchley the brain-bender, but... wait. It sounded like Mark hadn't been with Benchley.

"Were you with Benchley and Thomas in Springfield?"

"For a couple months, but then..." Mark stuck his hands between his legs and squeezed his eyes shut, his shoulders trembling.

Shit. Jake shouldn't have asked. It was enough to know the boy was alive and safe. Jake needed to focus on reuniting Mark with his parents and rescuing Thomas and the other boy from Benchley. With that done, then he would find a way to punish Benchley and Reznik.

Mark started rocking back and forth, keening softly.

If Benchley and his helper were at the house where the boys went to hide, Thomas was talking and Benchley would soon learn that the files were here in Weston. And then he would come for them. No, he'd send his helper for them. Seth. And when Seth didn't find the files in the Impala, things would get ugly for Thomas and Andy.

Jake needed to save them before that happened.

"Mark?"

The rocking stopped.

"You said the connection dropped. Were you calling on their cell or to a landline?"

"A landline. There's no cell service out there."

"And the call dropped? Andy wasn't forced to hang up?"

"He was telling me what was happening. They were still outside when the call ended."

Good. Without cell service and with the landline down—it made sense for Benchley to disable it as he went in—if his helper, Seth, came to Weston looking for the files, he wouldn't be able to call Benchley. The man wouldn't know the files were missing until the muscle got back there.

Buying Jake some time.

"I need the address for the ranch where Andy is," Jake said.

"It doesn't have a real address. It's on a rural route, but I can get there."

"I need exact directions."

"What about Thomas?"

"Benchley took him." Jake sat back down. "That's how he found the ranch."

Mark's eyes went wide. "We have to save Thomas."

"I will. Thomas and Andy both."

"I'm going, too." Mark wiped his eyes and tossed the tissue on the table.

The doorbell rang.

Jake sprang up and opened the front door.

Paul stepped inside. "Jake, what's going on?"

"Dad?"

Mark's voice was soft and childlike.

Paul stepped around Jake and stopped in his tracks. "Oh my God."

Then he fell to his knees. "Thank you, thank you thank you."

Jake left them alone.

49

Benchley glanced at Seth, who shrugged.

"Who is Michael?" Benchley asked.

"Thomas's friend," Andy said. "We met him in DC, but Thomas already knew him. He came in from Denver."

Denver. Benchley had sold a lot of boys that way over the years. Boys who broke down or got too big or otherwise started to show their age. That's where he'd sent his entire inventory other than Andy when Reznik screwed up in DC. He'd kept Andy only because he'd been absolutely sure of his loyalty. But he'd been wrong and that one mistake had cost him the files when Andy helped Thomas escape from the basement.

He slapped the boy again. "Where is Michael now?"

"He went back to Weston looking for Thomas because he didn't call. But—"

Benchley raised his hand.

"No. I'll tell you! Someone else did call."

"Who?"

"A cop called using Thomas's phone. Michael said the guy was a good cop. One we could trust."

Damn it! They had missed the phone when they took Thomas. "Was the cop from Weston?"

"Yeah. Michael was going to talk to the cop if he didn't find Thomas."

It had to be the same cop. The one with the Mustang. Benchley waved Seth over. "Tape his mouth, then bring in Thomas."

While Seth did as he was told, Benchley stood up and stretched the kink out of his back. Soon Seth had Thomas taped to a chair at the kitchen table where he could see everything Benchley planned to do to Andy if Thomas didn't talk. Benchley dragged another chair around and sat down, scooting forward until their knees touched.

Thomas's eyes were clear now, and his skin had lost its pallor. His metabolism had burned off the drug, but Benchley wasn't going to give him any more. The concussion and the chemicals were a bad combo. And he had other tools.

"Remember, Thomas, when I have the files back we go on our way and you and Andy are free. So tell me where they are, or Seth starts in on both of you." Benchley nodded toward Andy. "Him first."

Thomas looked that way, then his eyes shot around the room, looking, no doubt, for his friend Michael.

Seth straddled Andy, then slapped him so hard blood sprayed from his face. Thomas jolted in his chair. Seth laughed. Andy snuffled and whimpered, his legs curling up as if that could protect him.

Perfect.

Thomas pulled his eyes off the scene and locked them on Benchley. The boy was breathing hard now, his breath clean, almost sweet.

"You understand me?" Benchley said.

Thomas nodded, then licked his lips. "The files are in Weston."

"Where?"

"Right before you came I put them in the Impala and parked it in a garage a few blocks away."

"Boss, we saw that happen, remember?"

Shit! Seth was right. This bastard was telling the truth. They'd been so close. "Why?"

"That cop came asking me questions. He put us together—you and me. I was worried he would tip you off."

"He put us together because you stole my damn car. What were you doing in Weston?"

Thomas looked away, his eyes locking on Andy stretched out on the rug with Seth hunkered over him. Hesitant, but he would talk because he knew what would happen if he didn't.

"Mark's parents live in Weston. I was hoping they would help us."

"Mark? Mark Siebert? That kid from downstate?"

Thomas nodded.

"You ran into Siebert in DC, didn't you?

Another nod.

The shock of finding out he was alive had to be the trigger that destroyed Thomas's programming. Which in turn destroyed the entire enterprise.

All because goddamn Reznik had been obsessed with Mark, found him in Denver, and brought him to DC. Benchley had no doubt about that part.

"What did you tell his parents?"

"The truth. Or some of it."

Benchley's stomach flopped, but he swallowed and kept his face calm.

"Where *exactly* is the Impala?"

Thomas told them, and Benchley made him run through it several times to be sure Seth had it right. Then Benchley walked Seth out to the car and got his pistol from the glove box before sending the boy on his way. Seth could handle getting the files, and with the gun, Benchley could handle his two prisoners without the young man's muscle. He pulled back his belly and stuck the gun inside his waistband. The cold mass gave him some of the comfort that Seth's departure took away.

Finally, he pulled out his phone to call Reznik. Until he had the files in hand, he needed to keep in touch so Reznik wouldn't decide he had to take over. But when he dialed the congressman's number, there was no ringing. He checked the screen: no signal. Not a single bar.

He went back inside. "No cell phone service out here?" he asked Thomas.

"Not within a couple miles."

Shit. And he'd torn the landline out of the wall on the way inside. Reznik wouldn't like Benchley going dark on him. He'd think the worst—that Benchley had gotten the files back and planned to use them, including the one he had on Reznik.

That would drive the congressman crazy. And then who knew what he might do?

50

———————

Jake took the stairs to the basement. He'd developed a fascination with guns when he first became a cop: the mechanics, their precise manufacture, and how they sounded when he worked the slides and magazines and cylinders. And he loved shooting them at the range. So he started a small collection, which now sat unused in a gun safe he installed under the stairs.

Unused, because his fascination ended when he experienced firsthand how easily a gun escalates conflict.

And how it ends a human life in an instant.

He spun the dial through the combination and pulled the heavy door open, the scent of gun oil wafting over him. He pulled the little Glock from behind his belt and set it on a shelf in the safe. It was a fine gun, but he wanted more firepower. He pulled out his old duty Glock, a G22 in .40 caliber that held fifteen shots, and a twelve-gauge pump shotgun. A lot of firepower, but it was better to have it and not need it, than need it and not have it.

He took the guns to the workbench and checked them over, making sure they still operated smoothly after the years they'd sat unused. The G22 felt familiar in his hand because he'd fired thousands of rounds from it at the range. On the job he'd pulled it maybe a dozen times, and he'd fired it only the once.

He filled two magazines for the pistol, slotted one into the gun, and racked the slide to load a shell into the firing chamber. Ready to go. Then he put the Glock, the spare magazine, the shotgun, and a box of double-aught buckshot in a black nylon bag. He closed the safe and spun the dial and had the brief feeling that this could be the last time he did so. Two people had already been killed in ways that displayed the strength of the resources aligned against him and the desperation that drove the men directing them. The thought made him queasy, and he considered putting the guns back in the safe and just taking the Sieberts into the station.

But it would take time to explain it all, to develop an operational plan, and for other jurisdictions to be brought in. And that was assuming the bosses would even buy his story. He didn't have any real proof. Both men's deaths *and* Miller's disappearance could all be explained. Had, in fact, already been explained: Miller left town, Greer committed suicide, and David Smith was killed by his prison lover. Mentioning Reznik's name would only make it worse. Everyone would go into ass-covering mode.

But the files would force them to act. And Mark—he was the guts of the story. With Mark sitting in front of them, the chiefs would feel like they had to do something. And what would that something be? They'd probably send some under-trained rural deputy sheriff out to the ranch for a well-being check. He'd run into something he couldn't handle—a hostage situation, maybe even a black ops killing machine.

More people would die.

No. Taking the Sieberts into the station wouldn't work.

Jake slung the heavy bag over his shoulder and started up the stairs, the ugly weight bouncing against his back.

He had to admit—just to himself—there was another reason he didn't want to take the Sieberts into the station. If the chiefs actually did buy the story he'd be drained of information and pushed aside for SWAT to handle it. But it was his trip to Mount

Logan that triggered this mess. He needed to balance that, to make it right in some small way.

If he didn't do that it would eat at him.

Forever.

His phone buzzed when he was halfway up the stairs. Grady.

"Houser."

"Cooper called. He's headed to the parking garage because the camera caught a guy breaking into a car. Sounds like it was the Impala."

Shit. Jake didn't have time to waste explaining himself.

"Did dispatch identify the guy?"

"No, but I have a screen capture. I just sent it. You should have it any second."

Jake's phone vibrated in his hand, and he opened the message. The attached photo was a wide-angle shot showing a man stepping away from Miller's car—but it wasn't Jake. It was someone much bigger. This had to be Benchley's muscle.

"Thanks, Grady."

"What do you want me to do?"

"Whatever you would normally do."

Jake ended the call and hustled up the stairs, holding the bag against his side with one hand.

He found the Siebert men sitting with their chairs pulled close together. Paul held both Mark's hands in his. Both had tears on their cheeks.

Paul looked up when Jake came in. "Mark tells me we need to save his friend, Thomas."

"He's more than a friend, Dad."

Paul smiled when his son called him *Dad*, then turned to Jake, his face serious. "What do we do, Jake?"

Jake showed Mark the picture on his smartphone. "Who's this?"

"That's Seth. Where's that from?"

"He's here in Weston, which means he's not at the ranch with Benchley. Could Benchley have more people with him?"

Mark was shaking his head before Jake even finished the question. "Thomas said it's just him and Seth."

If Jake moved fast, he might be able to stay ahead of both Seth and the black ops killing machine—and save Thomas and Andy.

"I need to go right now." Jake stuffed the files into the bag with the guns.

"We're going with you." Paul's voice was firm.

"That's a bad idea, Paul. This bag is full of guns."

"I know how to use a gun."

"But have you ever pointed one at a person?"

Paul stood. "I need to do this, Jake. I need to help my son save his friend. And I need—" His voice broke, and he gulped back a sob.

Jake understood. Paul needed to get back the piece of himself that he'd lost when his boy was taken. Through vengeance. Jake understood that feeling because his own need for vengeance for his wife's murder had never been satisfied. But it was a bad idea to bring an amateur into this.

"Let me do this for you, Paul. I have the experience."

"We're going."

"What about Linda?"

"She's home with Annie and the boys."

"Did you call her?"

"I'll call her when we get back."

Jake knew everything would be forgiven when Paul returned with Mark. But what if they *didn't* come back from this?

Either way, he had to get moving. Right now.

"Let's talk in the car," he said.

He hoped they'd see it his way before they got there. When he told them about Reznik's blacks ops asset, perhaps they would. But just in case he couldn't talk Paul and Mark out of helping, he went back down into the basement and grabbed another shotgun and another pistol from the safe. Three guns were better than one, even if all the Sieberts could do was point theirs.

51

———

When Jake saw what Mark was driving, he decided to take that vehicle. The Bronco's weight and off-road capabilities made it the best option for where they were going and what they might run into.

He put his bag on the floor in the back seat, then got behind the wheel. Mark sat up front and Paul rode the middle of the back seat, leaning forward with one hand on the back of his son's seat. Jake took Washington north through the downtown, the glittering Christmas decorations doing nothing to lighten the mood, then Diehl west to Winfield and north to the East-West Tollway.

Paul's cell phone dinged as they pulled onto the highway heading west.

"It's a text from Linda. From Mom." He held it out. "Asking what Jake wanted to talk about. I'll tell her you wanted background on Mount Logan politics."

That would work as well as anything. When Paul brought Mark home to her, the lie would be forgiven.

While Paul texted back, Jake thought about their phones. Between their built-in GPS receivers and the notification services included in many apps, the phones were laying down a trail of

248

cyber breadcrumbs that someone with the right resources could follow in real time.

The congressman had those resources.

"Turn off your phones," Jake said. "People can track us through them."

"Who could do that?" Paul asked.

"I'll explain, but please shut them down."

Jake shut off his own phone, then eyed Paul in the rearview mirror, deciding how much to tell him. He had to warn him about what they might be walking into: about Benchley, and Reznik, and the asset in the Suburban. He couldn't sugarcoat it or Paul wouldn't understand the danger. And maybe the full truth would scare him into staying in the car and letting Jake handle this.

"Mark was abducted into a string of underage sex workers run by a guy named Stan Benchley."

"I wasn't abducted. I ran away," Mark said, again with absolute conviction.

"Why would you run away, son? We..." Pain tightened Paul's voice until it faded away.

Mark turned in his seat and put a hand on his dad's arm. Paul kept quiet, his eyes glittering with tears, while Mark explained that he'd always known he was different than the other boys. Little things. How they played games. What they talked about. And as they got older, the differences became bigger, more obvious. He didn't know that it was because he was gay. He just knew he was different.

"Then I met Thomas." Mark's face lit up.

They met at the video arcade the morning he left, and he knew right away what he was feeling. Finally understanding himself was such a gift that he didn't want to lose it.

"So when Thomas asked me to go with them, I didn't even hesitate." He twisted in the seat and licked his lips. Two classic signs of deception clustered together. All, or part of that, was a lie. Mark's subconscious knew it, even if he couldn't acknowledge it.

"Who was with him that day?" Jake asked.

"Mr. B was driving the van. Tracy and Seth were in the back."

Not Blake Reznik, Jake noted. "Tell me about Tracy."

"Who's Tracy?" Paul asked.

"The man who confessed to killing Mark."

"You mean David Smith?" Paul said.

Jake looked at Mark.

"I was... sent to Colorado before that happened. I only just found out about it."

"You didn't see a paper or a TV or have access to the Internet?" Jake asked.

Mark shook his head. "Colorado wasn't like Mr. B's place. It was... harder. I don't want to talk about it."

"How did you get away to come home and see Mom that time?" Paul asked.

"What?" Mark look confused. "I never came home."

"Mom thought—" Paul stopped. "Never mind."

So Linda Siebert's encounter with Mark Siebert two years before *had* been an hallucination—or perhaps a well-designed lie to convince Jake to help them. It didn't matter now.

"Where is Congressman Blake Reznik in your story?" Jake asked.

"The *congressman*?" Paul practically shouted, before calming himself. "How was that asshole involved?"

Jake ignored the question. "Mark, do you know Reznik?"

"Yes. I met him almost right away. And he came out to Colorado some. And I went to Washington a few times."

"Jesus." Paul put a hand on his son's arm. "I'm sorry, Mark."

"A while back, Thomas and I were both at the same... party. In DC. That's how this whole thing started."

"Explain that part of it," Jake said.

"I was there for Blake, and Thomas was with another guy. Anyway, he saw me and freaked out."

"So you and Thomas..."

"We found a chance to talk, and he told me about Tracy

confessing to killing me. Thomas and Tracy both thought it was true. Mr. B. can do that to you. Make you believe things."

Like you voluntarily becoming a child prostitute. "And you decided to do something about it," Jake prompted.

"Thomas had a friend who helped. Lowell. He got me out of Colorado and brought me to Illinois. Then Andy helped Thomas escape from Mr. B's." Mark shrugged. "Then we decided to get Tracy out of prison."

A chance meeting in Washington, DC unraveled Benchley's entire operation. "Was the congressman more than a client? A part of things? A partner with Benchley?"

"Thomas thinks so."

Jake told Paul about the files full of compromising photos of men with political and economic power, and his theory they were leverage Reznik used to help him get elected and re-elected.

Paul's teeth ground together and his voice shook. "I'll kill the—"

"Dad! We need to save Thomas. And Andy. That's what's important. Our future. Not our past."

"He's right," Jake said. "Except for the 'we' part. Reznik and Benchley both have a lot of power, and they've been very active doing cleanup." He explained about David Smith's death, Greer's supposed suicide, and the man in the black Suburban. It was an ugly summary.

Mark choked back a sob. "I just can't believe Mr. B would kill Tracy."

"He's protecting himself." Jake switched lanes as they approached the tollbooth by the Wolf River. He tossed out a couple of quarters, then gassed it as they left the harsh glare of its lights. "Once you reveal yourself, people would have asked Tracy some tough questions, and Benchley didn't want him answering them."

If Tracy could have answered at all. His mind and memories had appeared broken.

Mark's hands clasped at his chest, his eyes closed, and silent tears glistened on his cheeks. His lips moved silently. Praying, maybe. Couldn't hurt.

"You make it sound like Benchley and Reznik are doing separate cleanups," Paul said. "Aren't they working together?"

"For some of it, maybe, but snatching Thomas the way Benchley did was very risky. If he and Reznik were working together there, he would have waited for the operative."

"He's desperate," Paul said. "Couldn't wait."

Jake nodded. That sounded right. "It's about the files for Benchley. One of them is on Reznik. Benchley has probably been using it to keep Reznik on a leash."

"Then the operative won't be out there and we'll only have Benchley to worry about if we there before Seth gets back from Weston," Paul said.

"That's best case," Jake said.

"Worst case?"

"We get there, and both Seth and Reznik's man in the black Suburban come in behind us."

* * *

As they approached the Orchard Road exit, Jake pulled into the right-hand lane and put on his blinker, slowing to the posted ramp speed. A few vehicles back, a small sedan followed his lead and slowed enough not to run up on him.

"This isn't it," Mark said. "We go all the way to the Peace Road exit." He swiveled his head to look behind them. "You can still cut back over. There's room."

"Okay." Jake waited another hundred feet, then pulled the steering wheel left, the big tires biting into the pavement then skittering as they passed through the loose bits accumulated on the pavement between the highway and the ramp. The suspension bottomed out as they hit the low point between the two, then they were back in on the highway, accelerating through the underpass.

Jake's eyes found the mirror. The car behind them, an Accord, stayed on the ramp. He checked the other vehicles behind and around them, but none were suspicious. They were in the clear.

"Once Mark has shown me the house, I'd like you two to drive into town and bring the police back out with you," Jake tried one last time to keep the Sibert men safe.

"Thomas doesn't trust the police." Mark's voice had more energy when he talked about Thomas.

"Paul, you a have a daughter and five foster boys who need you. And Linda. And there's a real chance that we might not live through this."

"They do need me," Paul said. "You're right. But I've also got my son back, Jake. Something I never thought would—" Paul shook his head. "Mark's back, and this is what *he* needs from me."

"Thanks, Dad."

Paul put a hand on Jake's shoulder. "You don't need to worry about me. We're doing the right thing. You know that."

But even the right thing can go wrong.

* * *

Drill was impressed by Houser's maneuver with the Bronco on the off-ramp, but not surprised. When Houser cleared every room of his house, Drill knew the man expected someone to come after him. That's why Drill had put RF transmitters on all three cars while the men were inside talking: that way wherever they went, he could follow at a comfortable distance. And when Houser had come out of the house with a heavy-looking bag over his shoulder, Drill knew that bag must contain the files.

So he'd followed the bag—and the men.

After Houser made his dramatic swerve back onto the highway, Drill simply kept on going up the exit ramp, parked on the shoulder at the top, pulled out his sat phone, and called up the tracking app. The Bronco an easy to follow yellow dot pulsing its way west along the highway. Drill texted Spec. *Houser had a second visitor and now all three are westbound on the tollway. Houser carrying heavy bag that likely holds the files.*

He got a return text almost immediately. *Good. Probably headed to a house outside Sycamore where Mr. Red's ally was taking the man he snatched up in Weston there.*

The ally again.

Great.

52

———

Jake followed Mark's directions and exited onto Peace Road. He took it north as it skirted DeKalb, then struck off through the country heading west. Traffic thinned out to nothing and the county blacktops eventually gave way to gravel roads, the stones rapping against the underside of the SUV. There were no streetlights and the moon was often obscured by cloud cover. It was a land of widely spaced properties—farms, orchards, and confinement hog operations—screened with rows of evergreen trees planted to block the wind that whipped across the flat land.

Jake was good with directions and could picture where they were in his head as if on a map. Finally, Mark told him to head down a narrow lane that cut north. The road was more dirt than gravel, rutted and pot-holed, and Jake drove slowly. The Bronco handled the terrain with creaks and squeaks of its suspension, bouncing them in their seats.

"You get used to the smell," Mark offered.

Jake doubted he'd ever get used to that barnyard stench, and he didn't want to. "Tell us about the ranch," he said. "The layout of the buildings, what the land is like, the neighbors."

"It's a nice old one-story house. All original woodwork and

very country. It's set back from the road like all of these. No real neighbors." Mark waved out the window. "It belongs to one of Andy's... friends."

"I need more, Mark."

"It'll be on the right. Behind a row of big trees with a sign that says 'Lenzo Hogs.' The gravel driveway goes past the house to a big garage then over a small hill to the pig buildings. You can't see them from the house because of the hill."

Jake checked his watch—a few minutes before midnight. "Will anybody be there with the pigs now?"

"Probably not. Andy says the people who work the pigs only come in the morning."

"Tell me about Andy. And Seth."

Mark nodded, then bit his lip. "Andy is a nice guy. He's been with Thomas at Mr. B's. I remember Seth from when I was... first joined them. He was one of us, but now he's Mr. B's guy. And after Andy locked him in the basement, he's probably pretty mad about that. And he's big and—"

"Seth's in Weston," Jake reminded Mark. His voice had been winding up into a shrill whine as he talked about Seth. Benchley was alone there with his two captives. He would have them tied up or maybe locked in the basement. And Andy might already be dead because Benchley didn't need him to find the files.

"Is there a basement?" he asked.

"No. This is it!" Mark braced himself against the dash but Jake didn't even slow. The gravel driveway and the "Lenzo Hogs" sign flashed by in the Bronco's headlights as they continued on by.

The place wasn't a ranch with a capital R. No wrought-iron sign with the name arching over the driveway, and no white-painted fences holding in well-muscled horses. Just a low house backlit by a yard light between it and the outlying garage, and a gravel driveway extending behind it and curling around a low hill.

Then the giant evergreens along the road blocked their view, and Jake took his foot off the gas and let the Bronco glide to a stop.

* * *

Benchley's gaze followed the headlights as a big SUV cruised slowly past the house, the evergreens backlit in the wash of its headlights. The light faded into the night.

"How much traffic do you get out here?"

"Some," Thomas said.

Benchley leaned close to the window for a better angle. The lights were gone. Nothing to worry about. He hoped. Being alone out here in the boonies was getting to him.

He checked his watch again; Seth should be on his way back with the files by now. He needed to finish this before Reznik's man got involved. And now that Benchley had gone silent, Reznik's man would be coming for them using surveillance technologies the public didn't even know existed.

Benchley walked around Andy on the floor and stood in front of Thomas, one hand resting on the butt of the gun in his waistband.

"If Seth doesn't bring those files back it's going to get ugly. Understand?"

"I do." The drug cocktail had completely burned off and Thomas's eyes were clear. Benchley had fed him two bottles of water and a banana, and the boy looked better. His skin had color and the sheen of sweat was gone.

"Ugly for you, and for Andy, and for your friend Mark."

Thomas's head jerked up. "I told you the truth about where I hid the files."

"We'll see." Benchley sat down and leaned in close. "We all want the same thing here."

Thomas raised his eyebrows.

"We all want me to leave here while you and the boys are still alive." Benchley smiled and patted the gun. Thomas tracked the movement. That was about all guns were good for, Benchley thought. Threats. Once you pulled the trigger, the threat was gone.

It was better to get directly into their minds. "And that is completely up to you."

Thomas's brow furrowed and his gaze wavered. He wanted to believe; Benchley could see that plainly on his face.

Benchley smiled again, and Thomas looked away.

53

———————

Jake kept his foot off the gas as the Bronco rolled past the end of the evergreen windbreak. Ahead, a pair of fat metal silos gleamed dully in the moonlight filtering through the wispy cloud cover. He shut off the headlights and angled the Bronco off the road, dropped down and across the shallow ditch, and parked by the silos. He popped open the overhead light cover and removed the bulb so it wouldn't go on when they opened their doors.

Then he faced the Siebert men. He planned to post one Siebert as a lookout to warn about anyone coming in behind them, and the other would hold a gun and go in with Jake. A show of overwhelming force to convince Benchley he didn't have a chance. The bigger the show of force, the less actual violence they would need.

In theory.

He gestured to Paul. "Haul that bag up onto the seat."

Paul lifted the bag and set it on the back seat with a soft clank of metal.

"I brought a pair of shotguns and an extra pistol. Benchley is alone and we'll have numbers, so just aiming one of the shotguns at him should be enough. Plus, he's after the files and we have them. He'll want to trade. But you need to be ready, because anything can happen."

"I've used a shotgun before," Mark said, looking from the bag to Jake. "Hunting when I was a kid."

"And he was a good shot," Paul said, putting a hand on his son's shoulder.

Shooting a man was a hell of a lot different than shooting a pheasant. Jake hoped neither Siebert would learn that tonight.

"Let's get out and regroup on your side of the car."

Jake eased his door open and stepped into the night. The wind blew in hard and cold, pelting him with bits of grit. He shut his door gently, quietly, and circled to the downwind side of the boxy vehicle. Paul and Mark were already out, their doors left open.

Jake reached inside the Bronco and dragged the nylon bag across the bench seat. He pulled out the long guns and handed them to the Sieberts, then pulled out the boxes of shells.

"This is exactly like the one Uncle Lenny had," Mark said. He nestled the gun in the crook of his arm with the barrel pointed down, looking like the practiced hunter he claimed to be.

Jake handed the box of shells to Paul, and the Sieberts loaded their weapons, smoothly slotting the shells into their guns. They knew what they were doing. Jake then pulled the extra Glock 17 from the bag and confirmed it was loaded, even though he'd loaded it himself an hour before.

"Paul, would you rather use this? It holds seventeen shots."

Paul settled the long gun in the crook of his arm and took the pistol. "A Glock. No safety, right?"

"Right." Glocks had several layers of safety mechanisms built into the firing system, but no external safety switch. If there was a bullet in the pipe, when you pulled the trigger, the gun fired. "Pull the trigger and you're shooting."

"Pass," Paul said, handing it back. "I've never used one, and tonight doesn't seem like the time to learn. I'll stick with what I know."

Jake put the extra Glock back in the bag, then stuffed the extra magazine in his back pocket. He zipped the bag closed around the files and slung it over his shoulder. After shutting the doors gently, he motioned for the men to draw close.

"We're here to trade the files for Thomas and let everyone go their own way." Jake patted the bag hanging over his shoulder. "Benchley's likely to be tense, pumped up. Just pointing that shotgun at him should be enough to shut him down." A twelve-gauge barrel pointing at you looked like the tunnel to hell. "But if he points a gun at you, use yours first."

"Seth's not here, right?" Mark asked, licking his lips and looking around.

"Right. But he could show up soon."

"You can stay with the car, son," Paul said. "You've done your part by getting us here."

"No." Mark shook his head and adjusted his grip on the shotgun, scowling.

"Let's go," Jake said.

He pulled the Glock from his waistband, then led them down into the shallow ditch and back the way they'd come. The ditch wasn't deep enough to block the wind, which had whipped up to a low howl and soon chilled his face and hands. His heartbeat accelerated and adrenaline pumped through him as his body readied for what lay ahead. The feeling took him back to his days on patrol and the domestic calls he'd handled on Chicago's west side. Most involved booze and a web of relationships too complex for an outsider to fully understand.

He glanced back to see how the Sieberts were doing now that they were in motion. Mark trailed behind Jake, a death grip on the shotgun, his face taut and determined. His dad followed a few paces to the rear, his head swiveling like they were sneaking through the jungles of Vietnam.

Alert and ready.

Thirty feet short of the driveway Jake pushed through the evergreens and stopped at the edge of their cover to observe the house. The thick stand of trees blocked the wind, and the air was almost still. He squatted on the spongy pine needles. A low porch spanned the entire width of the house. Two dark windows on the left, the front door in the middle, then a wide picture window on the right. A soft yellow light glowed in the wide window.

Mark and Paul pushed through the heavy branches behind him.

"Those windows on the left are bedrooms," Mark whispered, pointing. "There's another bedroom and a bathroom behind them. The right side of the house is basically one big room with TV area in the front and the kitchen on the backside with the eating area in the back corner. There's another door back there."

"What does that front door open to?"

"Right into the big room, but there's a computer desk blocking it."

"Stay here while I take a closer look," Jake said.

He left the Sieberts at the edge of the pines and snuck up to the corner of the house. He climbed onto the porch, sidestepping close to the house to avoid squeaks, the bag bouncing against his back and the Glock cold in his grip. He edged his head over to look through the picture window.

The room beyond was large but sparsely furnished. Just a couch under the window with a recliner off either end of it, and a flat-screen TV hanging on the wall to the left. A hallway beyond the TV led to the bedrooms—a light was shining back there.

Jake edged his head farther into the open window glass, and the kitchen came into view, a dinette set in the back corner. A country-style lamp hung over the dinette, and another glowed from the near corner of the room that Jake couldn't see.

A chair from the dinette faced this way. Thomas sat duct-taped to the chair, the dull silver tape wrapped around his torso so many times he looked like a mummy. The left side of his face was swollen and there was dark flaky blood on his shirt collar. But his head was upright and his eyes were open.

Movement in the corner of Jake's eye. He ducked back, his mind working on the afterimage. It had been a person on the floor.

He looked again. A man lay stretched out on a rug in front of the couch, duct tape wound around his ankles and strapped over his mouth. Arms taped behind him. That must be Andy. His chest rose, and then his entire body twisted in a brief struggle against his bonds before giving up.

Both men were still alive. They weren't too late.

But where was Benchley?

Jake ducked down and crept back to the corner of the house, then continued around it, the yard light bright in his eyes from its tall pole beside the distant garage. The side of the house had one window near the back, and light spilled through it. Jake crept to the window, shuffling through mulch and dead flowers, and eased his head up. The curtain material was thin and he had a good view of the dinette, Thomas taped to the chair, the kitchen beyond, then the hallway to the bedrooms.

A man stepped into the hall from a room at the other end of the house. His hand swept over the wall and the hallway light went out.

"When's Seth coming back with the files so you can get out of here?" Thomas said. His voice came through the single-pane glass clearly.

The man stepped into the kitchen. A white guy, maybe sixty, with a bushy gray mustache straight out of an '80s music video. Benchley. He was short and slight with a little paunch.

He stopped in front of Thomas, clasped his hands together, and rested them on the butt of a gun wedged into his waistband. An old Browning 1911A semiautomatic pistol, the military's workhorse for decades. Jake had one just like it in his gun safe. This one was well used, with most of the bluing worn off the metal. The 1911 was a single-action pistol and couldn't be fired without being cocked. Benchley's gun was not cocked.

"If you'd told us where the files were when we were in Weston, we would have settled everything then and there."

Jake ducked down, then circled the rest of the house. The kitchen door was unlocked and a back bedroom window slid up silently. He left it up, finished his scouting, and rejoined the Siebert men under the branches.

"Well?" Paul's voice was hoarse from excitement.

"Here's what we're looking at."

54

According to Drill's GPS, the Bronco had stopped in the middle of a field at least a half mile from the nearest road—but as Drill threaded his way toward the blip, he realized that many of the little roads out here didn't show on the GPS map. He zoomed out and found the roads depicted formed a perfect grid, with Houser's blip centered in a grid box. He drove toward the blip until he was aligned directly south of it, then stopped.

He was in the middle of an intersection, with a thin dirt track leading straight north through the rural expanse. The ripe stench of cows or pigs drifted into the car. He'd spent time in most of the world's armpits, but the smells here rivaled them all. He checked the screen again. The Bronco was still there. Sitting still.

This was it.

He pulled the Accord forward a couple hundred yards onto the wind-flattened weeds along the shoulder and turned off the engine. As he unzipped his duffel and took out his go-bag, the sat phone buzzed on the dashboard. He answered, hoping for some useful intel.

"Drill."

"Report." The congressman barked with an abruptness that

265

told Drill the man had restored his confidence. Probably with bourbon; all the DC big shots liked their bourbon.

Drill pulled the phone away from his face, found the right app, and triggered the recorder. "I've located their vehicle on a dirt road west of Sycamore. They must be at that house you said your ally was headed to." Anything else would be too much of a coincidence. "I'll be approaching and engaging as soon as we hang up."

"I want those goddamn files."

"Do you have any intelligence from your ally on how many people are in the house and whether they have guns?"

Drill didn't have a gun with him and had done dozens of jobs without one. They were loud and made a mess that was hard to control. But if his target had a gun, it changed his approach.

"No. Stan Benchley, my ally, was helping me recover the files. He has a helper and they have the man who stole the files with them. But Benchley has stopped communicating, so he may have gone rogue."

Rogue. The line sounded rehearsed and about as true as a campaign promise. But whether it was true or not, Drill was going to run into at least six men at the house: Benchley's three and Houser's three. "Understood."

"And do not look inside the files! They contain sensitive defense plans and codes. You are *not* authorized to look at any of it."

"So you've said. Spec?"

"I'm here."

"You good with this?"

"Mr. Red has the reins."

My reins, Drill thought.

"Spec, please be explicit. Is Mr. Red directing this operation?"

"Confirmed." Spec's voice was clear.

Confirmed. Drill pulled the phone away from his face and verified the recording app was still rolling.

"Describe Benchley," Drill said.

"Mid-fifties with a thick gray mustache. Retired Army colonel. Intelligence, not combat."

"And his helper?"

"Seth. Big, strong, and young. But mentally slow."

"Any other instructions? Level of force authorized?"

The congressman lowered his voice to a whisper. "Extreme prejudice."

Straight out of a Vince Flynn thriller.

Drill considered asking Spec for confirmation that he was now authorized to kill whoever it took to get the files, but Spec was on the line. If he objected, he would speak up.

He didn't.

"Understood."

* * *

"Like we figured," Jake said, "it's just Benchley, but he's got a gun. A pistol. Thomas is taped to a kitchen chair, and Andy is taped up on the floor in front of the couch. Both of them are alive and conscious. So we're going to go in fast and strong and take control. Now, while we have numbers and surprise on our side. If that fails, we'll trade the files."

He turned to the younger Siebert. "Mark, me and your dad will go in. I want you to stay out here on watch. Hunker down back under the branches of the tree closest to the driveway."

"And if someone comes?" Mark looked off into the dark front yard and back to Jake. His face glistened with nervous sweat despite the cold.

Not if, but when. Seth *would* be coming. But with a little luck they would be done before he got here. And if they'd read the relationship right, Benchley would keep Reznik's man away. So they should only have Seth to worry about. An amateur.

"Fire a warning shot. That should scare Seth enough to slow him down, then one of us will come back to help you."

Mark nodded and adjusted his grip on the shotgun. "Please save Thomas. And be careful, Dad."

Paul pulled his son into a hug, their guns clanking together, then released him. The boy scrambled away, disappearing into the dense shadows under the trees.

Jake then went over his plan with Paul. They would go in separately. Paul would enter through the back bedroom window and make a noise to attract Benchley's attention. Jake would watch through the window in the back door and bust in loudly at that point, redirecting Benchley's attention and scaring him into the realization that he was surrounded. He'd either fight or give up, and if he fought, it would be directed at Jake, not at Paul.

Jake wanted both Siebert men to get back to Linda in one piece.

* * *

Drill gazed across the barren field. It was carved into straight rows, its crop already harvested, corn stubs casting shadows in the thin moonlight. He stepped into a furrow and walked along it, the dirt clods shifting and crumbling under his weight. The rich smell of earth that rose up partially masked the stench of manure.

Ahead and to his right, a yard light glowed. According to the GPS, the Bronco was there.

He continued until he drew even with the light, now partly blocked by a row of tall pines, then he began crossing the rows, stepping high to avoid the corn stalks. A sudden gap formed in the clouds, and bright moonlight glinted off something north of the pines. Drill dropped into a low crouch and waited, but when nothing moved or made a sound, he crossed the remaining rows, angling toward the reflection, high-stepping over the stalks, his travel silent in the soft dirt except for an occasional rustle when he stepped on a cornhusk.

He found the Bronco parked by a pair of silos. He circled the vehicle carefully, and when nothing moved he approached it.

Empty. He opened the doors one by one and searched for the files, but didn't find them or the heavy bag Houser had carried.

Drill closed the doors, then moved south in a low crouch along the shallow ditch toward the house sheltered behind the pine trees.

As he approached the driveway, the *zup-zup-zup* of a zipper sounded in the shrubbery between him and the house. He froze and turned toward the sound. He waited, then crept toward the streaming splash of a man urinating. Drill darted forward, weaving through the branches catching at his face and clothes. The pisser had his back turned, but Drill could see it was the small man who'd driven the Bronco to Houser's house. On the ground behind him was the dull gleam of a long gun with a fat barrel. These people were armed. But once Drill took that shotgun for himself, things would be more than even.

He waited for the man to finish, partly as a courtesy and partly to avoid getting pissed on or dick-whipped. The man shook it off, bouncing in his boots, then put it away and zipped up.

Drill deftly reached around, pinched the man's neck in the crook of his elbow, and squeezed, cutting off the flow of blood to his brain. Within seconds the man was out and Drill lowered him to the ground.

Quick, easy, and silent.

He pulled a syringe from his go-bag he wore around his waist and dosed the man with the M98. It would keep him down for at least an hour —probably longer given his size. Department-developed drugs didn't go through rigorous testing, so a guesstimate was the best he could do. He flipped the man onto his stomach and turned his head to the side so he wouldn't choke to death if he puked in reaction to the drug, then stabbed the needle into the ground, broke it off, and put the syringe back in his bag.

He hefted the shotgun the boy had left on the ground. A pump-action Remington. Twelve-gauge. He racked it slowly over and over to count the shells. Six. He reloaded it and racked a round into the chamber. A handgun would be easier to handle in the house, but it didn't have the scare factor of the Remington. Houser's suburban cop experience probably hadn't prepared him for a close-quarters firefight with a twelve-gauge. If he had to, he could fire the shotgun into the television. The noise and damage would shock the hell out of the amateurs inside and give him a few extra seconds to get the upper hand.

Headlights appeared, approaching from the south, the lights jiggering as the car maneuvered the rough road. Drill crouched and froze, waiting for the vehicle to pass by.

55

Benchley paced the living room, eyeing the two boys. They were both afraid—Benchley knew fear and read it easily—but not in the primal way they had feared him in the beginning. Their fear then, quivering through their young bodies, had been so delicious as he took away their innocence and taught them how to make men happy.

But as the reprogramming took hold, the need to use fear for control diminished, and with it, so did his own pleasure. By the time the new programming was in full effect and the boy believed that what Benchley asked him to do was exactly what he himself wanted to do, Benchley's pleasure was of a different kind. More academic. The satisfaction of a job well done in building another boy who would do what was asked of him.

Until his brain matured and he became susceptible to outside influences. Like what happened to Thomas when he went to DC and saw Mark Siebert there, still alive.

Damn that Reznik!

"Seth has the files by now," Thomas said.

"Maybe." Benchley yanked the pistol out of his waistband. "Why don't we have a chat while we wait."

Thomas's eyes tracked the gun, but it didn't appear to faze him. "We have nothing to talk about."

"What about those goddamn tweets?"

"That wasn't me," Thomas said, his smile twisted with hatred.

Maybe the boy hadn't sent the tweets. But he knew who had. These little shits.

"Did you know hogs love to eat meat?" Benchley asked. "You can throw a dead cow in the pen and within a few hours there's nothing left but a stain on the ground. They crunch through the bones and all."

Ah—and there it was. A shadow of those old primal fears flickering across the boy's features. A spike of pleasure shot through Benchley from his toes to his fingertips.

But then Thomas closed his eyes, and when he reopened them the hatred was back.

The light in the hallway popped on.

Benchley swung his head toward the light, then down to verify that Andy was still on the rug.

The light must be on a timer. But a timer on a hallway light set to turn on after midnight... that didn't seem likely.

His hands were suddenly slick with sweat, and he took turns wiping them on his pants while the other hand held the gun.

A long squeak of a door hinge sounded from down the hallway.

That was definitely no timer.

Maybe Mark had come back and snuck in through a bedroom window?

Benchley wiped his hands again, then edged across the floor to line up with the hallway. He drew up his shoulders and held his pistol in two hands.

The light winked off.

Benchley took a short step forward but could see nothing in the hallway's shadowed depths. He brought the gun up, hands trembling, gun wavering.

"Who's there?"

* * *

Drill stayed crouched low as the headlights approached. The car slowed and turned into the driveway, gravel skittering from under its tires. The lights swept over him as the car took the turn.

It lurched to a stop.

Shit!

The driver's door flung open and an immense man sprang out, running straight for Drill.

Drill brought the shotgun up, then flipped it and gripped it like a pugil stick. If he fired the weapon he'd lose the element of surprise he'd need to take on the men in the house. He'd have to handle this the old-fashioned way.

* * *

Jake had turned the knob and then held the door, waiting for Paul to get into position. When the light flicked on in the hallway, Benchley flinched, his focus shifting toward the light. And when the light went out again, he raised his gun, finger around the trigger. But he still hadn't cocked it.

Jake eased the door open; the groaning hinges announced his entry.

Benchley turned, the gun dropping along his thigh, a smile spreading across his face. "Seth," he said, a relieved sigh around the word.

"Freeze!" Jake shouldered the door hard, and it banged against the wall as he jumped into the room, Glock trained on Benchley. Paul emerged from the hall, leading with the shotgun.

Benchley gasped, then started to bring his gun back up when headlights swept across the window. He turned toward the lights, and the boy on the floor lashed out with his legs and kicked Benchley's feet from under him. Benchley lurched and—

BLAM!

56

———————

Drill saw his chance.

When the gun discharged inside the house, the giant paused in his mad rush and turned toward the sound. Surprised, trying to decipher what it was and what it meant. But Drill already knew exactly what it was and what it meant. A twelve-gauge shotgun had fired large shot. Aught, maybe double-aught. It would have ripped apart whoever it hit.

Drill stepped forward and hit the big man in the throat with his gun barrel, then whacked him in the back of his head with the stock. As the man fell, Drill dropped the gun and spun the big man to the ground in a chokehold, the pressure on the carotid artery putting him out in seconds. Drill quickly dosed him with M98, then snatched up the shotgun and headed for the house. He needed to go in now, while the people inside were stunned by the noise.

And the gore.

* * *

Jake dashed across the kitchen toward Benchley. The man pushed up to his hands and knees, his head came up, and he raised his pistol toward the hallway.

Toward Paul.

Jake kicked Benchley in the side, a sharp crack as a rib broke. Benchley gasped and rolled away and the gun fell from his hand as he wrapped both arms around himself and groaned. Jake swept his gaze to Paul in the hallway, who was holding the shotgun vertically in front of him, smoke swirling from the barrel.

Jake kicked the loose pistol toward Paul, then dropped to a knee and grabbed Benchley's throat with his left hand and pressed the Glock to his temple. Blood was pooling on the floor under the man's head.

"Hold still," Jake said, his words sounding muffled after the shotgun blast.

Benchley squirmed, his face twisted in pain. Then his eyes fluttered and closed, and he went still, his body unclenching. But his chest moved, in and out. He wasn't dead.

Jake found the source of the blood: a shallow three-inch-long groove in Benchley's scalp above his ear. A graze. It wouldn't kill him.

"I didn't mean to shoot," Paul's voice shook, but made it through the cottony fog now clearing from Jake's ears. "I—his gun came up and he lunged. I thought he was going to shoot. My brain didn't register that the guy on the floor tripped him."

Benchley jerked, arms clutching his chest, gasping. His eyes fluttered open, then closed. He was out again.

"Let's free these two, then get moving," Jake said. He found a couple of knives in the kitchen, and they started working to remove the tape binding the two prisoners, Jake working on Thomas, Paul on Andy.

"Where's Mark?" Thomas asked.

"Outside."

"Those headlights," Paul said, then gestured toward the front window, glowing from the exterior light source. "They didn't just drive by."

Shit.

"Seth must be here," Jake said.

* * *

Drill had sprinted to the house then soft-stepped along the side of it. He found a blast hole from the shotgun through the wall, but shredded insulation blocked him from looking through it, so he continued to the back door and peered through the window.

Houser was sawing at the tape binding a man to a chair while the other man who'd ridden here with him worked on the bindings of a man sprawled on the floor. A second man on the floor—the gray mustache said it was Reznik's "ally," Benchley—had blood on his face, but he was breathing.

Drill went in quick and low with the shotgun out in front of him.

57

Jake sawed at the layers of duct tape on Thomas's wrists with the kitchen knife. It was dull, making for slow work.

"Stop!"

Jake froze.

A stocky man dressed in black stood in the open back doorway holding a shotgun.

Aimed at Jake's head.

Jake slowly pulled his eyes off the gaping barrel and up to the man's face. It wasn't the big young man from the parking garage video. This guy was smaller and older and completely calm.

The congressman's black ops hit man had found them.

Jake glanced at his pistol. He'd set it on the table—too far away to do him any good.

"Put your hands up!"

Jake raised his hands, his eyes still locked on Black Ops. "You must be Reznik's fixer."

"Drop the knife and kick it to me."

Jake dropped the knife and kicked it clattering across the oak floor. He lowered his hands, thinking about the pistol.

"The hands stay up, Houser."

Jake put them back up, momentarily surprised the man knew

his name. But why wouldn't he? Jake hadn't been undercover in Mount Logan.

"You, too." The shotgun swung toward Paul.

Paul stood, dropped his knife, and kicked it toward the man.

"Now both of you back up and sit on the couch." He gestured with the gun. "On the ends."

Jake and Paul sat, sinking so deep into the old cushions that it would be impossible to get up with any speed.

"Hands on your knees."

They obeyed.

Black Ops propped the shotgun against the wall and snatched up Jake's pistol from the kitchen table. He eyed the load indicator, then rubbed a thumb over it. Satisfied, he waved it back and forth across his five captives.

"What did you do to my boy?" Paul asked.

"The little guy out front?"

Paul nodded.

"He's fine. Just put him out." He tested Thomas's bindings.

Paul's face flushed, and he leaned forward. "If you hurt my boy you'll wish you hadn't."

"I told you he's fine."

The voice was as calm as a Sunday Bible study.

"Who are you?" Thomas asked.

Black Ops ignored him.

Jake caught Thomas's eye and shook his head. *Just be cool.*

The man stepped over to Andy and checked the tape binding him. Andy twisted away from the man's touch.

Black Ops looked around and spotted Jake's nylon bag on the floor by Thomas. He grabbed it and put it on the table, edging around to put his back to the doorway.

"When the congressman sent you after this file he probably told you it was full of national security secrets," Jake said. "But that's not what's in those files."

Black Ops tugged the bag's zipper open and looked inside.

"Nothing in there is about national security," Jake continued. "I've looked through it all."

The man raised an eyebrow.

"We all have." Jake had the man interested. "Pull out the file with Reznik's name on it and see what this is really about." Jake hoped Black Ops cared. About the country and its people. And about right and wrong.

Black Ops moved around the room and rechecked the bindings on Andy and Thomas.

"I can tell you what's in there," Jake said. "If you aren't *allowed* to look."

Black Ops circled back around behind the table, then set the gun down, yanked a phone off his belt, and checked its screen. The phone was much thicker than the norm—a satellite phone.

"That accordion folder contains blackmail files kept by the mustached man on the floor," Jack said. "Inside are individual files on politicians and businessmen with pictures of them having sex with underage boys."

The harsh language drew only a nod from Black Ops. Then he set the phone on the table and picked up the gun.

58

Drill kept his face impassive, but everything Houser said echoed his own doubts about this op. He knew the Mount Logan part of it had been all about protecting the congressman, and now it sounded like the files were more of the same. Protecting the congressman from a sex scandal was *not* a legitimate operation; it was politics. And Drill's job was supposed to be above politics.

He picked up the accordion file, carried it over to Houser, and dropped it in the man's lap.

"Show me."

* * *

As the fat bundle of files hit Jake's thighs, Black Ops turned sideways to keep all of them in view. His face was a stone mask, his eyes never still, his gaze sweeping around the room. Giving nothing away.

Paul pushed against the couch and shifted his weight forward, but he was so deep into the cushions that Black Ops was able to step over and shove him back with a hand on the top of his head before he even had his feet under him.

"Sit down or die."

"It's going to be okay, Paul," Jake said. "Thomas, Andy—be still."

Jake unwound the string and folded the flap over. He pulled out Reznik's file and held it up. He hoped the photos would be enough.

Black Ops stepped forward, and Jake leaned to make the handoff.

"Nothing in that file has anything to do with national security, domestic or international," Jake said.

Black Ops took the file, circled back behind the kitchen table, and stood there with the back door open behind him. The casual disregard for the doorway worried Jake. The operative had said Mark was fine, but maybe he wasn't. Maybe he was dead and the operative lied to lower tensions. He almost asked, but he didn't want the answer. The wrong answer could start them down a path of destruction he hoped to avoid.

"Nothing in that file has anything to do with national security," Jake said again.

"So you've said."

Jake took the hint and shut up.

The man's face stayed blank as he opened the file and shuffled through the photos with his left hand, the gun still sweeping back and forth across the room with his right. Rock steady. He spread the photos across the table. His eyes darted from photo to photo, swept over his captives, then back to the photos. Finally he chose a few and held each under the light hanging over the table, angling them back and forth. He grunted something Jake couldn't make out, then shuffled the photos together and back into the file.

He picked up his phone.

Here we go, thought Jake. A spike of doubt tore through him. Maybe the file would only confirm the man's mission.

Maybe protecting the congressman from possible blackmail *was* his mission.

59

———————

Drill had kept his face a mask as he examined the photos, but anger heated his blood until his ears burned. Some of these boys hadn't even hit puberty yet.

He lifted his gaze from the photos and locked eyes with Houser. The suburban cop was completely still, waiting to see what Drill would do.

He picked up the sat phone, started the recording app, then called Spec.

"Did you get it?"

The congressman again. Where the hell was Spec?

"Put Spec on. Right now."

The tone changed as the phone went on speaker.

"I'm here," Spec said.

"So, now, Mr. Drill." Reznik's voice was gravelly with anger. "Did you get it?"

"I don't know."

"What does that mean?"

"The cop has a thick accordion file here with a lot of separate files inside it. Tell me which one you want and I'll make—"

"No! Don't open the files. That's an order! Bring them all."

Drill's eyes found Houser's. He'd heard the congressman's voice. It had carried through the room.

"Protocol requires me to confirm asset acquisition before extraction." Not true, but the congressman didn't know that. If Spec was playing this thing straight, he would speak up.

Spec said nothing.

"Is Benchley there?" Reznik asked. "He can confirm it."

The congressman had called the man "rogue" less than an hour ago. Now he was an ally again?

"He's here, but unconscious. There are a lot of people here. So I need to get this done and get out of here. Tell me what's in the file you're looking for."

"What do you mean, a lot of people?"

"Five inside the house and another two outside."

"Seven people? And just you?" The congressman's voice was now breathy, frantic. "Have they seen inside the files?"

"Houser says they've all looked through them."

"Kill them all," the congressman croaked, his voice suddenly hoarse.

Houser flinched, then sat up straighter and nodded as if to say, *There you go. Now it's up to you.* The cop was betting everything on a patriotic assumption that a covert American intelligence operative wouldn't kill Americans on American soil to protect an American congressman. Houser had to have figured out that Drill had already done that when he killed Greer.

This guy had balls of steel.

"Did you hear me, Drill?"

Drill had heard him, but he'd still heard nothing from Spec. Spec was hanging them both with this. Drill for the killings and Reznik for ordering it.

Drill couldn't imagine the messed-up dynamic that had led to this. He considered asking for Spec's direct authorization, but decided that might give away that he knew what was going on. And he was covered; he had Spec on the earlier recording authorizing Reznik's direction and on this one acquiescing to it. But still, this was crazy.

"Repeat."

"Kill them all and don't look in the files."

"All seven?"

"Yes, damn it. Do your duty!"

Drill always did his duty. The congressman thought his duty included killing seven people to protect his political career.

Did it?

Asking that question was Spec's job.

Drill's job was to take orders and execute them.

Point and shoot.

Seven people. Americans.

"Understood."

He ended the call, checked the recording, and put the phone back on his belt.

60

Jake kept still, his eyes locked on Black Ops. Hoping for some indication that the killer, a man whose profession was based on taking orders, might, this time, disobey them.

Black Ops came around the table and stood in front of the couch. "Read me the names on the other files."

Jake read off the names. All state and local politicians and businessmen. Reznik was the only one with a national profile.

"Some of the boys in the pictures are a lot younger than these two here." Black Ops gestured at Thomas and Andy. "Where are these younger boys?"

"Denver," Thomas said. "Mr. B—Stan Benchley, there on the floor—he sent them all there when this started."

"Are they going to come back?"

"None ever have before."

Black Ops squatted next to Benchley and shook his shoulder. Benchley's mouth gaped open and saliva strung to the floor. "I'm not sure he's going to make it."

Jake hoped he was wrong about that, but he probably wasn't. Killing was what the operative knew.

Black Ops stood. "I'm going to tell you how it's going to be. If you don't follow through, I'll find you. Each of you."

His hard gaze swept around the room and landed on Jake. "You *don't* want to ever see me again."

* * *

Drill kept the file on Reznik and walked back to the Accord. He didn't care what Houser and the others did with the rest of the files, as long as they stuck to the deal they'd made. Drill would handle the congressman, they would handle the little man with the gray mustache and his big helper, and no one would say a single word to the press or anyone else. They all understood the consequences of breaking the deal, and Drill was confident they would comply; Houser would make sure of it.

The Accord was where he'd left it. He reversed course, and when he got to the main drag running between Sycamore and DeKalb, he drove south into the college town, checked into a worn-out motel, and caught a few hours' sleep. In the morning he took a long shower, washing off the stench of the barnyard. It had gotten so deep into his clothes that he threw them away. He had a nice breakfast at a townie diner, then went to an office supply store and used the equipment in the business center to scan the entire Reznik file.

He emailed the scanned images and the audio files he'd made on the sat phone to his lawyer. The lawyer was his failsafe. The man would hold the files and release them to the press if Drill didn't make contact at set intervals. The lawyer was capable and trustworthy, and after once looking at an earlier such package, he knew better than to repeat that mistake.

Then Drill sent the photos and audio files to Spec at the man's personal email address with a short message: *Mr. Red has to go or my failsafe releases the photos and audio files.*

Spec would do the right thing. The audio files were too powerful.

Back in the car, Drill used the sat phone to ask an analyst friend with the agency—a guy about to age out like Drill—to work up a profile on Stan Benchley and any connections he had in Denver. Then he stole a fresh car from the student parking lot at the university: a Camry with a lot of miles but a comfortable leather seat.

He headed west.

* * *

Jake drove Paul and Mark back to Weston in the Bronco. The adrenaline surge had bled away, leaving him jittery and exhausted, so he took the back roads, fearing the straight and smooth interstate would put him to sleep. They dropped south of the highway and then east through the country to Kirwin and on toward Weston. Mark woke on the way, but he was groggy from whatever Black Ops had given him and lay in the back seat resting his head in his dad's lap. Paul told his son what happened in the house and that Thomas and Andy were safe. The whole way he kept stroking Mark's head and wiping the tears from his own eyes.

The deal they'd made with Black Ops hadn't settled well in Jake's mind, but he'd had no choice but to accept it. Black Ops had held the guns and the files and all their lives in his very capable hands, and Jake had no leverage and no room to negotiate. And in the end, Jake had to admit that even if he sought justice, he had no courtroom-worthy evidence against either Benchley or Reznik. Justice could only be served outside the system.

And it would be. Thomas, standing over Benchley's unconscious body with hatred burning in his eyes, had said he would "take care" of the mindbender so he would never hurt anyone again. It had been very clear what that meant. Thomas had also convinced them that after Benchley was gone, Seth would quickly fall back in with the rest of them.

And Black Ops left Thomas with the files.

All except for Reznik's. Black Ops had kept that one, and he promised the congressman would get what he deserved.

Jake believed him.

It bothered him that these arrangements left him with no justice to deliver himself. But it was best for the boys. There would be no trials where they had to tell strangers what had happened to them. The boys—Thomas and Andy, and even Seth—would stay hidden with Lowell Carr until they heard the promised news about Reznik. And Mark would do the same, but with his parents. After that, each would have to choose his own way. They were adults and could go where they chose, whether that was home or on to a new future Carr helped them find. If they went home, their reappearances would generate some media buzz, but if they told a boring story about running away, then kept their mouths shut, the media would lose interest quickly.

He came into Weston on New York Street and then cut over to Hillside at the high school. As Jake pulled to the curb in front of his house, he saw a woman sitting on the front stoop, hugging herself against the early morning chill.

Linda Siebert.

"Mark?" Jake nodded toward the house. "Your mom's waiting for you."

61

———

The fog in Benchley's head swirled and bunched and, finally, released. But with consciousness came the pain, pulsing with every beat of his heart, rushing through his entire body to slam against the side of his skull. And a second pain, a rhythmic one that spiked in his gut, over and over. Both pains melded together until nausea rose up within him and he spewed.

The mess ran up his face and dripped from the top of his head.

He was upside down.

He twisted, and his arms flopped and bounced in rhythm with the gut pain. He realized he was being carried, and the hard point of a shoulder was driving into him on every step.

The last few hours came back to him all at once. *The shotgun blast!* His hands came to his head as he remembered the searing pain before the blackness.

"He's waking up." A familiar voice. Andy.

"That's too bad," said the man carrying him. Thomas.

Benchley struggled, but Thomas just gripped his legs tighter and kept moving.

Now Benchley felt the cold air against his face. A gravel road passed below him. He turned his head and saw a building approaching, and just past it a thin line of orange below a light gray sky. Shuffling and stomping and snuffling came from inside the building. Then the smell. Pigs.

Andy ran ahead of Thomas and opened a metal service door. They stepped through, and the animals immediately broke into a frenzy, squealing and bumping against the boards of their pens. Thomas walked the entire length of the building, the animals getting bigger as they went. At the end, he dropped Benchley on the hard-packed floor and squatted next to him.

"I'm giving you this end that you threatened for me because you worked so damn hard to turn me into a monster like you. It's a tribute, I guess."

"No!" Benchley wasn't sure he'd said it out loud.

"You can't throw him in there conscious," Andy said. "No one deserves that."

"You hear that, Benchley?" Thomas shook his head. "Andy still cares about you."

Thomas stepped away, and when he came back within Benchley's range of vision he was carrying a shovel. He raised it, and it came down against Benchley's head with a dull explosion of pain. That brought the fog back, billowing and darkening and closing in at the edges of his consciousness.

Then he was being hoisted and heaved over the boards. He landed with a thud.

Before the darkness took him, a soft flat wetness brushed against his face, his nose, his ear. Just as he drifted away, a crunch came from his leg, and another to his hand.

And then he was gone.

* * *

Jake ushered the Sieberts into the house, out of the cold and away from the early-morning commuters stirring in the neighborhood. They sat at the card table in the kitchen, their chairs pulled close together. Mark took the attention well, letting his mom kiss him and hold his face and rub her hands over his shoulders and back, repeating over and over, *Thank you, God. Thank you, God.* Paul leaned back in his chair, his smile wide, watching them.

Jake hung back for a minute then edged around them to the basement door and took the guns down to his workbench. He unloaded them and cleaned them and put them back in the safe. He put his duty weapon back in the pocket of his windbreaker. When he was done he sat on the high stool in front of the bench, not wanting to interrupt the reunion upstairs or disturb the sounds they'd brought to his house.

Wonderful family sounds. But they dredged up a painful longing for a family of his own.

He'd had his chance, with Mary, before her murder took that away from him. Now the best he could do was help other families, like the Sieberts. By doing what he was good at.

Finding the truth. And avenging the dead.

Chairs scraped against the floor above his head, then the front door opened and closed. Footsteps across the floor and down the stairs.

"Jake." Paul stood at the bottom of the stairs, his smile still wide, dark circles under his eyes but a flush in his cheeks. "Thank you." He shook his head. "I had no idea... no hope even, that this would be how this ended."

"We're even," Jake said.

"Never. Not after this." Paul turned away, then came back and pulled Jake off his stool and gave him a long hard hug.

Then he left.

62

———————

Jake spent the last few days of his week off moving back into his Spring Street property. After seeing the Sieberts together in his Main Street house he'd decided that living there alone, he would always feel what was missing; he didn't want that hanging over him.

The Spring Street property had been the headquarters for his dad's landscaping business for decades. It was nothing like a house, and so it would, hopefully, never give him that missing-out feeling.

And now that he'd decided to make it his permanent home, it was time to get started on some projects. He'd previously converted the second floor of the offices into a bachelor pad with new windows and skylights. Now he moved on to planning upgrades to the flooring, cabinets, and countertops—and after studying the shop area, he decided to finish half the floor with rubberized sport flooring and install a basketball hoop, some aerobic equipment, and weights. He would have the walls spray-insulated and install a pair of heaters to keep the worst of the winter's chill out of the place. Not homey, but functional and convenient.

Mark was holed up with his parents and sister and foster

brothers. Paul said he was doing well. Thomas called to say Benchley had been "taken care of" and would never be seen again. Seth had shrugged off Benchley's "sudden disappearance" as Thomas predicted and joined Thomas and Andy at Carr's ministry in Rockford. Apparently he had already become the building's handyman.

On the last day of his time off, Jake took a long run, then showered and stretched out in his favorite leather recliner to watch one of the NFL pregame shows. But the talking heads laughing over one another's football predictions were hard to follow, and his mind continually drifted to Mark, the other boys, and Benchley.

And Reznik.

Jake was far past thinking the only justice came from a court of law, but still had trouble with how they'd ended this because people were going unpunished—the men in those other files, the men in Colorado, and whoever had allowed Reznik to corrupt the operative's agency. But justice wasn't always perfect, and Carr had been very right about one thing: the boys and their futures were far more important than those men and their pasts.

His cell phone rang, and he muted the excited babble of the TV. The caller ID said "Unknown."

"This is Houser."

"I kept my part of the deal."

Black Ops.

"What did you do?"

"Turn your TV to CNN."

Jake flipped to that channel. They were showing an exterior shot of a large brick house dusted in snow. The scroll on the muted TV read: *Illinois Congressman Blake Reznik found dead from apparent suicide. Sources in the intelligence community say he was under investigation for arson and insurance fraud in the destruction of a home allegedly used for love connections by the congressman and his political allies.*

Jake unmuted it to hear the voiceover. Reznik had shot himself with a gun once registered to his wife. He'd left behind a suicide note that simply said, *I'm sorry.*

Dead and disgraced. Justice, of a kind.

"How'd your end shake out?" Black Ops asked.

"As promised. A job well done, Mr. G-man."

"Except for Detective Greer." The man's voice was heavy.

"And the men in Denver."

"I'm taking care of them now," Black Ops said. "But you won't hear about that."

Jake smiled as Black Ops hung up. Justice served.

He spent a few more minutes watching the CNN coverage and thinking about Greer. Could Jake have done something different, something to have saved the man? Maybe, maybe not.

He had to accept that.

A few minutes later his cell rang with another call. He saw the name on the screen and decided to take it.

"This is Houser."

"*This* is McKay."

Jake smiled. "Well, well. Calling on Sunday. It must be personal."

"I have good news about Jeffrey Storch."

"Oh?"

Jake already knew about the bags of heroin found in the man's car after a CI tip. Of course he knew: he planted the drugs he'd bought from Smoke, and he delivered the hot tip using Smoke's CI number. Smoke should get a nice little chunk of cash out of it.

While Anna told him the story, he tried to think up a clever line to lure her over. But it was a short story, and when she'd finished he still hadn't come up with anything.

"Is he willing to roll over on the next guy up the chain?"

"Not yet. Claims he's being framed. But he'll come around."

"I'm sure he will."

Jake fell silent and so did McKay, two single people with a long Sunday stretching ahead of them.

"How about coming over for the Bears game?" Jake said at last. "It's on at noon. Have a few beers. Order a pizza."

"Sounds like you're inviting over one of the guys. Is that how you think of me?"

Absolutely not. "Let me try that again. How about red wine and something Italian?"

He could hear the smile in her voice. "I could be persuaded to do that."

The invitation was his only persuasion. He upped the offer. "Red wine and lasagna."

"And garlic bread?"

"Sure."

"I'll be over in a half hour. I'll bring the wine."

As Jake headed to the kitchen to defrost some food, he felt a big smile stretching his face. Maybe he wasn't met to be alone after all.

PREVIEW OF JAKE HOUSER MYSTERY #4 - PAST MADE PRESENT

CHAPTER ONE

Detective Jake Houser leaned harder, his foot on Alan Mitchell's back, pressing him into the oil-stained gravel. The junkyard's Dobermans sensed their master's distress and started barking and howling. Jake shot a glance that way when the one with the red-hued fur launched itself against the chain-link fence of their enclosure. The gate was latched and the fence was tall. He was safe.

"That's assault on a police officer," Jake said. "I'll let that go if you tell me where she is."

"I don't know!" Mitchell scrabbled at the ground. "I keep telling you."

The problem was, Jake believed him. It might be the only thing the man had said that turned out to be true. Everything else he'd told Jake about Kate Ballard—where they met, where they spent time together, and who else they spent time with—had turned out to be lies. They met here at the junkyard when Kate Ballard was buying a cheap taillight assembly before her mom noticed the damage to her car, not at a party at a mansion in Weston. They spent time together in the trailer at the back of the junkyard, not going out to dinner and movies. They saw no one else, not all her friends from college as he'd claimed.

Kate Ballard wasn't even in college. She was a high school senior who went missing the Friday night her spring break began, ten days ago. Kate's mom called in her disappearance the following Saturday morning, and Jake had worked it ever since without developing a single solid lead. One friend was sure Kate had hitchhiked to Colorado to go into the backcountry with her dad, but spring break was over and Kate was not back and her dad was still in the mountains. Unreachable.

So Jake kept coming back to Mitchell, the secret boyfriend no one knew about.

Jake pulled his foot off Mitchell and the man scrambled to his feet, wiping off gravel that was stuck to his face. Blood began to well from small wounds on his chin.

"You're crazy, man." Mitchell backed away, Jake following him, step for step. The air smelled of old oil and dog crap.

"Run through it all again." A cold spring wind whipped across the junkyard, whistling and howling through the twisted wreckage of hundreds of cars. Mitchell backed into a stack of rusted fenders. He startled, glancing behind him as if there might be a monster there. When he turned back around, his eyes wide with fear, locked on Jake's. *I* am the monster, Jake thought.

"All what?"

"Everything," Jake said. "How you met. Where you went. Who you saw. Everything. For every time you saw her."

Mitchell started babbling. He'd already run through it at least three times so was getting better at keeping things straight. But Jake interrupted him anyway, forcing Mitchell to jump forward and backward in the chronology to test everything the man said. Nothing new came out of it.

"And I swear I thought she was in college, man."

"She wasn't."

"I know. I mean *now* I know because you told me. But she told me she was in college. North Western College. And the way she talked made me think that was true, man. She was super smart."

There! "*Was* smart? What *is* she now?"

Mitchell shook his head, backing up again, rising on his toes against the stack of rusted metal. "I just meant back when I talked to her she sounded smart. She still is smart and alive and everything as far as I know." A trickle of blood ran from one of the little wounds and Mitchell flicked at it, smearing it across his face. He looked at his finger. "I'm bleeding, man. You gotta leave me alone. I called *you*. Remember? Why would I do that if I did something to her?"

Mitchell *had* called in. One of the few calls to the tip line that had gone anywhere. But that didn't mean he was innocent. Some criminals liked to insert themselves into the investigation of their crimes. It happened all the time.

"You called in, but told a lot of lies."

"But now I've told you everything!" Mitchell's voice rose even higher. The dogs howled. "The whole truth and nothing but the truth."

Jake believed him. Which meant he had nothing. He fished his sunglasses out of his shirt pocket and put them on. "I'll be back if I find out otherwise."

Mitchell's gaze slipped around, trying to see Jake's eyes through the dark lenses. "You won't, man. I'm telling you. She and I were over months ago."

Jake said nothing, letting the silence stretch until Mitchell swallowed, his Adam's apple bobbing. Jake spun and walked through the yard and out the gate to the parking lot. Back in the Mustang, he checked his phone. One text from Erin. Her official title was Civilian Investigative Support but she was a lot more than that including his eyes and ears at the station. He avoided the place and the constant political boil as much as possible.

Braff wants to see you right NOW!

Jake texted back that he was on his way and headed for Weston and the station.

#

Jake survived the greetings gauntlet that now occurred every time he came into the station. It had become a thing a few months before when a new front desk sergeant started announcing his presence over the intercom whenever Jake showed up. He didn't like it.

Deputy Chief Braff's door was open and Jake found his boss behind his desk with Detective Callie Diggs sitting across from him. Callie and Jake had a romantic history together, but all that remained was a casual friendship and the habit of calling each other by their first names. Jake stopped in the doorway. "Callie." He nodded to her. "Want me to come back later, Deputy Chief?"

"Get in here, Houser. And close the door."

Jake did as he was told. Callie greeted him with a small, sorrowful smile.

Not good.

"What is it, Chief?"

"I'm cutting you off on this Kate Ballard thing. You—"

"It's not a thing. She's missing. She—"

"Do *not* interrupt me."

Jake closed his mouth.

"I've read your case file. You have no fresh leads and working your old leads has turned into a harassment complaint." Braff picked up a pink message slip and shook it. "Alan Mitchell's boss claims you smashed the boy's face into the ground and stood on him."

Jake returned Braff's hard stare. "Mitchell took a swing at me."

"Then why didn't you haul him in?"

"Because I deserved it," Jake said. He'd pushed the man as hard as he'd ever pushed anyone.

Braff frowned. "Do I need to worry about you and this guy?"

"No."

Braff crushed the paper into a ball and tossed it in his trashcan.

Then he propped his elbows on his desk. "I need you back on the opioid thing."

"But I—"

"I gave you the weekend. Today is Monday. I kept my side of the deal. Now you backburner this."

"We can't just quit on her, boss. She's out there—"

"Yes. She's out there. But we have zero evidence she's out there against her will. She's eighteen so *can* be out there, doing whatever she wants to do."

"She's still in high school. And her mom is sure she *is* missing."

"Her mom is a miserable drunk who doesn't even know what day it is."

"We can't hold that against her daughter."

"I am *not* holding it against her daughter. I'm holding it against her credibility. And her best friend is sure she's in Colorado visiting her dad."

Jake fumed, but Braff was right. Jake had no new leads and he wouldn't be able to disprove the friend's hitchhiking to Colorado story until the dad returned from the mountain survival course Kate supposedly went out there for. That trip would explain why her phone was off and her social media accounts had no new posts.

"When the dad gets home we'll all sigh with relief. Or ramp back up." Braff leaned back. "Diggs will brief you on what's going on in the task force. There's a meeting tomorrow morning. Be there." Braff's gaze dropped to the paperwork on his desk. "You're dismissed."

In the hall, Callie grabbed Jake's arm. "I can take the task force meeting, Jake. You can keep on with—"

"No." Jake shook his head. "Braff's right. Until something new pops, her dad comes home or her body...uh, she's found...I need to step away from it."

CHAPTER TWO

Eddie Shaw checked his word count for the day: nineteen thousand six hundred and forty-two words. At this rate he'd be done writing the book by noon Thursday and could spend that afternoon and all day Friday cleaning up the manuscript. Five days to write a first draft. It would beat his personal record by six days. But writing these books was the easy part. Finding the right crime to write about and convincing the people involved—victims and witnesses and suspects and cops and coroners—to talk to him was what took time. When the research was done he spent a couple weeks letting it all percolate until he found the narrative thread that tied all the threads together. Then he banged it out. Presto. A true crime book of the Eddie Shaw brand chock full of illicit sex and sudden violence.

His phone rang. Caller ID said it was his agent. He considered letting it go to voicemail, but he'd played that game too many times recently. He took a deep breath and answered.

"Hey, Gavin." Eddie got up from his desk and took the phone over to the window. He squinted against the sun, and gazed down at the afternoon bustle along Court Street.

"You're avoiding my calls." Gavin Ellison spoke with that rapid-fire New York urgency Eddie hated.

"But I got your text, Gavin." It had reminded Eddie of his blown deadline and finished with "and we need to talk." Gavin used that phrase when he had bad news. Eddie didn't like bad news.

"And?"

"They don't need to see the first three chapters. I'll have the whole thing to them by the end of the day Friday just like the contract says. I *am* a pro, Gavin." Eddie had learned that saying his agent's name sometimes softened him.

"Professionals don't miss deadlines."

Eddie ground his teeth, but said nothing.

"I've re-assigned you to one of our newer agents." Gavin paused, but Eddie had nothing to say. "The missed deadlines,

Eddie. Those are my deadlines, too. My promises. My reputation. I can't—"

"I understand," Eddie said. Gavin had stuck by him through a long slow decline in sales.

"I *am* sorry, Eddie. But you'll like your new agent. She's young and full of energy. Her name is Haley Jones. She'll call you."

The line went dead. Gavin had hung up on him. Eddie put his phone in his pocket, his gaze finding the movie poster centered on his wall. *Trackside Hunter*. His first book. His big one. Gavin had landed Eddie that book deal and negotiated the advertising budget that propelled the book to number eight on the New York Times bestseller list. Then Gavin sold the story to Hollywood and the real fun began— fancy dinners, morning talk shows, long lines at his book signings. Gavin had helped deliver that, but Eddie had done the work. Chasing the interview that freed a man and put the real murderer behind bars—a train-hoping serial killer whose crimes, until Eddie's book, had never been recognized as linked.

Eddie shuddered at where that work had taken him. He'd nearly been killed twice while working hobo camps that most people thought had disappeared after the depression.

Since then he'd focused on lesser stories. Stories that didn't put him at risk. Stories with emotional hooks he amped up with titillating photos and evocative captions.

Since then, he'd played it safe, relying on his writing to thrill the reader when the material didn't do it. And that suited him.

He frowned, flexed his hands, and got back to work.

Acknowledgments and a Historical Note

Like book #2, this novel started as a NaNoWriMo (National Novel Writing Month) project, this one in 2014. Although I "won" the challenge by writing 50,000 words in one month, the book was far from done. It took thirty thousand more words, four years, and dozens of drafts to turn that rough beginning into this final product.

I would not have been able to write this book without the continual support of my wife, Diane, and our children, Meghan and Jack. Writing a book is an all-consuming experience that sometimes leaves me looking like a zombie when away from the computer as I mentally work through a plot point or piece of dialog. Diane has put up with a lot of those moments!

Diane also read an early draft of this book and provided me with valuable input. My primary beta reader for this book was Peter Thompson, whose ideas and suggestions were a big help in bringing this book home.

I again enjoyed the help from the following professionals, without whom this book would not look as good, or read as well, as it does. Thank you!

Ron Edison, Developmental Editor.
    David Gatewood, Line Editor.
    Jeroen Ten Berge, Cover Design.

Historical Note: This book was in part inspired by the real life disappearance of Johnny Gosch from West Des Moines, Iowa in 1982. Don't google his name unless you have a strong stomach and a few hours to spend down the rabbit hole.

ABOUT THE AUTHOR

Bo Thunboe is a suburbanite—born and raised—and still lives in Chicago's western suburbs. When bad eyesight killed his dream to fly helicopters for the Marines, he went to college. It didn't go well, and a few lost years later Bo was out in the world laying bricks and repossessing cars. Then he met his wife, Diane, got his head on straight, and went back to college, where he earned a BA in Economics and a JD from Northern Illinois University. (Go Huskies!) After a couple decades spent lawyering he is now a full-time writer.

Please visit www.thunboe.com to sign up for news and to learn more about Bo and the Jake Houser Mystery Series.